MW00981767

 FriesenPress

Suite 300 - 990 Fort St
Victoria, BC, V8V 3K2
Canada

www.friesenpress.com

Copyright © 2021 by Josh Stettner
First Edition — 2021

All rights reserved.

No part of this publication may be reproduced in any form, or by any means, electronic or mechanical, including photocopying, recording, or any information browsing, storage, or retrieval system, without permission in writing from FriesenPress.

ISBN
978-1-5255-8601-9 (Hardcover)
978-1-5255-8602-6 (Paperback)
978-1-5255-8603-3 (eBook)

1. FICTION, SCIENCE FICTION, CRIME & MYSTERY

Distributed to the trade by The Ingram Book Company

POSITIVE MEMORY

WHAT IF WATCHING YOUR MEMORIES COULD SOLVE A MURDER?

JOSH STETTNER

CHAPTER
ONE

Dillon Murphy walked into his favorite local coffee shop shortly after dinnertime. His dark chestnut eyes made contact with the twenty-something barista across the counter, who smiled back at him.

"Hello, Mr. Murphy. What can I get you today? Are you having your usual, or will you mix it up today and try one of our new summer flavors?"

Dillon figured she was probably getting paid to sell him some fancy seasonal drink that the company was trying to push on the public. Shares in the coffee giant had taken a swing toward the negative due in large part to Dillon and various news outlets exposing the dangers of excessive caffeine use. This scare caused a large percentage of the population to either scale back on consumption or stop drinking caffeinated beverages altogether. Drug companies held the secret that excessive caffeine increased generalized anxiety and panic disorders. For many years, they paid off neuroscientists and members of the government, because antidepressant drugs were readily used to combat these symptoms. Dillon didn't care though. He just wanted his coffee.

"No thanks, Carla," he said in his calm, somewhat sarcastic tone. "I'll just stick to my cinnamon dolce latte, no whipped cream."

Dillon paid for his drink before checking his sleeve phone. He knew he was late, and staring at the time didn't help. He had a text message from his son: "goin to Shy's, don't wait up, don't tell mom! luv ya."

Being a father to an eighteen-year-old was a lot harder than Dillon had imagined. He vaguely remembered telling his foster parents that he was going

1

to do things differently than they had done. How he was going to be a "cool" dad—one who understood the youth of today. Well, "today" was now years passed, and Dillon knew that, if his foster parents were still alive, he would be eating his words.

"One cinnamon dolce latte, no whip."

Dillon adjusted his tie as he checked himself out in the reflection of the glass where the coffee machines sat. He grabbed his cup of advertising from the bar and headed straight out the door. He forgot to give his usual thanks for his usual drink.

As he ran across the busy intersection, a horn honked. "Use the crosswalk, you idiot!" a man in a grey Toyota yelled.

Can't that guy see who he's talking to? Dillon wondered.

As he entered his apartment building, Dillon was thankful that he hadn't gotten rained on. The overcast sky looked a bit gloomy. The rain was the only thing that he detested about living in the big city. His wife, on the other hand, had many reasons to dislike it; Dillon could just never figure them out.

He scanned his thumb as he got into the elevator. The entire building had recently been renovated, and the scanning technology was added. He watched the lights on the numbers go up one at a time. Mesmerized by it, Dillon remembered that it wasn't very long ago that the lights in his old apartment would have only moved up a couple of notches. He would have gotten off the elevator and walked over the drunk and drugged-up neighbor named Edwin, who was never quite able to make it back to his apartment before passing out.

As the final number lit up for his private floor, he checked his hair in the mirror behind him, ran his fingers through it, and smiled. He was gorgeous. Electrifying. Who didn't love Dillon Murphy? Dillon looked at his wife through the mirror as the doors to the elevator opened.

"Where the hell have you been? And where is Jacob? I'm freaking out here. You don't get home until now—my God, love, you're an hour late! What do you have to say for yourself?"

"Jillian, my sweetest angel, why the anger? Are we not two souls careening through earth with nothing but love and reality TV to keep us from killing each other?" Dillon stepped into his home, kissed his wife on the cheek, and removed his tie and suit jacket.

Jillian frowned and tilted her head away from the kiss. "What the hell is that supposed to mean? Are you patronizing me? And where the hell is Jacob? You'd better not tell me he's seeing Shyla!"

"Jillian, let's calm it down. Jacob is sleeping at a friend's house tonight. I'm sorry I'm late. I really needed a coffee. You know I'm stressed from my earth-shattering story. I'm still trying to figure out how to put it together. What's for dinner?"

Jillian looked at her husband as if she were going to kill him. Her eyes seemed to pierce his sarcastic yet giant heart. She walked toward the kitchen and asked the housekeeper to put the dinner on the table. Jillian was not a fan of having someone in the house with them for four hours a day to clean and cook, but Dillon, her loving husband, felt that it was the least he could do for her. She worked just as hard as he did, although Dillon would be the first to say that it didn't matter how hard she worked when he was the one on a major Internet network service. The network started out by fact checking misleading stories from other stations. Now its premise was delivering the truth every weekday, or whenever someone had time to stream it. TTN (The Truth Network, as it was aptly named) had over thirty million subscribers and was the biggest source of trusted news for the American masses.

The housekeeper, Edna, a heavier-set woman in her later years of life, set the food on the table. She had prepared enough for an entire family to be eating it over an hour ago. It was now a slightly overcooked version of itself. The disappointment in her eyes made Dillon dejected enough to apologize for being late. He didn't understand why she should have a problem. He was paying her for whatever she did no matter how many people were eating or how cold the lasagna was getting.

Edna tidied up the dishes in the kitchen and then prepared to leave for the day. Four hours was more than enough for her tired body, and she had already mentioned she would like to cut back. The wrinkles on her face looked like a map of Alaska, with lines like rivers moving toward an ocean.

"Where is my little girl?" Dillon bellowed. "Does she have ballet tonight?"

"Dillon, she stopped doing ballet three weeks ago. She's upset and holed up in her room." Jillian swung her hand toward the hallway. "Oh, and her boyfriend broke up with her today."

"Are you serious? What the hell is wrong with that boy? I told him if he hurt my little girl in any way . . ." Dillon couldn't finish his sentence.

"He didn't hurt me, Daddy; I broke up with him!" his daughter yelled from her bedroom. "He kept treating me like an incompetent woman. Plus, I found out that he kissed my ex-best friend. And the next time you want to talk about me, try doing it quietly, *okay?*"

Rebecca slammed her door. She had dark red hair just like her mother, which accentuated the fire that was burning in her heart.

Jillian turned back toward her husband before taking a bite of the vegetarian dish, which looked almost untouched on her plate. "Are we bad parents, or is this normal?"

"I'd like to think that this is normal," Dillon replied.

"I just don't understand why she has to have an attitude. There is something wrong with that generation, Dill."

Dillon didn't like when she called him Dill, but that was the last thing he cared about at that moment. His food was cold, and he wasn't even hungry. He excused himself from the table and walked out onto the deck.

The apartment building was old but felt newer after the renovations were done, both inside and out. The balcony was framed in glass and the flooring was redone. Dillon just couldn't get over the gargoyle that sat perched at the top of the building right next to him. It was only an arm's length away, staring down at the traffic below. It wasn't the tallest building in the city, but thirty floors felt high to Dillon, who was clandestinely afraid of heights. He called the gargoyle George.

Jillian walked out onto the balcony with two glasses of chardonnay. The patio lights danced in the wine as the grey sky above dulled their facial features. She handed one glass to Dillon and stood beside him, looking over the railing at the lake just a few blocks away. Mountains surrounded the city on either side, creating a valley. Jillian loved the lake. She would walk on the beach in the summer, kicking sand into the water, hoping she would grow to love this city as much as the city had grown to love her husband. Being married to Dillon wasn't easy. She was always Dillon Murphy's wife, and they were Dillon Murphy's children. No one in the family felt like they got to be their own person, which was part of what made it difficult for the household.

"Dillon, where is our son, really?" Jillian leaned against the railing, her eyes piercing the side of her husband's head. "Please tell me the truth. I won't get upset; I swear. I just want to know if he's with her or not. Is he?"

"You promise you won't get upset?"

"If you're asking me, then I already know the answer. And no, I'm not going to get upset. I just don't like him going over there. And, well, when the kids are busy, I feel like there's more reason for you to focus on work."

"Jillian, you can't stop young love. It's a beautiful thing. Look at what happened to us!" Dillon put his arm around her shoulders. "We fell in love young, and now look where we are. You're unhappy, I'm a sexy news personality, Rebecca is heartbroken, and Jacob is a horny teenager who better be using the essential tools."

"Shut up! You always make a joke of everything. It's ridiculous." Jillian smiled as she slapped Dillon on the arm. He knew he could always make her smile. Two small dimples seemed to exude seductively from her face when she did.

"Let's go for a drive," Dillon exclaimed. "What do you say? We have a nice new convertible from the company, and we haven't really used it. It's still a few hours until bed. We can go get some of that plant-based ice cream and drown our family issues in it." Just as Dillon finished his sentence, a drop of rain hit his cheek. They would be driving with the convertible top up.

CHAPTER TWO

"Honey, your father and I are going to go for a drive. Do you want to come with us?"

"No!" Rebecca replied from her room.

"Okay!" Dillon echoed.

Jillian grabbed her purse, and the two walked to the laundry room. Dillon looked at himself in the mirror and fixed his hair as they got into the elevator. Jillian shook her head, and an annoyed sound came out of her mouth.

"What?" Dillon asked.

"Nothing, Mr. Perfection," Jillian retorted as she smirked and coughed up a short laugh.

The elevator moved quickly. Dillon smiled at his wife and kissed her. The doors to the elevator opened to reveal an old couple looking perturbed at the sight. Jillian blushed, and she and Dillon strode hurriedly toward the parking garage doors. Dillon opened them and headed directly to their brand-new silver-and-black Porsche convertible. Dillon pressed his fingers on the car door sensor to unlock his side. Jillian put her finger on the sensor on the passenger side, but the door remained locked.

"Even the car lacks chivalry," she joked.

Dillon sat in the car, and a voice came through the fifteen-speaker system. "Good evening, Mr. Murphy," it said with an English accent.

"Good evening . . . car. Can you unlock the passenger door please?" Dillon asked.

"Of course, Mr. Murphy."

Click.

Jillian opened the door and sat in the soft black leather seat. The headrest adjusted automatically to her height. The car smelled like new carpet and expensive cologne. A bra sat on the floor in the back seat.

"What the hell is this, Dill?" Jillian asked, picking it up.

"I don't know, Jill! You know I just got the car! I swear on our lives, this has nothing to do with me. Honest to God."

Jillian grabbed the bra, opened the door, and walked over to the garbage and recycling room a handful of stalls away. She vehemently threw the bra at the can and missed. A four-letter word echoed throughout the concrete parking garage.

When Jillian returned to the car and slammed the door, she looked at Dillon with convicting eyes. "One hundred percent, that has nothing to do with you? Why didn't you notice it?"

"Jill, one hundred percent. It's black. The interior is black. Honest, I swear."

"I only believe you because it looks like an old woman's bra. Not that I would put it past you." Jillian still wasn't 100 percent sure.

The car was an electric vehicle that ran on solar power. If the top was down for any length of time, however, Dillon had to plug it in. At least that's what the good-looking, older HR manager who explained the car package at work told him. He got stuck on words like "Porsche" and "convertible," and he only saw what was below the neckline. The remainder of the conversation just kind of melded together into a soup-like substance in his head.

As the car slowly pulled out of the parking garage, the driving lights and wipers automatically came on.

"Would you like me to control the vehicle?" the voice asked.

Dillon had been in driverless cars, but he didn't fully trust them yet.

"Take control of the car, please . . . car."

As the two drove toward the grocery store, Jillian respectfully communicated her choice of soft jazz, which immediately started playing.

The sun had finally set through the broken clouds behind the mountain when the Porsche pulled into the parking lot at the local grocer. The happy couple liked to shop there, because they felt like they were supporting the people in the community and not some large conglomerate that had a CEO making all the money at the end of the rainbow.

Trying to keep dry, Dillon jogged slowly through the lightly spitting rain to the entrance.

"So, what kind of ice cream are we getting, love?" Dillon asked.

"I'm thinking I'd like something with chocolate and fudge," Jillian replied.

"Your wish is my command."

Dillon ran down to the freezer aisle in his expensive, black Armani suit pants and collared white shirt. Jillian thought he looked like a casual car salesman, although she would not dare say that to him. It made her smile for a moment.

Dillon reappeared from the aisle before Jillian could make it there, holding a two-liter tub of fudge-brownie ice cream. Jillian salivated at the thought of it melting in her mouth. It had been a stressful few months for her family, and the thought of this momentary luxury was more than enough to satisfy her. If only temporarily.

Dillon noticed the clothes his wife was wearing as they stood in line to pay. She had on a tight-fitting dress that appeared to grasp at her curved hips and almost melt around her waist. She said it was called a "picnic play dress," whatever that meant. He was somewhat turned on by the charcoal-colored fabric that fit her so effortlessly.

Dillon waited for Jillian to look at him before he awkwardly reached into his pants pocket with two hands, pulling out one finger to create the appearance that he was going to pay with a counterfeit digit. Jillian laughed. Even though she knew it wasn't possible to scan a dismembered extremity without a black-market device, she still worried someone would be watching and take him seriously. Words weren't always needed with Dillon. Jillian often said he could have been a mime if his news career didn't pan out. He always had some form of facial expression to go along with how he was feeling, and many times it was a dead giveaway that he was trying to lie to her.

"That will be ten seventy-five please," the cashier said as she looked up. "Hey, I know you! You're the guy from TTN! That is so cool. My parents watch you, like, every day. I don't like the news. Personally, I find it depressing." She continued to speak as if Dillon were listening as he scanned his finger to pay.

They were used to Dillon being noticed. Jillian wished it didn't go straight to his head.

As the two sauntered out of the store, Dillon walked ahead of Jillian and opened her car door.

"I guess chivalry isn't dead after all," he said.

"Get in the car, you idiot." Jillian said, laughing and shaking her head.

Dillon jumped into his seat and activated the motor. He continued the music selection Jillian had picked out, and the two started home. As the streets illuminated from the light system within the roadway, Jillian's uneasiness about how her life was going kicked back in. The ice cream wasn't going to make her problems go away. It might for an hour or so, but all her feelings were going to come right back directly afterwards, and she was going to be 300 calories greater for it. As Jillian turned to Dillon to discuss her troubles, she noticed a disturbing look on his face.

"What's wrong, Dill? You look worried."

"When I push the brakes, nothing happens! We aren't slowing down!"

Jillian didn't know if he was joking or not, but this was not funny. She started to feel sick to her stomach. "Are you serious? This is not funny, you asshole! Not fun—"

"I can't stop! I can't stop, Jillian!" Dillon cried. "Car! Stop . . . the car! Stop yourself! Please!"

"The brakes are not working," the car replied.

"No kidding!" Dillon yelled. "Car, call the police! Now!"

"Calling the police," the car replied in a calm tone. "The call could not be completed," the car said politely a moment later. "Would you like me to try again?"

"*Yes,* please! Call the police! Call 911!"

"The call could not be completed," the car said. "Would you like me to try again?"

"Oh my God, oh my God, I tried all the brakes! We're coming up to a light, and there are cars ahead. There are cars ahead!"

Jillian screamed in terror as the car missiled toward the intersection. She wished the cars sitting there could see how fast they were approaching and get out of the way. She prayed they would move or realize something was wrong, but they didn't do either. They just sat there at the red light that never seemed to change.

Dillon had never seen a light stay red for so long. It was as if some power greater than them was doing this on purpose, toying with the fact that they were unable to end a drive that was supposed to alleviate Jillian's stress momentarily, not exacerbate it. Dillon looked at Jillian and saw fear that he had never seen on her face. She was screaming, and as Dillon watched her panic, he started to become aware that this could be the last few moments of their lives. He felt sick with fear. Jillian's terror-filled scream echoed from window to window. As the vehicle approached the stopped cars that awaited the never-changing light, the steering wheel started to turn the car off the road to avoid a collision.

"I love you!" Jillian cried.

The Porsche turned sharply into the densely wooded area to the right of the road and flipped into the air.

Everything moved in slow motion but went so fast it felt like a lifetime crammed into a matter of seconds. Dillon cranked his head without even trying and watched Jillian as the car roof slammed down hard to the ground, sliding into a hulking oak tree that seemed to fight back against the car's impact.

Dillon looked around, confused, as blood dripped from his nose and mouth. His head was caught between the steering wheel, the air bags and the roof. He could feel nothing except for the exertion of air that forced its way out of his mouth but struggled to arrive.

Then everything went black.

CHAPTER
THREE

As Dillon partially came to, he heard voices. He couldn't feel anything. He could only see a pale, blurry face talking to him, asking him questions. He didn't understand what was being said. He tried to speak, but apparently, nothing came out because no one answered him. It was all so confusing.

Instantly everything went black, and then gold. The indistinguishable words thrown at him echoed into nothingness. Peace took hold of Dillon.

He found himself in a canoe on a wide river surrounded by tall trees. The wind danced from leaf to leaf and eventually through Dillon's hair. The smell of fresh air and water blended together to form an intoxicating aroma that calmed and relaxed his entire body. He sat there, floating. He could think of nothing except the immediate sound of birds calling to one another and water splashing against the banks. Nothing could be better than this. How could it?

The canoe floated past a large rock in the middle of the river. It was magnificent. It glistened with the spray of the water that was striking it. The water began moving faster. It didn't bother Dillon. He felt so alive as the air rushed past his face.

Much farther down, smoke lifted up past the trees. The smoke was insignificant to his immediate surroundings, so Dillon didn't give it a second thought. The canoe continued to gain speed down the river. Dillon looked onward. The plumes of smoke appeared to be getting bigger. The smoke drew closer and started to take over a large portion of the sky. It floated in front of the sun, turning it a dark orange. Dillon stared at it, hoping it would become bright again and pierce the smoke that blanketed it. Instead, the smoke became even more prevalent, overlaying the trees and all that surrounded it. It seeped into his nose and mouth, dripping into his lungs, causing him to start coughing.

He looked around. The trees were glowing a blazing red. He was surrounded by fire and heat. The treetops were like medieval farmers carrying torches toward the outcast, pushing him out past the city limits.

The water sped even faster, and Dillon fell into the back of the canoe. He lay there, looking up, unable to see where he was going or what was waiting for him ahead. The air became too thick to see past his fingers, which were covering his burning eyes. He choked on the only substance he could breathe. It felt like he was taking his last breath.

CHΛPΓER
FOUR

"I'm looking for my parents!" Jacob was shaking as he spoke to the reception-ist in the Emergency Room. "They were just in a car accident. Please, where can I find them?"

"What is their last name, son?"

"Murphy, Jillian and Dillon Murphy."

"Come with me, young man. Bring your friend."

"No, my sister."

"Bring your sister with you."

The siblings followed the ER administrator through the department, their faces pale like half the patients who were staring at them. One man, lying in a bed, moaned about needing water. He looked like he was in his mid-twenties. Jacob Murphy thought it was a drug overdose. He didn't care, though; all he could think about was the phone call he'd just received and the police escort he and Rebecca were required to take.

The lights of the ER felt like they were draining the energy out of the room. Row upon row, they seemed never-ending, irradiating the very path they walked.

They continued on past patient rooms and down a hallway that seemed small for a hospital into a room with no windows. It looked like a waiting area, but not one for awaiting something good. It had an ominous feeling, like the floor was stained with tears, and the walls were scratched from fingernails.

The two kids sat down in identical chairs and stared at the nurse who entered right after them into the claustrophobic nightmare. An old coffee table sat in front of them with an empty paper cup on it.

The nurse looked at the kids for a moment before relaying her message. "The surgeon will be in to see you shortly. Can I get you some water?"

The kids shook their heads, and the nurse walked out of the room. The siblings couldn't tell what the news might be as they attempted to read the nurse's expression. The lack of any positive assurances unsettled them both.

Jacob was hit with another disturbing realization. He was the older of the two. If, inconceivably, his parents were gone, he would have to take care of his sister. He couldn't imagine that thought. He couldn't imagine the very notion that he may never see his parents again. He thought of the last time he'd told his parents he loved them.

Jacob slid his chair right beside Rebecca's and put his arm around her as she slouched with her head almost in her lap.

"It's gonna be okay, sis," Jacob said in an unconvincing tone. "It's gonna be okay. They're gonna be okay." Jacob hoped he wasn't lying to her.

As the two sat there, time stood still. There was a clock in the room, but it didn't move—or at least it appeared that way. Minutes, hours, or days passed until a doctor in light-blue scrubs opened the glass door and came to sit next to the children.

Jacob's heart raced as he prepared to hear the very words he feared, the words that could change the course of their lives forever. Jacob swore the doctor could see his heart pounding through his sweat-soaked shirt.

As the kids waited impatiently for the news, a woman entered the room. She sat opposite the doctor. Her blonde hair hung past her shoulders. Jacob thought she was beautiful, and if circumstances were any different, she would have lingered in his mind for more than a fleeting moment.

"You're the children of Jillian and Dillon Murphy, correct?" the surgeon asked.

"Yes," Jacob choked. "Yes, we are." The words barely fell out of his mouth.

"I'm Dr. Paul Felding. Across from me is our resident psychologist, Dr. Kristine Jamison." He hesitated before he spoke again. "Kids, I have regretful news about your parents. They both sustained major trauma to the chest and head in the accident." Dr. Felding paused as if he didn't know how to say the next part to them. "Your mother died shortly after we got her to the hospital. We did everything we could, but we couldn't save her for you."

Rebecca began to cry. What she had just heard didn't make sense. This couldn't be true. The words she had heard were not meant for her. This had to be a mistake. It couldn't be her own mother who had left her when she needed her the most. How could the world be so cruel to punish someone for being a good and honest human being?

Dr. Felding carried on, welling up as he looked at Jacob and Rebecca as if they were just children. Because, at the root of it all, that's what they were in that moment. Children.

"There is hope for your father. He isn't responsive, but he's alive," Dr. Felding continued. "As I said, he's badly injured in the chest area and suffered trauma to his head. There is still a chance he could die. The next twelve hours will be critical for him. He just came out of surgery. I'll look into when you can see him, but I can't promise it will be anytime soon. Kristine here is going to spend some time with you. She's a psychologist, and she specializes in family cases such as these." As he got up to leave, he placed his hand on Jacob's shoulder. "I'm sorry."

As Dr. Felding walked out, Jacob held his little sister tightly as she cried. He could feel the pain that she was feeling, but he had to be strong for her.

Water crested on Rebecca's shoulder; Jacob was crying too.

CHAPTER
FIVE

Jacob stood in the entrance of his father's walk-in closet. He had to pick out a suit for his mother's funeral. Jacob was almost a legal adult and was already as tall as his father, if not slightly taller. There were many suits to choose from; it felt like he was in a department store. Being on the news meant never appearing to wear the same one twice.

The closet was a circular room with reddish hardwood floors. The walls were a shade darker than the flooring, and the dimmed LED pot lights around the edges gave the room a cozy feeling. A mirror covered a portion of the wall directly across from the entrance.

A hand-carved wooden table sat in the middle with a glass case on it for all his dad's watches. Soft red-velvet couches surrounded the table and created a circle within the rounded room. Jacob weaved his way from the door. When he arrived at the mirror, he looked at the reflection that glared back at him. It was difficult to look at himself and be completely honest. Inside, Jacob longed for normality.

He stared at the eyes peering back at him, the ones he couldn't shy away from. He told himself that he wanted to be strong. He wanted to be strong for Rebecca and for his father. He wanted to be strong for his own peace of mind, because breaking down now only meant admitting to the pain.

It was a funeral, so Jacob would have to have to wear something black. He walked over to the black suits, pulled one out and placed it on the red velvet couch. He sat next to it, his face in his hands, sobbing.

* * *

Jacob sat in the front pew of the church with Rebecca directly beside him. She'd donned her black dress and black funeral hat, the veil covering her face. Her eyes looked swollen from the lack of sleep and the endless river that flowed constantly down her pale skin. Jacob had practiced his eulogy over a dozen times, but he was still very nervous. He wanted to remember his mother and share a note about the impact she had had on his life.

As the priest went through God's reasoning for death, it didn't soothe the pain in Jacob's heart. Each mourner spoke about the experiences they had with Jillian, but all Jacob could think about was how surreal this was. It was a nightmare that wouldn't end. He wasn't scared as much as he was confused and angry.

It was his turn to go up. Rebecca patted his leg as he stood up. She wanted to let him know she was with him, even if she was sitting away from the podium.

"Ehm... Sorry." Jacob coughed into the microphone. "Mom . . . I miss you." Jacob paused as he looked up at the people staring back at him. He didn't care that they were there. He wasn't talking to them.

"You were the realist of the family. You made sure we kept our feet on the ground when our heads started to make us float away. Well, mostly Dad's." The mourners aptly chuckled. "You had just the right balance of being your best without letting people get the best of you. I shudder to think of who I might have become without your strength and guidance. Many times, I would bring an issue to Dad about girls or about guy things, but he usually made a joke of the situation to calm my nerves. It generally worked, and I would smile. Unfortunately, my problem would still be there no matter how hard I laughed about it. You were there for me when I needed advice, and you listened to me and took me seriously. Even if it was something that wasn't very serious—like when Rebecca took my stuffed animal, Charlie, because she had lost hers and couldn't sleep. You understood how it made me feel, but you also made me understand how Rebecca was feeling, and I was happy to let her have Charlie if it would help her fall asleep."

Jacob smiled at Rebecca. "One of my fondest memories is when you took Becca and me to the library with you. You told us about how you used to read novels on paper when you were a child and how you would march into a building and find thousands upon thousands of pages. How you loved the smell of old, musty books when you walked in. I'll never forget that moment, because for that instant, I felt like I got to know what you were like when you were our age."

As Jacob spoke, a tear pushed out of his eye, dripping down his cheek.

When he finished, he stood there, looking at the faces in the church before making his way back to his seat.

He hugged Rebecca, sat down, and stared at the closed coffin.

It was sinking in.

CHAPTER
SIX

It was the last day of October, just before class started for the morning. Jacob was now in his first year of university. He'd always been a smart kid. It wasn't just his boyish good looks that got him a scholarship for the first year. Jacob was also athletic and creative and had a knack for saying the right things at the right time, a trait that seemed to be genetic.

Jacob walked into class and tossed his backpack and tablet on the desk at the back of the room. That was the spot he kept choosing in all of his classes. It had become difficult for him to concentrate on what the professor was saying or what the class was discussing or debating. He kept quiet and imagined that, for the most part, people didn't even realize he was there.

Shyla Winters also attended the school. She was the same age as Jacob and had also done well in her final year of high school. She was taking a completely different set of classes than him, so they didn't get to see each other much, except for the afternoon break they shared for forty minutes on Thursdays.

Jacob didn't speak much to Shyla after the accident. He used to feel comfortable with her, something he had never felt with anyone. He even wondered if he had been in love with her. However, Jacob pulled away from everyone other than Rebecca after his mom died. He couldn't imagine losing anyone else.

Jacob was staring at his tablet when his class started. It was his last one of the day. Throughout class, Jacob kept going back to the PAstREAM website.

He couldn't focus on his work. He was convincing himself to finally try it out. The thought of being able to let go and be happy for sixty minutes seemed worth the price of admission. He wouldn't have to think of anything other than a memory.

Ever since PAstREAM and other brain-level function enhancement companies became overnight sensations in the US, things had continued to change. The world was becoming even more high-tech, and new mind-altering technologies were readily available at a fast pace.

Jacob remembered when he first heard about PAstREAM on the news as a pre-teen. Eight years ago, his father was the only reporter in the country who had access to the equipment and to the test site at the first PAstREAM head-quarters. It was one of the stories that helped propel TTN to reach a wider audience than it had with just leaked information and fact checking. It also expedited the growth of PAstREAM to the conglomerate it became. Dillon's story still ran on the PAstREAM website, although it was now embedded on the history page. Jacob clicked the link for inspiration and motivation to pay for a session, but he also did it to see his father doing what he loved. The story filled the screen, and his father's voice filled the earbud that was facing away from the teacher.

"Two of Harvard's top students were hard at work on a project that the school has repeatedly claimed they were unaware of. The dean of Harvard said that any projects the students worked on outside of the establishment are not illegal and that they have the right to their creative outlets as long as it does not hinder the institution in any way." In the video, Dillon walked over to a table with an electronic headset on it. The camera followed.

"The students created a memory device, one that will change the way millions of us will remember our lives. For the first time, these students are giving us a glimpse into the equipment and their inspiration." Dillon reached over to pick up the apparatus sitting on the table next to him. "It rests on the user's head like a halo while microscopic needles penetrate the scalp. The memory device is called PAstREAM, a play on the words "past" and "stream," because it streams the users' memories to them in real time. Hippocampal ensemble dynamics carry a code like a time stamp to the brain when new memories are created. This makes it possible to pull the memories in order and play them back in 4D, using lenses that are placed over the eyes. People are already lining up outside the new PAstREAM building just to spend an hour on the machines. Although it's priced so the average person can use it, there is a long wait to get in. The inventors are planning to expand in the very near future. The twenty-three machines they have created so far are running twenty-four hours a day."

Dillon finished his report for the station with a final thought that had made him famous. "Can you imagine being able to re-watch your wedding day or your honeymoon? The birth of your child or your first kiss? What if you could watch the best days of your life, all through your own eyes, exactly as you remembered them? Everyone has a moment, just don't let it make you forget your future. For TTN news . . . I'm Dillon Murphy."

Jacob put down his tablet and rubbed his forehead. He decided today wasn't the day for memory watching. He felt selfish, thinking about using it when he considered Rebecca and how she was faring.

Jacob cleaned up his desk and was the last student to leave. He took the path that led away from the Business Administration building where he was taking his financial courses. His dad had always pushed him to be smart with his money. He was now going to study it.

The air was cool in the autumn breeze. It had a crispness to it, and Jacob felt the bite on his exposed skin. When he inhaled, he felt the cool air fragment into his lungs. The sunlight on his face improved his mood.

Jacob got to his bus, scanned his city pass at the terminal, and found a seat next to a girl with enough piercings to cause an airport metal detector to overload. Passengers were required to sit in alternating seats, if there was room, to maintain social distancing. There was a new virus scare sweeping the globe, albeit not as deadly as the last one. As the bus started to move, Jacob could only think of Rebecca. She would already be at the hospital.

Jacob had stopped looking forward to visiting his father. It frustrated him. He was especially troubled by Rebecca. Visiting their dad drained her. She was with the man who raised her, every minute of every day. She was Daddy's little girl, and now she acted like he was all she had left. Jacob felt guilty that he wasn't doing enough for her. He didn't know how he could. He had tried so many times to get her to go to school or spend time with a friend, but she wouldn't leave. She would comb their dad's hair and brush his teeth every morning. Their grandma had tried everything she could to get Rebecca to go home and start living her life again, but she was too old and frail to force the issue. Her mind was failing, and she had just moved into a care home.

When Jacob got off the bus at the hospital, he walked toward the front entrance. If he looked up along the front of the building, he would often see Rebecca, with her red hair, sitting on the window bench four floors up, but he didn't see her this time.

Jacob took the elevator. He'd read the same sign for months: "Critical Care Unit—Long-Term/Short-Term."

Jacob always hung a left down the Long-Term Care walkway. It was a newer section of the hospital and had a sign-in tablet at the front desk. Jacob didn't like scanning into it. He wondered if he and Rebecca had set a record for most scans.

Jacob pushed the door open and walked into Unit 401. It had a bathroom and a tiny living space with a TV, and a couple of comfy black recliners—the luxuries of having a top-tier health plan. He walked up to his dad but didn't see Rebecca anywhere.

Dillon was lying in his bed. He had been in a coma for four months.

Jacob sat beside his dad. He knew if he waited there with him for any amount of time, Rebecca was sure to show up. Jacob grabbed his dad's hand and squeezed it, hoping he would feel the love that Jacob was pushing through their touch.

The door opened, and Rebecca immediately looked at Jacob. She appeared dreadfully tired.

"How was he today, sis?" Jacob asked, knowing full well it was an irrelevant question. Rebecca would have called or texted him if anything of note had happened. That didn't stop her from answering with mild enthusiasm.

"Well, his eyes were really moving today. He must have had a great dream. The doctor thinks his mind could be starting to become more active."

"Did Grandma come and visit today?"

"Yes. Her care worker helped. She wanted me to tell you that they're serving perogies tonight if you want to go over for dinner."

"Will you come with me?" Jacob asked as he looked at her. "At least get some food in your belly, sis. I'm worried about you."

"Jacob, you know I'm not going to leave Daddy here alone. What if he wakes up?" Rebecca gave him an angry look, scoffing at the idea. "No, I can't take that chance. You need to stop asking me. It's, like, every day."

Jacob didn't want to tell her that he didn't think their father was ever going to wake up. He sat down on the chair in front of the TV, turned it on, and began to watch the baseball game. He didn't know how hopeful he could be anymore. He missed his dad, and he especially hated seeing Rebecca like this.

CHAPTER
SEVEN

Thanksgiving had passed, and holiday shoppers were finally getting into the swing of things. Snow christened the ground, and snowflakes kissed the skin of those who dared brave the cold. Christmas was near, and people everywhere were getting into a festive mood. Time seemed to be riding on a sleigh toward that magical day.

The first week of December came and went, but there was no great feeling of the approaching holidays for Rebecca. She had lost fifteen pounds since the accident. She ate when Jacob forced her to or when she wanted to make her stomach pains go away. Christmas this year would be distressing.

Jonathon Winters entered Dillon's room. He was wearing an expensive duffle coat, and his shoes seemed overly polished. Jonathon was always at the top of trends. He dressed for success. His dark skin made his white shirt appear bright in the dimly lit room.

Jonathon was Dillon Murphy's best friend. They started together at TTN years ago in their hometown. Now Jonathon was the general manager in charge of it all while Dillon was the face of the network. Rebecca felt uneasy about Jonathon, because she never really understood if he had a motive for their friendship. Maybe it was just the apprehension her mother had felt with him, but Rebecca trusted her mother's intuition.

Jonathon mentioned to Rebecca on several occasions that they wanted to interview her father if he woke up. She would always fix his sentence and say, "*When* he wakes up."

"How has he been lately, Becca?" Jonathon asked.

"His mind appears to be getting really active. He's even mumbling, which is new." Rebecca looked happy for a moment. "He's showing some great signs."

"Where's your brother?"

"He had school and should be back any time."

"How has school been for you?"

"Well, I only have two classes I need to pass right now, and I figure I can still get through grade eleven if I finish strong before my next semester. Dad has to be awake by then," she said with unwavering hopefulness.

She turned her gaze from Jonathon's piercing green eyes to look out the window at the people below. She thought it was astounding how, even in a hospital, people still had the Christmas spirit.

"Mr. Winters. How are you today, sir?" Jacob said as he entered.

"Jacob. Good to see you, son. It's been a while." Jonathon moved away from the window. "Look, I just wanted to see how you kids were doing. Everyone at the station—they're really worried about you. They started a fund in your mother's honor to raise some money for you guys."

"Mr. Winters," Rebecca interjected, "we don't want their money, we just want our dad to be back to normal."

Jacob didn't seem to like this response. "What my sister is trying to say, sir, is we really appreciate that you would do that for us. We don't expect people to give us any money." Jonathon aimed the credit chip, and Jacob accepted the scan for the added funds.

"Well, we are worried. And if you need anything, please don't hesitate to call me. I really do want to help."

With that, Jonathon left the room.

"Why does he have to come here?" Rebecca asked. "He doesn't care about Dad."

"Sis, why does it bother you that he's trying to help us? I don't get it." Jacob knew now was as good a time as any to talk to her honestly about the situation. "Dad isn't waking up. You have to start going to school and living your life again. I'm sorry that Dad is like this. I'm sorry that Mom died. But you can't stop living. You're all I have left, and I don't want to lose you too. You're too thin, and I'm honestly getting scared that you're just going to wither away if you don't start taking care of yourself. I'll sleep here every night if it means you'll go home and start focusing on yourself." Jacob started to tear up. "You're so frail and sad all the time. I love you, sis, and I can't bear to watch you do this to yourself anymore."

Jacob hugged Rebecca, and she hugged him back. She knew he was partly right, though she didn't want to admit it. She felt guilty that she was even thinking that way. Her dad needed her.

Jacob told Rebecca that he was going out for dinner but that he'd stay the night at the hospital. He promised to bring her back something fattening.

Her brother's words, although difficult to hear, were fairly accurate. She had to start getting her life back together.

She felt that her presence was helping in the healing process, but Rebecca knew her father wouldn't want her to give up on her own life. She had to start somewhere, and school was the best place for that. She would go first thing in the morning. She couldn't stay at the hospital forever, but she would return to her father every day after school.

Rebecca turned off the light and switched on the lamp next to her father's bed. His facial features were more prominent when the soft glow shadowed his cheek bones.

It was getting dark out already. The sun set so fast in the cold calendar days. The lamp and the TV were the only things illuminating the room. As Rebecca sat down to stream the new comedy she had been watching, she remembered it was time to move her dad's shoulder blades, which was a task in itself, to prevent bedsores. Rebecca walked over to her father's bedside and lifted his left shoulder. She adjusted his position slightly and placed a hydrocolloid dressing on the spot with the most redness.

As she rested him down, she grabbed the comb and brushed his hair into less of a bedhead look. She stared at her dad, noticing how much his appearance had changed since the accident. He looked frail and gaunt. Rebecca set the comb down and put her ear to his chest. She liked to hear his heartbeat. It reminded her that her dad was still alive. She didn't hear anything at first, but as she lay there, she felt her father's chest rise and fall. Relieved, she moved her ear over slightly to where she could hear his heart pumping. A calm feeling enveloped Rebecca. She lifted her head off his chest and turned to kiss him on the forehead. She stopped abruptly, starting at his pale face.

Her father's eyes were open.

CHAPTER
EIGHT

Jacob was eating at his preferred table in the restaurant his parents had taken him and Rebecca to on the very day they moved to the city. It was a peaceful eatery. The owner had worked as a personal chef for Hollywood stars in her early years. Pictures adorned the walls around the entrance of the bistro, each one of the owner standing beside some of the A-listers of her time. Going there was comforting for Jacob. Soft jazz music played in the background, a favorite of his mother's. She would sit in her loft on rainy days listening to it while reading her favorite authors and burning incense that stank up the house. Jacob wished he could go back to one of those moments with the smells of vanilla and lavender filling the air.

He thought about going to the PAstREAM building and watching one of those instances in his life. He felt his balloon of desire puncture with the reality that, in short order, he would be back at the hospital. He didn't have the time or the money to use such a lavish respite. He had to accept a banking chip from Jonathon for the account the office started raising for his family because of their money issues. There wasn't really any income, just a savings account that was slowly dwindling.

As Jacob got off the sofa bench at the table to go to the washroom, he bumped the cutlery to the floor, and it slid under the table. Irritated, he reached for it and banged his head on the way up.

"Ow. Shit."

Just as he got his fingers on the fallen cutlery, his sleeve phone vibrated. Immediately, a picture of Rebecca jumped onto the screen. Jacob answered it.

"Jacob!" Rebecca's voice was animated. It sounded like she could barely contain herself. "Dad's eyes opened—he's awake! You need to get here right now!"

"What? Are you serious? Did he say anything? I'm on my way!" Jacob couldn't believe what he was hearing. He was scared. What if his father had brain damage? How would he tell his father that Mom was dead? He thought instantly about Rebecca having to face these questions on her own and ran out of the restaurant without paying for his meal.

"I have to go!" he yelled to the waitress. "I'm sorry—I'll pay tomorrow. I'm really very sorry!"

Jacob raced down the sidewalk and across the street. He didn't get any answer from Rebecca on how their dad was doing. She just said to get over here immediately. She didn't have time to talk. Jacob wondered if his grandma knew her son-in-law was awake or if she would even understand. She was the only relative they had left, but she was not doing well mentally.

Jacob pushed the front door of the hospital open and sprinted past the front desk, skipping the scan-in. He was not going to stop for something so stupid at a time like this. His heart was pounding out of his chest.

"Jacob!" Rebecca yelled. "Come over here!"

The doctors and nurses on duty were all surrounding their father, thrilled with the news that he was awake. Jonathon was there too. He had asked the nurses at the front desk to call him if this moment ever came. He made sure to make it worth their while too. Instant access to the PAstREAM device would make the average person do almost anything.

"Has he said anything?" Jacob asked.

"Not yet," Jonathon answered for Rebecca.

Jacob wondered how Jonathon had made it there so quickly, but the thought was short-lived. As he walked over to the right side of the bed, he could see his father's face. His eyes were open, and he was blinking. He looked at Jacob without so much as a flinch.

"Dad, I missed you." Jacob couldn't stop the excitement that was building inside him. He sat beside his dad and grabbed his hand.

"Jacob, he's a bit confused right now," Rebecca said softly as if to avoid having her father hear what she was saying. "He hasn't said anything since he woke up. The doctor said this isn't abnormal for a coma that has lasted this long."

The doctor interposed himself into the conversation. "Now, although your father is awake, there are some things we need to do, and above all else, we must have patience. Sometimes people who have been in comas for some time can wake up and fall back into a coma again. I'm going to ask at this time that everyone except for the kids leave for now. We're going to start some tests on his brain function and see how awake he is."

Dillon looked almost lost. He showed no emotion or expression on his face. Jacob's initial feeling of excitement started to turn into anxiety. Now what? His father wasn't doing anything. Nothing here answered the questions burning in his mind. Rebecca still looked overjoyed that her father was awake, and that kept Jacob feeling positive about what was happening. At least their father was conscious, right? After months of stasis, that was a step in a good direction.

Rebecca's smile was intoxicating. Jacob stared at her. It was a side of her that had been missing for so long. He'd thought he would never see that smile again. Jacob didn't know why, but he started to cry. He wasn't sure if it was because he was realizing his father was awake or if it was seeing his little sister beam for the first time in what felt like a lifetime of pain. Life had tossed his family into a blender, and the emotions that had pirouetted in his mind over the last six months were overwhelming him.

Everyone left the room except for the kids and the specialist who had come on short notice. The siblings were left looking at the doctor as if to say, *"Fix him. We want to speak to him!"*

The doctor sat on the bed beside Dillon. "Dillon, my name is Dr. Stanley Richards. You can call me Stan. I was wondering if you could do something for me, Dillon. Can you blink your eyes for me three times in a row?"

Dr. Richards smiled and waited patiently. Dillon blinked slowly and opened his eyes. He repeated the action again and then repeated it once more.

"Very good, Dillon. That was very well done."

Rebecca looked at Jacob, full of delight.

The doctor proceeded to check Dillon's pupil dilation with his pen light before speaking again.

"Now, Dillon, I'm going to apply pressure to your fingernail here with my pen. I want you to blink three times again if you can feel it, okay?"

Dr. Richards applied pressure to Dillon's fingernail and watched his eyes. Dillon's eyes bulged slightly, and he blinked three times, a little bit faster than the previous time. Dr. Richards applied pressure to Dillon's big toe. Dillon blinked three times. Then Dr. Richards moved Dillon's legs and arms and looked for signals from him.

"Well, Dillon. Welcome back, sir. We will be doing some more testing with you tomorrow after you regain your bearings. I'm going to leave you now, but I'll be back first thing in the morning." Dr. Richards held his patient's hand and leaned in slightly. "It was a pleasure to meet you, Dillon. You have very wonderful kids here." He smiled before stepping over to Jacob and Rebecca. "Kids, I'm going to tell you a couple of things, okay?"

Jacob felt suddenly sick, similar to the feeling he'd had the night of the accident when the doctor wanted to talk to him and Rebecca, but it wasn't the same circumstance. He didn't know what made him feel this way. He ran to the bathroom and threw up.

He didn't make it in time and got vomit on the side of the toilet and on the floor. His face turned a bright shade of white. It looked identical to the shirt Jonathon had been wearing earlier in the day.

"Jacob, are you okay?" Rebecca asked.

"I'm fine. I must have eaten something spoiled at the restaurant. Sorry, sis," Jacob responded as he wiped his face with a towel. He moved out of the bathroom and told Rebecca he would clean it up after they spoke with the doctor.

"Are you alright, young man?" Dr. Richards asked.

"Fine, sir. Just an upset stomach. So, what do we do now?"

"Well, that's what I want to talk to you about. What I'm seeing from your father is very positive. He responded to my request, and he reacted to my pain stimuli. Now, I won't know more until we do some tests tomorrow. At this point, I can't tell you how he will be or what his life will be like. I ask that you give it some time. Be patient with him. We won't understand his final functionality instantaneously." He paused as he looked into their eyes.

Jacob was concerned, but he felt better after relieving himself of the acid build-up in his stomach, though his throat burned. The doctor's words encouraged him, but he was still worried about what the outcome of his father's life was going to be. The future was still so murky. Would he be the same person he was? Would he be able to play cards with Jacob again, or would he be destined to a wheelchair, sitting in a home while Rebecca wiped the drool from his lip?

Jacob thought he should continue feeling positive about the situation. His father was always positive, or at least he had been as far back as Jacob could remember. Jacob looked back up at Dr. Richards after staring at his dad, lying in the bed.

"Now, I'm going to leave for the evening," Dr. Richards said as he patted Jacob on the shoulder. "I'll be back in the morning to start helping your father progress forward now that he's awake. I ask that you keep things quiet here tonight and stay by his side. He may need your presence to keep from becoming too confused. Don't leave him alone. Call a nurse if you leave. And if he starts to show anger, fear, or sadness, that's normal. It's likely a sign that he's regaining cognitive function. Just keep calm, let him know that he's okay and that you are here with him." Dr. Richards put his hand on Rebecca's shoulder and looked at her as if he meant to say, *"This is a great day. Continue to smile,"* but he relented so as not to get the kids' hopes up.

Jacob watched as Dr. Richards walked out of the room, and the door closed slowly behind him. He looked at Rebecca and hugged her. The moment felt inconceivable. Dr. Richards seemed optimistic, so Jacob couldn't help but echo that feeling in himself.

Rebecca looked up at her brother. "I'm not going to school tomorrow." She smiled at him, knowing Jacob would think it was appropriate considering how the circumstances had changed since he'd boiled over in anguish.

"I won't be either, sis."

Jacob and Rebecca walked back over to their father. Jacob wanted so badly to talk to him, to tell him everything that had happened since the accident. The discovery of a planet that was identical to earth within our galaxy. The massive earthquake in the Midwest that killed thousands of people.

Their mom's death.

They were both nervous at the thought of telling him that his wife was gone. Rebecca seemed to decide that she was content enough to enjoy the moment that had been created for them on such a cold day in December. She sat beside her father and grabbed his hand. Dillon stared back at her, but it wasn't a look of joy, excitement, or even mellow enthusiasm. It was still one of confusion and unwilling acceptance of the environment around him.

"Daddy, it's me, Rebecca." She looked at him, hoping to see a spark in his eyes. "Remember when I was a little girl, and you used to sing the song you wrote about me? It was my favorite song. It always made me smile even though I thought it was silly, especially because of how you would sing it to me." Rebecca stared into her father's eyes and smiled at the only parent she had left. She hummed quietly until she found the right note that started the song, which had a country twang to it.

> When I was just a boy,
> The good Lord said to me.
> One day you'll be a daddy,
> And start a family.
> I didn't stop to think about,
> Just how that life would be.
> But when my little girl was born,
> It was there for me to see.
> She had red hair like her mother,
> Which scared me half to hell.
> If she's a spitfire like her mommy,
> My soul I'll have to sell.
> But when she looks me in the eye,
> Something funny happens to me.
> I pull out my wallet,
> And give her all my money.

Rebecca smiled, and perhaps her dad did too. It was hard to tell with his muted, expressionless face, but Jacob thought for an instant he saw something alive in him that they hadn't seen since he woke up.

For the rest of the night, Dillon lay motionless and watched his children moving around him. Jacob and Rebecca decided to alternate watching over their father, with one sleeping while the other sat beside him. As expected, neither of them could sleep.

It became apparent that, after months of endless slumber, their father wasn't about to close his eyes for any length of time other than to blink. As morning drew closer, and the sun polished the sky with a dark orange glow directly above the mountaintops, a sound emanated from Dillon's bed.

Jacob jumped off the chair that he'd curled into after convincing himself of the need for sleep at around 4:00 in the morning. Rebecca was asleep on the bed, her head laying on their father's chest while her legs dangled off the edge. Jacob nudged Rebecca and woke her up.

"Sis, I heard something. It sounded like Dad made a noise."

"Huh?" Rebecca lifted her head. Her red hair was a mess around her skinny face. "What, Jacob . . . What happened?"

"He said something. Look. He's looking around more too!"

"Dad. Daddy! Say something. Say something please, Daddy!" Rebecca pleaded.

"Ungh," was all Dillon forced out.

"Oh my God, Jacob! He's speaking!"

Jacob stood there waiting for him to say something else. Rebecca gazed at her father in anticipation.

His eyebrows tensed up on his face. It looked like panic was setting in. The kids watched as their father grew more and more uncomfortable. Jacob thought he looked like a scared animal who was being forced into a cage.

Dillon started to cry. He pushed out tears as he lay there, his eyes open wide. Rebecca and Jacob held their father and told him that everything was okay, that they were there for him. Their words did nothing to quell his anguish. It seemed as if he might be in some sort of dream where reality and fiction were clasped together like two little hands praying at bedtime.

Rebecca became worried and called the nurse to come in. In an instant, she entered, Dr. Richards right behind her. He must have been here early, planning Dillon's journey.

"Okay, okay. I don't want you to worry. He's confused, and now that he's awake, reality is starting to set in for him. When you have been in a comatose state for so long, you may not believe what you see. He is realizing that he's not dreaming anymore, and he's a little mixed up right now. Perhaps we can start our tests a bit early. If you kids don't mind, I'd like to take your father for a few hours. We're going to run some tests, including a functional MRI, to compare his brain function now to the scans we did in the months previous."

Dr. Richards checked Dillon's pupils with a penlight. "His pupils are dilating quickly, which is a great sign. They were a bit slower yesterday. Look, kids, I don't see anything here as of right now that is worrying me, so I don't want you to be worried either. Things like this happen. and from everything I can see, your father is progressing." He pocketed his light before offering a compassionate request. "I would highly suggest you two get some food in you. I'll have your father back here in a few hours. I promise."

Jacob and Rebecca hugged their father, who still looked shocked, though his tears had stopped. The kids grabbed their winter coats and walked out the door.

"I'm starving," Rebecca said matter-of-factly.

Jacob was happy to hear she was hungry for a change. That feeling alone made him hungry too.

CHAPTER
NINE

The nurses popped the wheels out on Dillon's bed and unlocked the bars that came up on the sides to prevent him from rolling off, as Dr. Richards prepared him for the fMRI. The nurses changed Dillon's gown and removed the feeding tube that nourished him.

Dillon's bed began its journey to the imaging floor. He looked around as the ceiling above him started to move.

The bed continued to the elevator. Everyone who had been with him since the kids left for breakfast were crammed into it, all of them wearing masks.

Dr. Richards pushed the button for the eighth floor and then leaned over to Dillon. "How are you doing, Mr. Murphy?"

"Ungh . . ." was all Dillon could muster.

"I have those days too," Dr. Richards joked.

It reduced the tension in the elevator. Everyone was staring at the man they had only known as having his eyes closed. Even though the nurses had been with him for many months, they had never gotten to know him. They only knew who he was from the news and as the lifeless body that required daily attention.

The elevator stopped, and the nurses pushed Dillon's bed out into the hallway. It remained there for a while as Dr. Richards worked with the technologist to get his patient in as quickly as possible. One of the nurses was explaining the noises that Dillon would be hearing and not to be alarmed by them. The words went in one ear and out the other.

Soon, Dillon found himself wheeled into a room with a very peculiar looking machine, at least from what he could tell from his reclined position.

The nurses bunched together around Dillon's bed, and each one grabbed a part of his body. On the count of three, they lifted his slender frame onto the scanner table and rested his arms and legs beside him.

The table slid slightly into the fMRI machine with Dillon's head resting around the opening.

Dillon started to become uneasy. He did not know what was going on, but he felt as though he was in some sort of trouble. He did not feel comfortable in this contraption, and it started to show. For the first time since the accident, Dillon started to move his arms and legs. It wasn't a violent movement of the extremities, but it was enough for Dr. Richards to notice. Dillon's head started moving when it was supposed to remain completely still.

Dr. Richards got the technologist to stop the scan and walked quickly to where Dillon was squirming. He slid out his patient.

"Mr. Murphy, you're a fighter. I love it. It's good to see you finding yourself again. Can you do me a favor?" Dr. Richards spoke as if he was talking to a child. "I'm going to put you back into this machine here, and I need you to lay still for a bit. Can you do that for me, Mr. Murphy?"

Dillon didn't say anything. He did, however, stop moving.

Dr. Richards rested his hand on Dillon's shoulder and waited a moment. When Dillon appeared somewhat comforted, Dr. Richards slid the table back in. Dillon lay still for the remainder of the scan.

When it concluded, the nurses put him back on his bed the same way they had taken him off. Dillon started to become more aware of what was going on, and a word actually trickled out of his mouth.

"Where . . ."

"Mr. Murphy, what did you say?"

"Where . . ."

Dr. Richards paused, waiting to see if anything else would come out, before responding. "Where indeed, Mr. Murphy. You're at the hospital, and we will be taking you back to your room in short order."

Dillon's neck felt stiff. He hadn't used his muscles for so long that they'd forgotten their purpose. He slowly moved his head in both directions with the help of a nurse. It felt good to loosen the tightness. Blood was starting to flow quicker into his brain.

He felt a sharp pain in the lower half of his body. He had the beginnings of a bedsore on the right side of his buttocks where the lack of movement caused blood to stop circulating. Rebecca had done everything she could to help the nurses move him around to avoid the sores.

As the blood flooded his brain, Dillon became thirsty.

"Water," he said, looking at a nurse beside him.

"Water? Doctor, Mr. Murphy wants water! He asked for water!" the nurse exclaimed excitedly.

She grabbed a biodegradable cup, filled it, and attached a lid and a paper straw. She placed the end of the straw into Dillon's mouth, and he began to suck on it, water splashing out of his mouth. Dr. Richards told the nurses to keep a close watch on his movements. The cold water hitting his stomach could cause him to throw up.

Dillon kept the water down. His mind started to feel loose. It had felt tight—so tight that he couldn't think of anything. It was like he was watching, but nothing was processing. Now he could feel his arms and legs, chest and heart, toes and fingers.

He could also feel thoughts forming in his mind. He started thinking. Thinking about how he felt at that exact moment. Thinking about the machine he had just been in, the doctors, and the nurses.

The thing that confused him, the thing that was really starting to make him feel anxious, was the fact that he couldn't remember much, if anything, before that moment.

He didn't know who he was.

CHAPTER
TEN

Dillon's bed was moved to a half-sitting position. He continued to drift in and out of sleep, wondering if this was just another vivid dream.

Three hours passed before he awoke again, this time with the realization that this dream wasn't changing.

Rebecca and Jacob had been watching him, ready to pounce at the chance to interrogate their father.

"Hi," Rebecca said, smiling, her eyes watery. She was so shocked that her father was able to look at her with more than a blank expression that she didn't know how to react. How could it be that the sleeping man she had been taking care of all these months was finally sitting up and aware? Rebecca was overjoyed but also terrified.

"Where am I?" Dillon sounded like he had a mouth full of marbles. He asked both kids, as if they were two people who worked with the doctor.

"You're in the hospital. You had an accident," Jacob said, holding back the urge to cry. He was conversing with his father. He hadn't known if he was ever going to get that chance again, and now here he was, face-to-face with him.

"Who are you?" Dillon asked, confused. He didn't know where he was or what was going on. He looked at his kids, but he didn't feel anything.

"Dad. It's me, Rebecca. Your daughter." Rebecca sounded worried.

"Okay," Dillon replied.

"And I'm Jacob. I'm your son. Don't you remember?" Jacob asked in the hope that he would say yes. He stared at his father, looking for the formation of his lips to read something positive.

"I don't remember," Dillon said.

Dr. Richards walked into the room. He saw his patient awake and looking at the kids.

"Where is Nurse Susan? I told her to tell me the minute he woke up again!" He seemed frustrated that the kids were talking to their father. He immediately went to Dillon's bedside and took control. "Mr. Murphy, so good to see you're awake."

"Doctor, he doesn't remember us!" Rebecca said, a panic-stricken look on her face.

"Kids, please . . ." Dr. Richard said calmly.

"Stop calling us kids, Dr. Richards," Jacob said. "We're old enough to be worthy of your respect, and we're old enough to hear the truth. If there's something you're not sharing with us, now would be a good time to tell us!" His voice was stern. The man he was becoming was on display for Rebecca and Dr. Richards to see.

"The problem," Dr. Richards said softly, "is that I don't know where your father is currently at. I need to spend time with him to see what sort of issues he may have. I'm not going to tell you something when I don't yet know myself. Your father has been through a very traumatic experience, both physically and mentally, and I need time to evaluate.

"I plan to do everything I can for your father to help him rebuild his normal functioning. I don't know enough at this point to be able to promise you anything except that I'll be honest with you, and I won't hide anything from you even if it may upset you. But you two need to promise that you will trust what I'm doing. Is that something we can work on together?" He looked at them with a half-smile and an authentic show of concern.

Jacob and Rebecca looked at each other before Jacob reached out to shake the doctor's hand. They knew they didn't have any other choice but to acquiesce to his request. They wanted to trust him.

"We can work together," Jacob said.

"Now I'm going to ask you kids . . ." Dr. Richards hesitated. "Sorry. I'm going to ask that you two stay in the room but not to say anything unless

I ask you to. There may be things said that will alarm you, but you must remain calm. We can discuss what we talked about afterwards. Understood?"

"Understood," they replied. They moved to the wall on the right side of the bed and sat down on two fold-out chairs. Jacob moved his chair closer to Rebecca's and patted her leg.

"Now, Mr. Murphy, I'm going to ask you some questions. Are you okay with that?" Dr. Richards asked.

"Yes," Dillon replied.

"Mr. Murphy. What is your full name?" Dr. Richards had a pad of paper and was preparing to write the responses down.

"I . . . I don't remember," Dillon said with a puzzled look on his face. He grabbed the water that was beside the bed and started to drink it. He drank it so fast that the water started falling out of his mouth, dribbling down the gown on his chest. Dr. Richards looked a bit concerned but retained a smile.

"More water," Dillon asked. He put the cup in Dr. Richards' lap before it landed on the floor.

Dr. Richards picked up the cup and handed it to Jacob. Dillon watched Jacob as he filled his cup and brought it back to him.

"Now, Mr. Murphy. Can you tell me, what is the earliest memory that you can remember in your life? Do you recollect anything about your childhood?" Dr. Richards' smile didn't waver.

"I remember playing with kids. Lots of kids—although I didn't like them much. They were all like me. They didn't have parents. They were loud, very loud. I did like one kid though. His name was Jules. He had white hair. His skin was very white. But his eyes . . . his eyes were red. Kids were afraid of him, but I wasn't. He was my friend." Dillon was looking directly at Dr. Richards, but it appeared as if he was seeing right through him. Then Dillon's eyes seemed to come back into focus and took in the details of Dr. Richards in front of him. The doctor's black hair was patched with grey and white. He was older than Dillon and seemed wise beyond his years.

"Well, Mr. Murphy, I must say that is an interesting story." Dr. Richards turned to the kids and asked them if this was something that was possible, or if their father was making up a story. Jacob answered first.

"Well, Dad was raised in a foster home by parents who had many other kids. Dad never told us that story, but it could be true. Did you ever hear that story, sis?"

"No." Rebecca was absorbed in her father's current state.

"Okay, very good, Mr. Murphy," Dr. Richards said as he turned back to Dillon. "Can you tell me the last thing you remember doing? Before today? Before you woke up?"

Dillon looked at his kids as if to force his mind to recollect something that included the two teenagers.

"I don't know," Dillon said.

Rebecca stared back at her father, and tears started to form again. Her heart sank almost as deep as it had when her dad was in the coma. How could he not remember? How could he not know who his own kids were?

Overcome with emotion, Rebecca stood up. "Daddy, please! Stop this. It's me, your baby girl! Rebecca! Daddy, you have to remember . . . you have to remember us . . ."

Rebecca fell to the floor. Her knees hit the ground, and she moaned in pain. The impact felt good. It took away some of the misery she was suffering from her father's lack of memory.

Jacob got down beside Rebecca and asked if she was okay. She had been through so much. He was scared for her, though he was thankful they were already in the hospital.

Rebecca nodded at her brother's question and got up in a squatting position. Dr. Richards and Jacob helped her back into the chair, and Dr. Richards called one of the nurses to attend to her.

Jacob watched his sister leave the room with the nurse. He didn't know whether to go with her or stay and continue with the progress, or lack thereof, that the doctor was making. Jacob thought about the fact that Rebecca was with a nurse and justified his feelings to stay with his father.

"Jacob, are you okay to continue with me here?" Dr. Richards asked.

"Yes, sir. Can I ask you one question though?"

"Of course. What's on your mind?"

"Is this . . . normal? Have you seen this before? I mean, have you ever seen someone wake up from a coma and not know who or where they are?"

41

Dr. Richards hesitated as if unsure how to answer the question. He kept his tone low once again. "Well, Jacob, to be honest, many different things can happen with a coma, and this isn't a daily occurrence for me. Some comatose people who wake up do not speak as quickly as your father has. It can take weeks or months, and many times the person is never the same. Every case is different. The trauma to the head plays a major factor, as does the length of time the patient is in the coma. I can't tell you much for certain until I get more information." Dr. Richards looked at Jacob, seeing that he wanted more concrete answers. "I do know you are concerned, and as I told you already, I promise to be as honest and forthcoming as I can. The best thing you can do is give your father time." Dr. Richards smiled insincerely at being questioned when he really didn't have any answers yet.

Jacob sat down in his chair. Dr. Richards turned back to Dillon, formulating his questions in hopes of finding out more about his current state.

"Mr. Murphy. How do you feel right now?"

"What do you mean?" Dillon looked confused. "I feel thirsty."

"Okay. I think that has been fairly evident with the amount of water you've been drinking." Dr. Richards grinned. "Tell me, Mr. Murphy. When you look around here in this room, when you look at your son sitting here—" Dr. Richards waved his hand slightly toward Jacob. "What feelings come to you?"

Dillon seemed puzzled by the question, but he did notice that he felt something. It wasn't *nothing*. He felt a pain in his stomach, and his head was pounding. He couldn't put it into words; he didn't know what to say. Dr. Richards and Jacob looked at him intently, waiting for a response. Dillon closed his eyes and let his emotions cross through his mind.

He was angry, because he didn't know what the hell was going on. He was frustrated, because there were two kids who seemed so desperate for him to remember them. He recalled being a child, and that made him smile.

Jacob watched as his father's face articulated the feelings he was rationalizing in his mind. Dillon was smiling when he opened his eyes.

"I would say I'm feeling a lot of feelings."

"Well, that is a very good start," Dr. Richards said with a cautious laugh. "Mr. Murphy, I'm going to ask you some elementary questions, and I want you to answer as best you can. If you don't know, tell me that you don't know. Don't try to guess, because it can mislead me. Are you ready?"

"Yes," Dillon said, nodding.

Jacob watched as Dr. Richards asked him simple questions, like "What's two plus two?" and "What color is my hair?" His father answered them all correctly except for the question about food. He didn't seem to remember what sushi was.

Hours passed, and Jacob grew tired. He watched as his father was politely interrogated by other doctors, including the cute psychologist they had met on the day of the accident. She looked more tantalizing than Jacob remembered, but he still didn't care enough to think about it for more than a few moments. Her presence brought on a Pavlovian response.

Rebecca returned and explained that she was dehydrated and tired and needed a nap and some fluids. Jacob's head became heavy as he sat there waiting for the next set of doctors to barge into the room and take over like crime investigators at a murder scene. His eyes started to feel like they had been open for days and just wanted to shut for a few minutes so he could rest and be ready for the expedition that awaited him. Jacob heeded their request, and in a matter of seconds, he was asleep sitting up, his head bobbing.

He awoke almost instantly, or so it felt. A hand was on his shoulder, and a face was peering at him, repeating his name.

"Jacob?" Dr. Richards lifted his hand when he saw Jacob's eyes open. "I'm sorry, but it's getting late, and I'm set to leave for the night. I do have some news I want to share with you and your sister, and I was wondering if you wanted some answers before I go." He looked tired. He had been there on and off with Dillon for the last fifteen hours, well past his shift requirements. It was dark outside, and the clock on the wall read 10:30. Jacob looked at his father and saw him fast asleep. The lamp beside his bed shadowed his sunken eyes. His father was as skinny as Rebecca.

"Of course. Yeah. I want to know." Jacob felt himself perk up and realized that whatever he was dreaming of was no longer available in his memory.

Rebecca was sitting beside him, wide awake.

"I told you I'm going to be honest with you," Dr. Richards began. "Here is what I know based on the results of the fMRI and the initial tests we ran on your father this afternoon." He tried to give the siblings equal attention as he spoke. "Your father, as you can tell, is suffering from a form of memory loss. Before you tell me this is an obvious conclusion, there's more to what

I'm about to say. From what we can see, it looks like your father is suffering from retrograde amnesia."

Dr. Richards looked at the kids' reactions. "Amnesia" was a word that seemed to only exist in movies and comic books. Dr. Richards received two sets of raised eyebrows and a look that urged him to continue on.

"Retrograde amnesia is the loss of more recent memories while still keeping distant memories. There is no set amount of time that this type of amnesia can be tracked back to. It varies from patient to patient. In this case, the older the memory, the less chance there is for it to become disrupted in his mind. That's why your father was able to recall his thoughts from his childhood. It seems that is as recent as he can currently remember."

Jacob asked the question that Rebecca was going to blurt out. "So, how long does it take for this to wear off? Could he wake up tomorrow and remember everything?"

"Good question. The brain is a funny thing. He could wake up tomorrow and remember everything, yes, but it is unlikely. There's a good chance he may never get his memory back." Dr. Richards kept watching for a reaction. Instead, he got two sets of eyes throwing darts. "On the positive side, your father was able to remember short-term memories, like the matching game you watched him play. He was also able to remember what color his popsicle was three hours after. These are very positive signs. Now, what is important to note here is that your father seems to have retained his procedural memory. Unfortunately, he's struggling with his declarative memory."

The confused look on Jacob and Rebecca's faces meant further explanation, "Procedural memory refers to things like skills and abilities. Like remembering how to ride a bike, although it will be some time before your dad will be able to do that, if at all.

"Declarative memory, which is the recollection of previous experiences and facts, is the memory function that your father is having trouble with. He cannot recall his name or the city he lives in."

"So how does he remember how to speak?" Rebecca asked, feeling foolish. "If he lost his memory, how does he know how to make a sentence?"

"That's a fair question, and it relates back to what I was speaking of. The skills your father learned should still be functional. That includes his speech and his ability to read and write. Many times, people with this type of amnesia do not believe they have these abilities, because they don't remember them, but when they try learning them again, they find that they are very quick to regain that skill."

Dr. Richards paused to stifle a yawn. He apologized for the tired response and told the kids that he needed rest and that they should get some too. There would be more work to do the following day.

As Dr. Richards left, the siblings sat next to each other, finally able to unwind in the comfy chairs. Jacob felt overwhelmed by what had transpired, but at the same time, serenity fell over him. His father was in better shape than he had been any other day since the accident. Even though his dad didn't remember him or Rebecca, he was awake and talking.

CHAPTER
ELEVEN

Jacob found himself standing in front of his school. He felt uninhibited as he walked into the university entranceway. His hair was perfectly in place, and his smile seemed to penetrate the eyes of every female he passed. He strode confidently down the hallway to his biology class, which was just about to begin.

Jacob was sexy. He wore his tight blue jeans, which were ripped at the thigh, and a hologram shirt that changed color depending on the direction someone looked at him. He was wearing his father's cologne—an expensive bottle from Paris that had an oaky smell to it with a hint of citrus. In a previous history class, he had studied a flower called the Youtan Poluo, which was said to bloom once every 3,000 years and represented the sitting of Buddha, symbolizing purity and divine birth. Jacob hated that class, but right now, he was a Youtan Poluo, blooming for the first time in his life, and everyone around him bore witness.

If Jacob's head were any more swollen in that moment, he would not have been able to get it through the doorway to the classroom. He walked past the students all the way to the front of the class. Girls stared in awe as he glided by, and his male classmates exposed a shade of jealousy on their faces. Jacob Murphy was a man, and he was about to show it. He walked right up to Shyla Winters, who was pulling her books out of her backpack. She beheld his presence with a shocked yet excited look.

"Jacob?"

Jacob put his finger on her lips to feign shushing her. It was not a moment to speak. The class watched as Jacob took Shyla with amicable force, gazed longingly into her green eyes, brushed her curly hair out of her face, and spoke softly into her left ear. "I'm going to kiss you now in front of all these people. But I don't care, Shyla. I love you."

Jacob held her head with his hand, closed his eyes, and moved in to kiss her. Their lips met, and Jacob thought he could taste her strawberry shortcake lip balm. The kissing became more passionate by the second.

As Jacob's lips Velcroed themselves to Shyla's, a hand rested on his shoulder. He heard his name being called, and the hand gently tugged at him, as if to gain his attention. Jacob didn't care, and he kept osculating his girl.

The hand shook his shoulder a little harder. Jacob's eyes opened, and when they did, it wasn't Shyla he saw but her father, Jonathon Winters. He was in the hospital room, watching Jacob caress the pillow that represented his daughter, although Jonathon was unaware of that fact. Embarrassed, Jacob slowly lowered the pillow as he eyed the person who had awoken him from such a splendid dream.

Jonathon jerked his head twice to tell his young acquaintance that he wanted to speak to him in a spot that wouldn't wake anyone. Jacob stood up slowly and checked Rebecca's face to see if she was still asleep, or if she knew what was going on. From the look on her and the drool that had pooled on the arm of the big comfy reclining chair, Jacob deduced she was still asleep.

He adjusted her blanket, so it covered her completely, then walked out to see the man who had caught him assaulting his pillow. Jonathon looked tired, and Jacob wondered what time it was. He looked at the clock in the hall, which read 3:17 a.m. Jacob looked at Jonathon, who was well-dressed for the middle of the night, and waited for him to say something.

"Jacob. How is your father doing?" Jonathon asked politely. "I heard he's speaking now. I thought you were going to tell me when that happened."

"Uh, I don't remember you asking me to tell you. Sorry about that." Jacob was shocked by the question. "Dad is doing okay. He doesn't really know what's going on, and right now, to be honest, he doesn't remember much."

"You mean about the accident?" Jonathon inquired.

"No, sir. He doesn't remember much about . . . anything."

"Really? About anything at all?" Jonathon frowned, his hands curling into fists at his side. "How could he not remember anything? Fuck!"

"Mr. Winters, why are you getting upset? Dr. Richards said he could still get his memory back." Jacob was baffled by Mr. Winters' obvious displeasure.

Jonathon backpedaled from his initial reaction. "I apologize, Jacob. You're right. I don't know what came over me. It's late—or very early—and I haven't had much sleep. I assume you haven't either. Look, do you need anything? Any money?"

Jonathon pulled out his wallet. He reached inside, pulled out a credit chip, and aimed it at Jacob. Jacob thought about taking it. He could use money to go to the PAstREAM building. But deep down, he felt like taking any sort payout for his own personal enjoyment from Shyla's dad was not something that would reflect well on him. Jacob motioned toward the chip and gently pushed Jonathon's hand away.

"I don't want your money, Mr. Winters. But thanks."

Jonathon put the chip back in his wallet.

"What about time at PAstREAM? I can get you in quickly with our TTN account." Jonathon's bribes had no end.

Jacob hesitated. He desperately wanted to use the PAstREAM device. "I . . . I shouldn't. But thanks."

Jacob opened the door and started walking back into the room when Jonathon, who wasn't done talking, grabbed him by the arm. "Jacob, is there any way I could get an interview with your father? People are concerned. We can show them how he has no memory. It might be important for others to see that."

"What are you going to ask him? What his first day after he woke up was like? I'll tell you now, it wasn't very exciting. Please, sir, just leave him be. You can come back and see him when he wakes up in the morning, but that's it. No cameras, no insinuating questions, nothing but the friend that he needs right now." Jacob felt out of place telling a grown-up the rules of engagement with his father, but he had to draw the line somewhere. He thought of how proud Rebecca would be of his stance against the man she didn't trust. Jacob felt differently about him now too. Things about Jonathon weren't quite as they seemed.

CHAPTER
TWELVE

Christmas came and went for the Murphy family. It did not feel like a time to celebrate other than to give thanks that Dillon was alive and awake.

Though it was painful and uncertain, Jacob and Rebecca were appreciative that their dad was now out of the hospital and back at home with them. The hospital bills had been getting more than expensive, and Jonathon had decided that his friend was capable of moving forward without the added cost.

For Christmas, Jacob gave Rebecca a new tablet capable of dictating a person's current thoughts when a wire was attached to the user's temple. When she used it on Jacob, Rebecca couldn't understand the jumble of words that ended up on the screen.

It was just another brain function invention that was taking over the tech world. There were legalities over these types of technologies, but companies pressed on, doing whatever they could to be the leaders in the industry.

As the weeks passed, the police continued to visit. They wanted to question Dillon about the accident and the events leading up to it, but getting any answers out of him was impossible.

It was an extremely difficult time for Jacob and Rebecca, having to deal with the loss of their mother and their father's recuperation. It was all the more painful having no answers as to why their parents' car had crashed. They'd filed a report and applied for their mom's life-insurance claim, but they were awaiting approval. The insurance company said they were still determining whether it was an accident, attempted murder, or something else entirely. They had no suspects, other than the company that supplied the work vehicle. The company vehemently denied any responsibility. Recently, authorities told Jacob that no one even knew where the car was anymore. It had gone missing, and they had been unsuccessful in tracing it.

The only arrest came shortly after the incident. The employee who had performed the review of the vehicle prior to Dillon getting the keys was detained for several days. There was no proof of any wrongdoing, and he was later released.

* * *

Rebecca stood next to the stove while her father sat on a barstool at the kitchen counter, waiting patiently for her to finish making supper. The beef stew would warm their bellies on what seemed like a cold, dark, never-ending January day.

Dillon had made a lot of progress, and he was starting to feel comfortable with his surroundings. Though he didn't remember it, hearing that this was his apartment and that this was his life didn't seem so bad. He was surprisingly happy. He had to report to work once per week as he prepared himself to continue his normal life. A desk job awaited him when he was cleared to return full-time. He also reported weekly to the hospital for testing and to see a psychiatrist.

Dillon felt fortunate. He had two kids who cared about him, and he was starting to care for them too. He had seen them do so much to make him feel like he belonged somewhere. He felt loved, and even though he didn't really remember what love felt like, he knew this was it. Rebecca was back in school and was doing well, and Jacob, although quiet about how classes were going, seemed to be settling into his routine too.

As Rebecca was turning off the stove and stirring the pot one last time, Jacob was in his room, deep in thought. They had brought their father home from the hospital one month ago to the day. Jacob still couldn't stop thinking about his father and what it was like living with a stranger who he'd known all his life. The irony made him chuckle.

He thought again about just letting go for an hour. About asking Mr. Winters for an hour at the PAstREAM facility. Maybe he should have taken him up on one of his offers.

Then it dawned on him.

Jacob soared off his bed, ran down the hallway, and slid on the hardwood floor with his socks as he got into the kitchen. Rebecca turned to see why he was acting like a doofus. Jacob was squeezing his head between his hands. It looked like he was trying to keep whatever information he had in his brain locked in tight, so he wouldn't lose his train of thought. His lips were moving, but nothing came out.

"Do you have something to say to us?" Rebecca asked.

"Do you see a lightbulb glowing over my head? Because I just had the most amazing idea!" Jacob said, ecstatic.

"Well, what is it?" Dillon asked.

"Okay, well, Dad, you may not remember this, even though you did a story about it on TTN, but . . ." Jacob hesitated for effect.

"But what?" Rebecca couldn't wait for his idea. "Just say it, you moron!" She thought he was going to say something stupid again, like the idea he'd had about topless sandals that would stick to the bottom of a person's foot with an adhesive. They would have a thin layer of memory foam in the middle and another thin layer on the bottom with rubber grip. When a person wore them, it would look like they were barefoot. Jacob's problem was that he didn't know how to get the prototype off his foot. The adhesive worked so well that it stuck for three days before a layer of skin had to be removed. Rebecca hoped it wasn't another one of *those* ideas.

"What if we took Dad to the PAstREAM facility without the doctors knowing so he could watch the important parts of his life? You know, to get to know himself again. He could see what his life was like with us as kids and with Mom—what his life was like before the accident! What do you think?" Jacob looked wide-eyed at both of them.

To him, it was the best idea he'd ever had, and he wondered why it had taken so long for him to put the two together: one who couldn't remember and the other that helped a person remember. It seemed so obvious. That is, until Rebecca put a different spin on it.

"Well, yeah, that's a great idea. But how would it work for Dad? He can't remember anything. How could they pull memories out of his mind if he doesn't even remember them happening? God, you are such an idiot sometimes, Jacob." Rebecca looked at him with dismay, as though she'd just won an argument that never happened.

"Okay, good point. But Dr. Richards said he could end up recalling his memories at some point. It's a possibility, which means the memories may still be in there, but his brain just can't connect the pathways to the information. It's worth trying, sis."

Rebecca nodded in agreement. Jacob was right; it was worth an attempt.

Dillon looked confused and frustrated. "If you're going to experiment on me, shouldn't I know what you're talking about? Maybe I don't want to get involved in this idea."

"Dad, PAstREAM might help you remember. It takes your memories of the past and replays them for you to relive again. If you stared at another woman on your wedding night, you would see that other woman and which part of her body you were checking out!" Jacob was excited to live vicariously through his father. At least his dad would get to use the PAstREAM device.

Just as quickly as the idea had dawned on Jacob, another reality hit him just as hard. How were they going to pay for such an experiment? A few hours in the device was moderately affordable, but this could take days or more. Jacob and Rebecca would have to find the money and figure out which memories their father should relive.

Rebecca stopped plating the stew. "I'll start researching important dates."

CHAPTER
THIRTEEN

Money. That was the name of the game. When Jillian died and Dillon didn't appear to be coming out of his coma, Jacob was given limited access to his parents' bank accounts—the cash flow, the line of credit, and the investments. It was all too dense of brush for Jacob to axe through at first, especially considering he was currently failing his financing degree.

Jacob was eighteen and was a legal dependent, but he never had access to this type of cash. Nor was he capable of accessing it entirely, now that his dad was awake.

Although it would wipe out most of his dad's investment portfolio, he had immediately thought about buying a Ferrari. An old red one, with paddle-shifters on the steering wheel and a CD player for his old-school collection.

Dillon had an old compact disc player that he kept packed away, and when Jacob was old enough, he pulled it out of storage and hooked it up for him. The old music that his father listened to was soothing to Jacob's ears. It was also entertaining, because the music from his father's generation didn't have advertising in it like modern music did. Dillon told him about how music became too commercialized. The government had fined record companies after a scandal that involved labels meeting behind closed doors and making rules about song lengths and what types of lyrics they were going to push.

Song lengths had decreased significantly over time. The whistleblowers who were on trial explained that they had an agreement with other record companies to keep the length of the songs at a specified average, a factor that benefited the corporate titans in a twofold system.

The first, they'd explained, was that the more songs they could play in an hour or a day, the more digital uploads there were, because more songs were being listened to in a shorter span. The cost of pay-per-month music sites had more than tripled in recent years.

The second benefit was the advertising that had found its way into the lyrics. Artists were paid handsomely if they dropped the name of a company or a product into their music. Record companies started mandating which advertisements would appear in the lyrics and taking the advertising dollars for themselves. It was a difficult battle between the artists and their possessors and was a major contributor in the corruption becoming public.

Jacob's dad wasn't immune to the circumstances that plagued the music industry either. Dillon was part of a business that was also looking to make money any way it could. Jacob recalled seeing his dad debating with his mom about being in similar situations when it came to what he reported on.

Jacob continued to manage the finances even after his father woke up from the coma, at least for the time being. He pulled up his father's bank account information and forwarded the data from his tablet to the wood-framed screen that hung on the wall over the fireplace, replacing the image of a painting that was displayed when the screen wasn't used as a television.

"Right now, you're sitting with a good chunk of cash in your account. You have some investments, which your financial advisor told me no one should touch until you're fifty-five. Apparently, we're planning to retire then." Jacob winked at his dad.

Rebecca had more pressing issues in mind regarding the money. "Who cares? We just need to make sure we have enough to take Dad to watch his memories."

Jacob stared at Rebecca as he shook his head with a furrowed brow and a sarcastic grin. "Sis, we don't want to waste too much money. If Dad is going to be reliving entire days or any long chunks of time, it'll start getting expensive. This is our future we're spending." Jacob winked again at his father.

"This is serious," Rebecca said. "If it works, let's not worry about how much it's going to cost." She felt money should be no object for such an undertaking. This could help their father remember.

"Now hold on a damn minute, kids," Dillon said. "This is my money we're talking about here!"

"Dad, first of all, don't call us kids. We have names. I don't want to have that conversation again," Jacob said. "Second, your concept of money is still a work in progress. Do you not trust me?" Jacob looked at him, his right eyebrow lifted.

"Very well," Dillon said through gritted teeth. "But you have limited access yourself at the moment, and this is only temporary until I get control back. And for your information, no matter how old you are, you'll always be my kids."

"Touché." Jacob pointed at his dad, making a gun with his finger and thumb. "Okay, what if we looked at it as if we were going to spend a good chunk of money on a nice vacation together? I'd say we could start with . . ." Jacob punched numbers into the calculator on the screen. ". . . forty hours in the PAstREAM device."

Rebecca thought for a moment. "That's a great start! Now, how do we prioritize what Dad watches and for how long?"

"Well . . ." Jacob said, thinking intensely, "you started the list. Let's go over it and decide which ones make the most sense and put time limits on them."

Rebecca looked as though she wanted to piggyback on that thought. "I also think we should do it in chronological order, so it doesn't confuse him. I mean, so you don't get confused, Dad."

"Don't you think I should try it out first to see if I actually do remember anything?" Dillon asked. "I don't want you to go through all this trouble only to discover that PAstREAM won't work for me."

"That's why you're the oldest one here. Good call, Dad. So, when should we test this theory out, then?" Jacob asked.

Rebecca smiled at him. "You think Mr. Winters can get us in quickly?"

"I can almost guarantee it!" Jacob became animated. He was going to get his chance to see how PAstREAM worked firsthand. His excitement turned to fear almost immediately. What if this didn't work for his father?

They would be back to square one and would have to consider that their father's memory may never return.

CHAPTER
FOURTEEN

Jacob sat in his three-year-old Honda Prelude. It was a remake of a car that had been in circulation in the late twentieth century. There was a certain panache about the old school that inspired him. The compact discs, the old cars. The feeling of what life was like at the beginning of the century. How amazing it would have been to live in the olden days when people received letters in a mailbox or carried a wallet full of plastic cards and paper bills. It was a time when families were allowed to have as many children as they wanted without a cap. The middle class still existed, and a person's privacy meant something, unlike the constant feeling of being tracked or monitored wherever a person went.

Jacob had spoken with Jonathon about getting his dad into PAstREAM right away, and it went over far better than Jacob had hoped. Mr. Winters had told him that there was usually a three- to five-day wait to get an appointment unless they waited in the standby line but that he could get them booked in right away. The only odd request was that Jonathon wanted to keep Dillon's profile a secret. Jonathon sent Jacob a chip with his account information and told him to make sure not to use his father's information or fingerprints anywhere, because there was a future story to be had. Jacob obliged, happy to get his father in.

As the electric car started and Jacob backed out of his stall, he looked at the passengers inside. Rebecca was sitting beside him, playing with the presets on the touchscreen. She was able to monitor the body temperatures of the passengers and adjust the seat vents.

Fortunately for Jacob, this car was not voice-activated like his father's last vehicle.

His dad was buckled in and was mashing buttons on the screen in the back, trying to select a video to watch.

Rebecca spoke quietly to her brother while their dad fiddled with the on-screen commands. "Jacob, I'm feeling extremely anxious about this right now for some reason. I'm scared."

"I know, sis. I feel the same way."

"If it doesn't work, it doesn't work," Dillon said from the back seat. "Listen, I have an idea."

Rebecca looked back at him. "Great. Let's hear it, Dad."

"I was thinking about what memory I should start with. I know you both made a list, but I'd like to pick the first one."

Jacob stared curiously between the road and his father in the rear-view mirror.

"I remember most of my childhood, but what about starting where I don't remember, when I was an adolescent? I don't know anything about myself past twelve or thirteen years of age. I really want to know who I was as an older teen, like you both are now. I think it would help me figure out who I am today."

Rebecca didn't like the idea. Selfishly, she wanted him to start at a time when he was married, and she and Jacob were born. She wanted him to remember and learn about what she was like. She missed her father so much and just wanted him to be back to normal. From her perspective, his life started when he was married and had a family, not when he was a teenager trying to find out who he was.

"But Dad, don't you want to know about your life and about us?" she asked, unable to hide her irritation.

"Of course, I do. You said we would have forty hours of this, and you're also the one who said I should start from the beginning and work my way through. I'm not looking to watch my entire teenage experience. Just give me an hour or two."

The car fell silent.

As the silver Prelude pulled into the parking garage at the PAstREAM building, Jacob felt uneasy but excited. They were close to finding out if this idea was going to work. As the car pulled into the parking machine, they got out, and Jacob pressed his thumb on the scanner. The car lifted into a parking spot on the sixth level. Each level held what looked like a hundred cars neatly placed beside one another. When it was time to leave, a robotic hand would pick out the car and lift it out of the sardine-can parking lot, putting it in the exit lane and forwarding the receipt to their device.

Jacob, Rebecca, and Dillon walked on the moving conveyor belt that ran to where all the patrons were congregating to get to the entrance of the massive building.

The walking conveyor and an escalator took them up a level and into a giant, dimly lit hallway. Security guards watched the people coming in and ID'd anyone who the facial recognition either couldn't pick up or identified as being too young. The government had originally set the age restriction to eighteen years old; however, PAstREAM had donated a large sum of money to government research, and the age limit was dropped to sixteen in all of the facilities around the country.

The conveyor pushed them deeper into the building. A series of rather magnificently immense paintings and portraits were organized methodically along the wall. Dillon marveled at the size of the pictures. He stared at one that drew his attention. The portrait was of a young man holding a goblet. It was the largest of the portraits, and for some reason, he couldn't stop looking at it. The young man's eyes seemed to follow him as he moved along the conveyor. The picture began changing as he shuttled past it, the silver goblet morphing into a knight in shining armor. The young man had been a peaceful-looking boy, but he transformed into a dragon, breathing fire at the knight. The knight's shield blocked what would have been the final blow of flaming death. It was like a dream turning into a nightmare.

Dillon's stomach started to churn. He had no idea where he was other than what his kids had told him and the news story they'd played of him explaining what PAstREAM did.

The conveyor kept moving, and a woman's voice spoke over the public-address system in the long hallway.

"Welcome to PAstREAM." The voice sounded soothing and immediately calmed Dillon's nerves. He looked at his kids, who were amazed at the visual stimuli they were experiencing.

Each painting transformed from something beautiful or peaceful into something troubling or even disturbing. As they passed, the paintings on the walls faded out of sight, and a large projection appeared in front of them in augmented reality, portraying a 3D movie that appeared to be someone's memory. They saw a scenario unfolding from the eyes of the memory's owner as they watched a young woman swimming in the ocean. It was a beautiful, sunny day on an empty beach drowning in white sand. The sounds of the waves echoed in the giant hallway.

A tranquil feeling washed over the Murphys as they watched what was unfolding. Dillon imagined himself behind the set of eyes, relaxing on some forgotten seashore.

The person who owned the memory looked left and right, confirming that he or she and the girl on the screen were the only ones for miles on the shoreline. The person watched the girl in the water. She was wearing a baby-blue bathing suit while the waves crashed upon her lightly tanned skin. Her dry blonde hair dampened as the spray from the waves misted her face. She was knee high in the water and looked back at the person staring at her.

Dillon felt like she was staring right at him.

The girl stretched out her hand, waving her fingers toward herself, urging the viewer to join her. She swam a little farther out into the open water. The memory's gaze did not leave her. The owner of the memory followed her every move and started moving toward the woman, walking into the surf.

Dillon didn't realize this augmented reality was moving along with them on the conveyor. He was too entrenched in what he was watching.

The owner of the memory's gaze looked down at their own feet directly underneath. The waves were cuddling the toes that sank into the soft, wet sand. Then the person in the memory peered back up to see his prey treading water.

Suddenly, the gaze moved quickly to the right of the woman—a tense change from the passive movements to which the crowd on the conveyor had become accustomed.

A long grey fin stood intimidatingly out of the water.

The crowd gasped.

The owner of the memory started running into the water, yelling to the woman.

The crowd was anxious.

Dillon felt fear in his heart.

Water splashed everywhere, and the memory became difficult to see. The person swam deeper, getting closer to the woman. The eyes made it to her. She was screaming and moving toward the outstretched hand while looking around hurriedly. The fin was nowhere to be seen. The hand was now pulling the woman toward the shore.

The people on the conveyor cheered, encouraging those in the memory to swim faster.

The vision kept looking between the girl and the shore. At one glance, the fin was back, and it was within striking distance.

The people on the conveyor screamed for the couple to swim faster, hoping to force a predetermined result.

The swimmers' speed increased as they made it to shallow water. The person in the memory looked back once more and saw that the fin had slowed and started back to deeper water.

The crowd was overjoyed.

The projection cut to black, and three-dimensional words floated in the air: "WHAT'S YOUR MEMORY?"

It was amazing. Jacob and Rebecca looked at each other in awe. Was that real? Was that someone's actual memory? Jacob instantly started thinking of all the crazy things that had happened in his life, like the fight he was in during his graduating year of high school. The winning basket he hit at his high school basketball tournament. The first time he slept over at Shy's when her parents weren't home. Jacob's mind salivated at the thought.

"What are you thinking about, Jake?" Rebecca asked.

"Ahh, the shark. That was crazy, hey? Do you think that was real?" Jacob avoided the real answer to her question. That was private. "Dad, how pumped are you right now? You're going to be reliving a memory, except it will seem like you're seeing it for the first time. That's so weird and awesome. I'm so jealous right now. Maybe you can give me one hour. Just one hour.

What do you say? I would love you forever!" Jacob was becoming addicted to something he hadn't even tried yet.

"Jake," Rebecca snapped her fingers in her brother's face. "Let's focus on one thing at a time here. Let's make sure this is going to work for Dad first before you start thinking about your own desires."

As the conveyor ended, they reached a stationary section where two more moving walkways branched off. A sign directed the crowd to the possible destinations. The left sign read "Main Lobby—Access to Hotel (If Staying at Hotel, Check-In to PAstREAM Here)" and the right sign read "PAstREAM Check-in and Standby."

The Murphy family traveled right to the check-in section, as Jonathon had told them to do. The conveyor began traveling slightly uphill. People started to run to get ahead. Dillon, Jacob, and Rebecca stayed where they were on the conveyor. Jacob was egging his family on to get moving, but the majority of the party did not want to join the rush of people who scraped by to get to the check-in.

"They can't be having us wait in a massive line, can they?" Rebecca asked. "It doesn't seem like good business sense to do that. No one likes waiting."

Patience was not a virtue for the current generation. They wanted everything right away, and they typically got it.

"We are scheduled for eight hours starting almost forty-five minutes from now," Jacob said. "Mr. Winters said we should be about half an hour early. Looks like some people just can't wait." He fully understood the ambition of those plowing forward.

As the incline leveled out, they saw the check-in area ahead. There had been no natural light since leaving the parking garage, and Dillon imagined there weren't any windows inside the building at all other than the hotel. With no view of the outside world, he was starting to feel like PAstREAM was a world of its own.

Digital screens of advertisements littered the walls around the giant entrance. Dillon wondered what the cost was to be on the thirty-second rotation.

As the Murphys walked off the conveyor, they saw row upon row of tellers who were ready to take names and payment. There were more than enough slots for those who had an appointment to avoid any chance of a major lineup. There was, however, a lineup of those patrons who had run up the conveyor past Jacob and his family. They were now waiting in line under an overhead sign that read "Standby Only (No Appointment Required)." The running now made sense.

Dillon walked up to one of the empty tellers, but Rebecca yanked him back. "Let Jacob check us in, Dad."

Jacob stood slightly ahead of his father and sister as he approached the kiosk, looking into the eyes of the woman behind the glass. She stared back at him.

"Good afternoon. Welcome to PAstREAM," she said from behind the window. Dillon leaned in behind his son. Something was off about the way the woman greeted them, and he wanted a closer look. He couldn't get past her movements.

Dillon took a few steps to the side and looked at the teller next to theirs. The exact same girl was behind the window, waiting for a customer. He walked over to the next teller, and it was exactly the same girl as the others.

"What the hell is going on? There's an army of identical women running the place!" Dillon said, shocked and amazed.

"Dad, calm down." Rebecca said. She didn't want attention drawn to them. "They're just robots. Let's just stand back until Jacob's done." She grabbed her dad's hand and brought him back to a reasonable distance behind Jacob. Although she didn't fully trust Jonathon, the idea of keeping her dad's presence as low key as possible was fine by her. Dillon was almost unrecognizable in his current state. His long hair, beard and gaunt face gave him almost a hippy look.

"Please place your thumb or chip onto the reader," the teller said.

Jacob pulled out the chip that Jonathon had given him and scanned it.

"Thank you. You're cleared for access. Please place your finger on the scanner to pay." The girl behind the counter smiled with some effort. Jacob thought her levers needed oiling, and it made him chuckle to himself.

After scanning the payment, the robot continued speaking to Jacob about the rules before explaining the final step. "Please choose an entrance. If you are familiar with PAstREAM, continue to the glass doorways under the central lobby signage. If this is your first visit or you need a reminder on how to use the PAstREAM device, please use the last three entrances at the end labeled 'To Orientation.' Guests may accompany the user through either of the two sections. Enjoy your stay here at PAstREAM."

Jacob walked past his father and sister. "Follow me."

On the wall above dozens of glass doorways was a giant digital clock and a sign stating "Central Lobby." To the right of it, where Jacob was leading his family members, were three similar glass doorways with a sign stating "To Orientation—New Users and Those Who Desire a Refresher."

Jacob stuck his hand out to his father and handed Jonathon's PAstREAM chip to him. "Before I forget, you might need this to use the memory machine. You can stick it to your finger."

Dillon took the chip and thanked his son with a nod.

"I guess we should go to the orientation before Dad's time starts," Rebecca stated.

As they walked to the automatic glass doorway under the orientation signage, they noticed another moving walkway. They looked at one another without saying anything, trying to figure out who was going to be the first to step onto yet another conveyor. Rebecca chose to be that person. Dillon and Jacob followed suit. The doors closed behind them.

Dillon had enjoyed the memory that played on the first conveyor as they came from the parking garage and wondered what glory awaited them in this one. Then again, he thought, maybe this was just a short ride with no frills. The company already had a chunk of his money and attention.

"So, what happens to us now? I mean, do we just carry on with Dad?" Rebecca asked, confused as to what she and her brother were supposed to do at this point.

"The teller said we can go to the orientation and central lobby even if we're not using PAstREAM. I'm sure they have a waiting area," Jacob said. "If not, we can always leave for a bit and come back once we find out if it works for Dad or not. I don't know if I want to sit here for eight hours."

Dillon noticed a light-blue glow up ahead. "Look at that. What do you think that is?"

Shrugs and raised brows were telltale signs that neither teen had the answer.

The three of them waited for what was fast approaching.

In a matter of seconds, the walls and the ceiling displayed blue water as if they were in a walkthrough aquarium. Dillon was awestruck. He had never seen anything quite like it, at least not that he could remember. Through the water to the left and the right, he could see the others who had entered in through the neighboring sets of doors. They looked cloudy through the glass, appearing almost ghostlike.

Dillon looked straight ahead. The path curved and dipped, so it was impossible to see how far they had to go or what was waiting up ahead.

As the conveyor moved them deeper into whatever cavernous belly they were destined for, a number of sharks, including a hammerhead and a great white, glided overhead. Jacob jumped up and slapped the glass to see if he could get their attention, but it didn't work.

After his initial amazement and seeing the awe in Rebecca's face, Dillon wondered if sharks were perhaps a theme at PAstREAM.

A school of beautifully colored fish swam to the left, causing Rebecca to gasp in wonderment. All kinds of sea life started to appear around them. Giant turtles and manta rays, jellyfish, and even a massive purple octopus. An orca whale swam by with fish sticking to its underside. The family members were captivated once again.

Jacob thought he saw a fish glitch ever so slightly, which made him realize this had to be another form of augmented reality.

Is anything real here? he wondered.

The conveyor bent to the right, and Rebecca continued to watch the underwater pageantry. The bright blue was abruptly met with a hit of black, cloudy water, like the start of a lightning storm rolling in on a hot and humid summer day.

In the black water that hugged the glass around them, the shapes of crying faces appeared. Dillon was starting to feel nervous. He watched his kids as their expressions turned from jubilation to utter despair.

"Why do they turn it so negative? This was a joyful passage, and now it's freaking me out," Rebecca said without taking her eyes off the dark water.

Dillon couldn't figure out what PAstREAM was trying to invoke in their patrons. Maybe this was some perverse way for them to demonstrate the emotions that he would surely experience while watching his own memories, feelings of happiness, joy, anger, and sadness.

Dillon grew concerned about what he was going to see and how he was going to feel watching his memories. A small part of him hoped this experiment would not work.

The blackness became blinding. Darkness overtook the passengers. They could barely see their hands in front of their faces, other than in the flinty glow of the black LED lights shooting up from the floor.

When a white light appeared ahead, it looked like the ride might finally be ending. As the conveyor took them to the light, the sound of running water grew with it. The moving walkway dipped, and they saw water pouring from the ceiling at the end, like they were headed toward the edge of a cave, ending at a waterfall.

"Is that real water, you think? Can't be. We'd be soaked going through it," Jacob said, answering his own question.

Dillon saw the outline of people walking on the other side of the pouring liquid. As they approached the water, he realized the moving walkway went directly through it. They would have to make a choice. Either start walking back against the movement of the conveyor or walk through the water that poured in front of the exit ahead.

Dillon looked at his kids, who didn't seem as worried as he was. He was going to have to step through the liquid wall, which looked, sounded, and even smelled real due to the mist in the air. He was going to hold his breath just in case. He felt a lot more optimistic about going through it than staying in the darkness that currently surrounded them.

Dillon walked into the wall of water. He emerged on the other side dry, finding himself in an enormous auditorium. There was no actual water; it had been another illusion. He realized in this newfound life of his that he should not believe everything he saw.

Jacob and Rebecca were right behind him.

"Can we do that again?" Jacob joked.

"Look at this place. It's surreal." Dillon's vocabulary had improved immensely since he had started reading books on his tablet. The words and pronunciations were still in his head; he just had to relearn a lot of the more progressive verbiage that he had used so profoundly while speaking to his mass audiences.

Other people were coming into the auditorium through their own exits, checking themselves to see if they were wet. Some, who had obviously been through it before, didn't even flinch. Dillon imagined that perhaps the water-fall was a test. If someone was too scared to walk through and would rather run back against the conveyor, they wouldn't be able to handle their time in the PAstREAM device.

As the three family members walked farther into the auditorium, they noticed dozens of people sprinkled in seats throughout, waiting for something to happen on the stage ahead. Dillon, Jacob, and Rebecca walked up to the sign and read the instructions:

"WELCOME TO PASTREAM. YOU ARE ABOUT TO ENTER AN EXPERIENCE YOU WILL NEVER FORGET. PLEASE FIND A SEAT AND PREPARE FOR THE JOURNEY OF YOUR LIFE."

The family congregated in the middle of the auditorium and found three seats beside each other. A timer was counting down above the stage. There were four minutes and twelve seconds left on the digital display. People were still filtering in.

As the time continued down, minute by minute, second by second, Dillon watched and wondered what else this place had in store for its new customers.

Finally, with only seconds left, Dillon counted down with his kids. Voices from other seats did the same.

"Four, three, two, one."

Everything went quiet. The lights that surrounded the auditorium started to dim.

Jacob wanted popcorn.

A few seconds passed before a woman's voice filled the room. It sounded like the same soothing voice from when they entered. "Welcome to PAstREAM, the world leader in memory streaming. Before you can enter your previous reality, please focus your attention to the stage for important information. If at any time you wish to leave, please exit using the door directly at the back marked "Exit PAstREAM." If you need help or assistance getting to the exit, we have associates available in red vests. Just press and hold the green button directly underneath your right armrest for ten seconds for assistance."

Everyone in the room looked for their green buttons, not to push but to be aware of where they were. The buttons immediately began glowing a bright green, making their hands light up under the armrest.

"Please enjoy your stay here at PAstREAM. In just a few minutes, you will be finding your way to a personal viewing room. If this is your first visit, you are required to watch the presentation on the stage in front of you, and when it is done, place your thumb on the scanner that is on the top of your left armrest, acknowledging your approval of the terms and conditions, to be granted access to your device."

A three-dimensional digital image of a height-restricted man appeared in the middle of the stage. He flickered. Music started to play—classical music that started with a flute and became a more complete sound with other instruments piping in. It sounded like a million speakers surrounded the audience.

The flickering image became solid. The digital man looked around at the people sitting in front of him. His smile was consuming. As Dillon looked around the room, everyone was smiling—including him.

The digital image started to speak. "Welcome to PAstREAM. We are so fortunate to have you here today. You will experience feelings you haven't felt in years. You will see things you forgot happened. You will witness moments of your choice exactly as they occurred. We are excited for you. We are thankful you are here. The only thing we ask is that you try to avoid painful situations. They can be a lot more difficult to watch than you might remember. We implore you to use sound judgement before and after you view a memory. Feelings and emotions can often manifest in you afterwards, causing you to behave erratically. Perhaps you watched a loved one die, a partner cheat, or your child curse your name. We remind you that you have already dealt with those emotions. Bringing them back to others after you watch them can be unscrupulous. Please remember that PAstREAM is for viewing purposes only and is not meant in any way for you to seek revenge or to recreate anger or sadness. So please, enjoy yourselves. I'll now demonstrate for you how PAstREAM works."

The little man bowed. While the audience clapped, another digital image flickered above him. A white semicircle object moved down toward the man. Thin, tentacle-like strings were flowing below it.

"Dad, what does unscrupulous mean?" Jacob asked, hoping Rebecca wouldn't hear.

"It means it wouldn't be fair," Rebecca interjected, proudly teaching her older brother.

The three watched as the tentacle-like helmet slowly made its way toward the digital man. His eyes were wide open as the tentacles started to tickle his scalp. The digital man placed two contact-like objects into his eyes. Quickly, the strands from the helmet disappeared into his head, and he began floating up toward the ceiling like a helium balloon until he hit the top of the auditorium and popped like a bubble. Drops of digital water rained down onto the stage.

The woman's voice returned. "Please place your thumb on the scanner of your left armrest. Thank you and enjoy your time at . . ."

Binary voices spoke at the same time, a mixture of the female voice and the digital male.

"PAstREAM."

Dillon scanned his thumb. Rebecca and Jacob did too, knowing they would love to use it as well in the near future. The lights came back up, and a large digital green arrow pointed toward grand wooden doors that took up half of the wall to their right. The kids and their father stood up and walked through them.

CHAPTER FIFTEEN

Rebecca stood just past the wooden doors that led from the auditorium to the small underground city that existed within the concrete walls. She had become one of the patrons who was so struck with amazement they couldn't move.

Dillon and Jacob kept walking forward with the crowd, unaware Rebecca had stopped.

"Where's Rebecca?" Dillon asked.

Jacob shrugged as they looked around. They spotted her soaking in the wonder that was the heart of PAstREAM. Rebecca walked out a little farther as other clients pushed their way into the colossal, circular, turret-style concourse. Dillon stood beside his daughter and looked around, realizing what she was feeling. The concourse had solid marble floors, and the ceiling had to be a mile high. Above them was another augmented reality movie of a familiar theme. A shark and a dragon appeared to be fighting each other while a golden goblet sat in the middle. The fight was half underwater and half in the sky. The blue colors blended into each other and looked natural considering the impossibility. Dillon admired the massive white columns that ran from the floor to the ceiling turret at equal sections of the rounded concourse.

Four passages were available for entry from their current position.

To the left, an entrance read "Hotel and Reality Room." One in the middle read "Waiting Room Only." The other entrance read "PAstREAM Users Only." Finally, to the far right, the entrance read "Mind Fuel and

Consumption." There was also a smaller entranceway beside where the Murphys had entered labeled "Washrooms."

Jacob was already walking toward the smaller entrance to relieve himself. The washrooms were just one giant, non-gender-specific facility. As he stepped inside, he created ripples and splashes on the digital aquarium beneath his feet. Different types of sea life were swimming below. Jacob felt weird having a turtle swim under him as he urinated.

He thought this had to be the most fantastical washroom in the world. It seemed a bit overkill, but he was glad he got to experience it.

Jacob washed his hands in the multi-user water fountain that expelled soapy water like a chocolate fondue. Clear water ran in the creek circulating at waist level for rinsing. Jacob noticed the view from the mirrors at shoulder level and above weren't even mirrors at all. They were a reflection of him, but it was a ghostly reproduction—as if they had taken his likeness and reversed it back to him in a three-dimensional image. Small cameras were visible above. Perception was its own reality in this facility, and Jacob knew it.

Jacob walked back into the colossal circle. He found his sister and father in the same spot, still gazing at the structure and battle above.

"Okay, so which way do we go now?" Dillon asked, ready to move on.

"Well, Daddy, I think we have to part ways. The entranceway to PAstREAM is over there, and I don't think we can go with you past the scanner. It looks like we're destined for the waiting room area." Rebecca looked at her father forlornly. She didn't want to leave his side.

"It's okay, honey," Dillon said with false confidence. "I'll be fine. I'm sure they have people who know what they are doing and can help me if I need it."

Jacob and Rebecca walked with their father to the entrance for PAstREAM users and stood in line with him as he waited to scan in. A large man and a well-toned woman, both in fashionable smocks, watched the scanning procedure and smiled with approval at each individual who scanned in.

The kids stopped just before the scanner, and Rebecca kissed her dad on the cheek. "Tell us all about it when you come out. That is . . . if it works. And remember, only one, maybe two hours of your youth. The rest of the time, follow this list." Rebecca handed him a folded digital sheet with dates and the context.

Dillon took out the chip Jonathon had given to them for preferential treatment and better pricing. He scanned it while watching the guard at the door. The light turned green.

"If I don't come back out right away, I guess you'll know it worked." Dillon shrugged as he spun away from his kids.

"Good luck, Dad!"

This was it.

This time there was no conveyor as he crossed the threshold from visitor to user. Patrons hurried past him, trying to get themselves to wherever Dillon was headed.

Dillon continued up a barely noticeable incline to a number of tellers ahead. The floor was covered with red carpet. The warmly lit walls and ceiling made Dillon feel like he was entering a cinema, on his way to the concession.

The teller he approached was the same robotic woman he had seen earlier. Beside her was a transparent glass door that appeared completely dark behind it. He watched as others walked past their tellers into the dark entrances before disappearing. Dillon wondered what kind of craziness he would have to face this time. Nothing would surprise him at this point, but he couldn't be sure.

Dillon said hello curiously, not sure if it was a social requirement to acknowledge the lifeless robot, even if it was hard to tell at first that she wasn't human. He placed his chip on the scanner. The teller asked him if he had any questions. When he said he didn't, she smiled. "Thank you. Enjoy your time at PAstREAM." The glass door to the right of her opened. "Take the elevator, then follow the floor to room 318."

Follow the floor?

Dillon walked into the blackness of what felt like a tiny closet.

The glass door closed, and a locking noise echoed in the tiny room. Suddenly, he started to move. Bright lights passed him again and again. The elevator was going so fast that he didn't have a chance to see what was in the doorways from which the lights were shooting out. He didn't even know for sure if he was traveling up or down, although from the weightlessness he felt, he assumed he was traveling downwards.

Finally, the elevator came to stop, and the door unlocked. Bright, square lights on the floor lit the colorless hallway. Dillon's eyes adjusted to the constant white light. The hallway stretched quite far, and at the end was a door with an "EXIT" sign above it. The ceiling was also higher than he would have assumed.

Dillon walked down the hallway, stepping on the squares of light, which each became slightly brighter than the others when he stepped on them. White electronic sliding doors lined the walls on either side. Small digital screens were embedded on each door with what appeared to be patron's names typed in them. Dillon looked at each one as he walked forward.

312 MICHAEL ROOSEVELT
314 ROCKY MIGINTY
316 ELLIS MERCHANT
318 USER OF JONATHON WINTERS

He had made it. The floor started glowing a bright green when he stepped in front of the entrance to 318. It would be hard to mistake which room he was meant to enter.

Dillon stared at the door. As he built up the nerve to scan in, he saw another man walk out a few spots down. His eyes looked like he had just been through something emotional.

"Have you been here before?" the man asked keenly.

"Um, no. This is my first time," Dillon replied.

"Well, keep it positive. The first time is something you will want to remember. You're going to love it! Have a good one."

The man walked toward the exit. The door opened and closed so quickly that Dillon couldn't tell where it exited to.

Dillon looked back at his door. The name was still there, along with the room number. He hesitated before entering. What if this didn't work for him? This was either the moment that was going to force his previous life on him, or the moment that he was going to realize there was nothing to remember, and his life would return to exactly the way it was before he entered the building. The latter option didn't bother him one bit. He tossed a number of thoughts around in his mind, realizing he couldn't go back now. He had to try.

He placed the chip on the scanner, and the door slid open. A calmly lit room with curved corners awaited him. A large screen took up the majority of the wall on the right.

Directly in front, an oddly shaped machine stood waiting. It had two metal plates about eight feet apart from each other, one a few inches off the ground and the other positioned high above it, supported by the back wall. A large piece of metal that protruded from the ceiling hung over the entire contraption. Dillon tried making sense of it, but it wasn't working.

The door slid closed behind him. A woman's face appeared on the large screen, her head taking up most of the wall. She was absolutely stunning, and Dillon was eager to hear what she had to say. Her black hair hung long around her brown skin, accentuating the enchanting blue eyes that hypnotized Dillon. Her lips were a ravishing red with a black tone to them. They started to move.

"Welcome to PAstREAM. We are excited that you are ready to mix past and present with your future. My name is Elizabeth, and I'll be guiding you today. Please scan at the console to begin."

Dillon scanned in.

"Do you require instruction?" Elizabeth asked. "If so, say 'yes.' If you have been here before and do not require instruction, say 'no.' Please make your selection now."

Dillon paused. It was his first time, and he definitely needed instruction. "Yes. Yes, I need instruction."

"Very good. To begin, you will need to remove anything that is on your head. If you have a hat or a headdress, please remove it now. You will also be required to remove any bulky clothing and personal belts. Please touch the green light at the back of the room to deposit any items, and put on a metal PAstREAM belt from the sanitization pod."

Dillon was not wearing anything on his head, but he did remove his jacket and belt. He looked behind him opposite the big screen and saw a rectangle on the wall glowing green. He touched it, and a door slid open. A spot to hang his jacket, as well as a spot for shoes and a small washroom with a toilet and sink, became available to him. Beside the washroom was the sanitization pod. He pressed the blue "open" light and took out one of the adjustable metal belts.

He looked back at the screen and stood silently, waiting for his next instruction.

"Please put the metal belt around your waist. It will self-adjust once activated."

Dillon put the metal belt around his waist and part of his lower stomach. It was much wider than the belt he had just removed. After putting it on, he felt the PAstREAM belt applying pressure as it tightened, but it wasn't unconformable. Padding lined the inside of the belt and squeezed around him, almost like memory foam, as it secured into place.

Elizabeth's red lips started moving again. "Please stand on the glowing footprints beside the PAstREAM device, and prepare for the next step."

Dillon put his feet on the brightly lit footprints, facing the screen. He heard a clicking noise followed by a circular bowl which came out of the floor, rising up on a retractable post. The bowl was tilted toward him and rose up to the height of his chest before coming to a stop. He looked into it. Was he supposed to do something with it? Dillon saw a watery solution inside.

Two small arms bent from the bottom of the bowl and poked out of the solution. It looked similar to the eyewash station Dillon had seen upon his reintroduction to safety training at the news station.

"Very good," Elizabeth said. "Place your face in the bowl in front of you. The bowl has a sensor that allows it to read your height. If the bowl is not in a position to suit your needs, you can say 'reposition' at any point, and the bowl will readjust."

Dillon stood directly in front of the bowl. "Reposition."

The bowl moved up slightly.

"Now, stare at the pink lights at the bottom of the bowl, keeping your eyes open. A soft solution will gently wash over your eyes. Please make sure to get the solution right into your eyes, or you will not be able to watch your memories while in the PAstREAM device."

After more than a minute of skepticism and procrastination, Dillon finally made up his mind. *What the hell, why not?* He put his face in the bowl and stared at the dim lights at the bottom. Instantly, a warm solution washed over his eyes. It felt soothing.

"Very good. In approximately three minutes, you will feel the solution start to thicken. This is normal and will allow you to use the PAstREAM device uninterrupted. You can peel off the solution at any time by pulling from the middle of the eye. You may also reapply as needed."

Dillon started blinking his eyes but found that the more he blinked, the less he was able to close them. His eyelids would spring back up easily. Soon, Dillon couldn't close his eyes at all; however, he could see perfectly.

"Shortly you will notice that you cannot blink. You're almost ready to use the PAstREAM device. The solution in your eyes will adjust to your required vision. You can also adjust the focus while in your memory."

Dillon stared at the woman and wondered if she could see him tapping the soft-shelled bubble that now covered his eyes. It was not on his skin, however. For some reason, the fluid completely dried away from the flesh of his face. Perhaps something mixed with the eye fluid to create a plastic bubble.

"Please go into the machine, and stand on the metal plate. Should you need assistance, say 'assistance,' and someone will come in and help you."

It seemed like an awful amount of work to get the machine going, but Dillon realized that the next time he came in, it would go a lot faster. He also wondered how someone who was physically disabled could use the device.

"If you would like an explanation as to what will happen to you, say 'explain.' If you would like to skip this step, say 'skip.'"

Dillon had no clue what was going to happen and felt there to be only one answer at this moment. "Explain!"

"Very good. You're currently standing in the PAstREAM device. In a moment, you will levitate. Above and below you are two metal plates made of diamagnetic pyrolytic graphite. The metal belt you are wearing is magnetic. Above the top plate is another powerful magnet to help pull your body up. You will not begin levitation until you pick up the handles that are directly in front of you."

Dillon felt like he was inside some kind of preposterous science experiment. Levitation? Magnets? There was little difference between the extremely creative and the systematically insane, and this was now bordering on both. Dillon looked around. Within seconds, a pole raised up in front of him with handles secured to it. As soon as he grabbed them off the pole, a quiet hum filled the room.

Dillon was suddenly floating between the two plates, only inches off the ground. He felt like he was flying.

"Very good. The handles will keep you steady during your levitation no matter what position you are holding them in. Should you drop one or both handles, the levitation will stop, and you will be set back down."

Dillon slowly started moving his arms above his head, out to the sides and in circles. He remained upright. It felt incredible. Defying gravity could be a money-maker in itself, let alone adding the memory portion to it.

"In thirty seconds, the PAstREAM device will lower onto your head and eyes with a stimulating sensation. Stay calm. If this is your first time using PAstREAM, you will feel a sharp pain in your frontal lobe that can last for up to three seconds. This is normal."

Normal? Dillon wondered how anything causing pain in his brain could be "normal."

The helmet contraption slowly lowered over Dillon's head but was not strapped in or secured. A cushion of air existed between his hair and the device. Dillon looked up and saw the tentacle-like strands lowering down onto his scalp like those he had seen in the auditorium presentation.

As the tentacles tickled his scalp, he smiled. Then came the short pain in the front of his head—he thought his brain was going to blow out the back—and then it stopped. It felt fine.

"Very good. Now for the last step. You will see two wires attach themselves to the coatings on your eyes, which will allow you to watch your memories from your point of view, as if you were there again."

The small snakelike wires did exactly that.

"Very good. Once the PAstREAM device is working, you will only be able to see your memory. Remember, you can say 'stop' at any time. If you require personal assistance, say 'assistance,' and someone will be in to help you."

Dillon stared through the lenses at the woman on the screen. He had come this far. He felt like this was going to happen, that he was going to be able to see the very man he had been and was trying to become again. Suddenly, a date popped up on the screen within his eyes.

"At the top of your handles are sensors that your thumbs can control," Elizabeth said. "Slide your thumbs up or down on either handle to choose the year you wish to watch. Swipe right, and scroll up or down to pick the month, then swipe right again to scroll through and pick the day. Triple-click the handles to submit the date. Should you want to change the date while in your memory, triple-click the sensor on either handle. Please be aware that once the memory portion of the device is turned on, your vision will go black."

Dillon tried to do some quick math to pick the date he wanted, but it took a bit longer for him to calculate than he had hoped. Finally, he entered in the calculated year, followed by a random month and day, triple clicking the sensor with his thumb. He waited. This was the moment to see if his memory would actually remember the things he couldn't.

Nothing was happening yet. His heart was racing.

"Very good. The darkness you should be seeing is yourself, asleep. This is the beginning of the day you have chosen. You can forward your way through the day by pressing the sensor on the handle on your right. The harder you press, the faster you can scroll through the day. The sensor on the left handle will allow you to rewind your day. If you wish to pause the moment, press both buttons simultaneously."

Dillon felt dejected. Nothing had gone black yet. He could still see the woman on the screen.

"There will be a small timer on the bottom right-hand side. It lets you know how much time you have remaining. Again, if at any time you want to stop the process or you need to get out of the machine, say 'stop,' and everything will end. Enjoy your moments at PAstREAM."

With that, Dillon watched as Elizabeth's face left the screen. A list of options and steps to using the PAstREAM device appeared after.

Dillon felt like saying "stop" right away. Nothing was happening anyway. He started playing with the sensors, hoping something would happen. Nothing did.

Then everything went black.

CHAPTER
SIXTEEN

With his eyes stuck open, Dillon watched the blackness of a past recollection. He was asleep in his memory. Dillon pressed the sensor on his right handlebar hard to fast-forward what he was watching, and quickly, the eyes in his memory opened.

The screens in his eyes made him feel like he was actually watching from his point of view, but he had no control over what was happening. He let his body relax completely. The weightlessness felt comfortable, and he could imagine himself functioning in the memory. He released the sensor.

A repetitive beeping noise echoed loudly in the vision. Dillon's hand appeared and smashed the buttons on the alarm clock. The beeping noise stopped. He rolled over in his bed and looked at a girl who lay beside him. She was asleep, apparently unperturbed by the noise. Her shiny red hair was a mess on her young face. Dillon's memory stared at her for quite a while before getting out of bed, walking to the bathroom, and looking at himself in the mirror.

Dillon pushed both sensors on his handlebars. The moment paused. He saw a younger version in the memory. A rather unsightly pimple was on his right cheek, and a small red dot graced his chin. His hair was quite a bit longer than he would have imagined, and it looked a little shaggy, his bangs covering part of his face. What was he hiding from? Everyone told Dillon that they knew him as confident and even a little bit conceited at times. Who was the kid he was staring at? It didn't feel like the person they told him he was, but it sure looked like him.

Dillon pushed both sensors again. The memory continued.

Dillon reached for his electric toothbrush and started putting toothpaste on his bristles.

Dillon fast-forwarded through small chunks. He didn't need to see himself brushing his teeth and using the amenities.

He was forwarding through himself shaving until the red-haired woman appeared and hugged him from behind.

"*Good morning, babe,*" *Dillon said.* "*Did you sleep well?*"

"*I would have if we didn't stay up so late.*" *Jillian's eyes lifted slightly for a moment.*

Dillon could imagine the feel of her touch as he watched her reflection in the mirror hug his younger self from behind. He immediately fell in love with the woman in the memory.

"*So, Dill, will you be skipping any of your classes, or are you going to be a good student today?*" *Jillian asked cynically.*

"*I think I'll be a good student today. I know how much you hate when I only show up for tests. I'm still passing, you know.*"

"*That's what you keep telling me,*" *Jillian said with a grin, stripping down and entering the shower.*

Dillon couldn't blink, and he was thankful for that. He was amazed at the sight. God, she was beautiful. He wouldn't be telling his kids about this scene.

Jillian turned the shower on, closed the curtain, and started to sing.

Dillon winked at himself in the mirror. He walked out of the bathroom into his studio suite. The small kitchen to the right of the bed was messy with crumbs dusting the table and dishes bursting from the sink. Clothes were strewn everywhere, remnants from the night before. Dillon grabbed the jeans that were half hanging off the edge of the mattress and put on the shirt that was lying comfortably on the floor.

Dressed and ready to go, he went back into the bathroom, applied some product to his hair, and messed it up.

"*Okay, babe,*" *he said, raising his voice so Jillian could hear him over the sound of the shower and the song she was singing.* "*I'm outta here.*"

"*Bye-bye, Dilly,*" *Jillian said lovingly.*

Dillon put his life in fast-forward as he watched himself walk out the sliding patio door and lock it behind him. He didn't want to watch himself walk. The clock in the bottom corner said he had nearly seven and a half hours left. Plenty of time for the first day of viewing his memories.

He wondered why he was already living with Jillian in the memory. He was about eighteen years old. Maybe she'd just slept over.

Dillon obviously didn't remember her in his new reality. She was a story his kids told him about, a vision from the video clips that he watched at home. Even though it was difficult for Rebecca to talk about her mother without getting emotional, she still spoke about Jillian every day.

Questions were swirling in Dillon's mind. How did he and Jillian get along? How did he treat her? He couldn't sense exactly how he felt about her at this specific time in his memory, but he was starting to feel something toward her just from watching this.

Dillon zoomed through the walk and the bus ride and kept his finger on the sensor until he met up with his friends at school.

Hundreds of kids were sitting on the lunch benches, waiting for the bell to ring. Dillon sat with his friends. Many of them were doing the homework they'd failed to complete the previous night.

"Dilly Bar! It's almost time for class, dude. Did the college girlfriend sleep over last night? Or did her angry mother come and pick her up?" A slightly muscular boy with short blond hair was sitting at the table, looking at Dillon.

"They both slept over," Dillon said sarcastically.

The other kids at the table looked up and chuckled. Dillon stared down the table at a beautiful young woman sitting with a group of girls. She had pale skin and curly blonde hair. When she looked over at him, he blew her a kiss.

She returned in-kind.

Dillon started to wonder just what the hell was going on. He had Jillian. What was he doing blowing kisses at another woman like that? How could he be such a jerk? He was annoyed. He also realized that the girl he blew a kiss to in high school was now the wife of his best friend, Jonathon Winters. At least they were just kids.

After reminding himself that this Dillon was still in high school, he decided to give his youthful self the benefit of the doubt.

Dillon pulled out his English book and started reading.

Dillon fast-forwarded again through the school day. He stopped at what appeared to be around 4:30 p.m., when Jillian got home from school.

"Jillian! I missed you. How's the day?"

Jillian put her purse down but kept her jacket on. She looked away. "Listen, Dill, we need to talk." Jillian looked frustrated. "Your friend sent me pictures of you and Dionna on Saturday night while you were 'at work.' What the hell, Dill? I thought we dealt with this already." Jillian's eyes started to water.

"I'm glad you brought it up. I wanted to talk to you too." Dillon glared at Jillian. "I don't know who told you about that, but I'll find out. And . . . I think I know what you're going to ask, and no, I didn't sleep with her." Dillon took a quick peek at Jillian's chest on his way over to her angry face.

"Dillon, I want to take a break again. I can't do this anymore. I care about you, I do—I just hate the lying and how egotistical you are about it! This time I really don't know if I want to get back together. My mom is right about you." Jillian grabbed her purse and left. Dillon didn't say a word.

He went to his dresser and pulled out the monogrammed, hand-carved wooden box that sat under his boxer briefs, out of sight from anyone who would have been in his room. Inside was a plastic bag of green buds and some rolling paper. Dillon prepared his medication and went outside to get high on the patio.

Dillon paused his memory. He could not understand what the hell he was watching. How could he have ruined his relationship with this wonderful girl and still go on to marry her?

He wondered if he should continue watching his younger years or move on to the list his daughter had made for him. He figured he would finish off the current day he'd chosen.

Dillon forwarded through the wasted moment of his younger life until he saw a man coming into view.

"Dillon Murphy!" a voice yelled at him. It was a gentleman with a bushy mustache that was obviously colored, because it didn't match anything else. He had to be in his late forties, maybe early fifties.

"Mr. Parrish," Dillon said nervously as he hid his bloodshot eyes by looking at the concrete beneath him.

"Dillon, what the hell are you doing? Are you high? I can smell that shit from my kitchen upstairs!"

"I'm sorry, Mr. Parrish. I'm just having a really bad day. I needed to clear my head. It's fuckin' legal man."

"Goddammit, Dillon, stop dropping the 'it's legal' shit on me. And don't fucking swear!" The man sat down in the lawn chair across from Dillon. "I can't keep turning

the other cheek. Personally, I don't care if you smoke that stuff, but the wife does. You know how our son died, and it scares her. She doesn't want anything bad to happen to you either. Clarisa and I have really gotten to care about you over the last two years, but you keep pushing our buttons. I don't tell her half the stuff you pull while she's at work. And the drinking, Dillon. You're too young to have that problem."

Dillon looked directly into the eyes of the only person who seemed to care about him at that point.

"I really care about you and Mrs. Parrish too, sir. And I'll remember this conversation. I'm not on some other crap; it's just weed. Anyways, I'm really sorry. I'm just not happy right now. I can't stop thinking about bad stuff. And I'm not drinking anymore, I promise. Just weed."

"Bad stuff? What do you mean, Dillon? Like suicide?"

"Well, no—yeah, kinda. I don't know. I just don't know what to do. I feel like no one gives a shit about me, but when they do, I just . . . hurt them." Dillon kicked a small stone from side to side.

"Dillon, you know, you should talk to your social worker. She's a really nice person who wants you to be successful in your life. I've had other kids like you live here, and they weren't as lucky to have someone who actually cared about them like she does for you. Like we do for you. Can you promise me you'll call her?" Mr. Parrish asked, looking concerned.

"I don't know. I'm kinda scared that if I tell her anything about how I'm feeling, she'll take me away from you guys." Dillon seemed to struggle, spitting out his words. "I'm too old to be put with another family, and . . . you guys are the first people I actually like."

"Well, that's the nicest thing you've ever said to me, young man. No wonder I keep sticking up for you," Mr. Parrish said, standing up. "You do have a heart. I think you just have to learn that other people do too. You can't keep pretending like you don't care about them—especially that girl you keep breaking up with. Honest to God, Dillon, I don't know why she keeps coming back. I hope you smarten up before you lose her."

Mr. Parrish went to walk away, but turned back to his young live-in. "Dillon." He waited for Dillon to look up at him. "If you need anything—if you need me—please come and see me. And would you please try a vaporizer or edibles?"

Dillon paused the memory, wondering if the tears behind his lenses would mess anything up. He imagined many users who watched their memories teared up. The kids had told him he'd been more emotional since the accident. He wondered if his old self would have felt differently while watching these memories.

Dillon triple-clicked the sensors to change the date. He had memorized a couple of the dates from the digital paper and decided he would start where Rebecca had wanted him to start: her first birthday party.

As Dillon entered the date and triple-clicked to get to the memory, the blackness from the start of the day entered his eyes. As he was fast-forwarding, the view in his lenses started to glitch. Dillon stopped touching the top sensors, but the lenses were still cutting in and out with flashes of light.

An image started coming in clearer. Dillon was viewing a memory, but something was definitely wrong. He was sitting behind a desk, somehow watching himself pace the floor beyond the desk. But how could he see himself? There were no mirrors. He must have been watching from another set of eyes. From someone else's memory.

The Dillon that was pacing the floor in the memory started speaking.

"It's the same thing Elizabeth told me. PAstREAM was designed to brainwash the masses, and you want me to report on that. Do you understand how crazy that sounds? I can't report that! What proof do you have?"

Dillon watched himself freak out to whomever this memory belonged to.

"Mr. Murphy," a voice replied, *"I'll not see it used for such methods. I created PAstREAM to help people relive memories, to appreciate the moments and people in their lives. Please! If we let millions of people know now, we can stop what is happening at these locations, but we have to act quickly!"*

The Dillon in the memory continued to pace around in frustration and panic. "Even if . . . Let's say I want to report it. I don't know if my boss will even let me. This is . . . this is crazy. It could ruin my career . . ."

The memory faded to black.

"Stop!" Dillon yelled.

The machine withdrew. The headset rose up, and Dillon's feet touched back down.

What had he just seen?

His heart was pounding out of his chest.

Dillon was done with this for today. He just wanted to see his kids.

CHAPTER
SEVENTEEN

Jacob and Rebecca were sitting in "Mind Fuel and Consumption." The tables were giant touchscreens, so the hungry diner could enjoy shared memory clips or surf the Internet while they ate. When patrons sat down, a menu would appear on the table screen directly in front of them. Jacob and Rebecca were able to choose something they wanted, scroll through all the ingredients and nutritional facts, and then secure their selection. Jacob searched through a multitude of options before settling on his favorite: lasagna. Rebecca chose a plant-based, gluten-friendly cheeseburger. She was famished.

Within less than a minute, a woman brought out the food and walked away without even making eye contact. This was the fast food they were used to. Restaurants had found out that they made more money by having servers work with the cooks to get the food out fast while the table took its own order. Speed of service became essential to keeping a restaurant open as people got used to having things instantly.

Rebecca and Jacob sat quietly as they ate, both stressed, wondering how things were going with their father.

"It's been a while; do you think that means it worked?" Rebecca asked Jacob with a questioning look.

"I would assume so, yes, but he's looking at his childhood first. Hopefully, it will work for him when he watches the most recent years."

The kids had passed some time watching other people's memories on the table screens.

As Rebecca started to devour the food in front of her, a pair of hands grabbed her shoulders. She turned her head quickly and almost choked on her burger after she realized her father was standing behind her. Jacob smiled and stood up, ushering Dillon to sit next to him. Rebecca chewed the remaining food in her mouth as fast as she could and then gulped it down.

"Daddy! Well? Tell us what you saw! Did you see yourself? Did it work? Why are you back already? Oh no, it didn't work, did it?"

"Well, yes. It did work. It worked quite well, actually," he said somberly with a half-smile. He had checked the waiting room thoroughly before finding his kids at the restaurant. Dillon was a touch perturbed by the wasted time.

"You look like you were crying," Jacob said.

Dillon thought he'd tidied up his swollen eyes. "Well, I, uh . . . I had to put these bubble-screens in my eyes, so that could be why."

"What did you see? Tell us everything!" Rebecca said.

"I need time to digest it. There was a lot, and it was all new to me. I did see your mom," Dillon said with a smile. He knew Rebecca would love to hear about her mother.

"You saw mom? What was she like? Wasn't she so beautiful? You kissed her, didn't you? She used to tell me that you guys dated on and off and broke up a million times." It was the first time since the accident that Rebecca could talk about her mother in this way.

"She was very beautiful. I can see why I fell in love with her." Dillon couldn't look into his kids' eyes when he spoke about her. He hadn't exactly picked the best memory to talk about.

Jacob jumped in, more curious about the device itself. "So, what was it like? Did you get to use the levitation?"

"Yes, there was levitation. The whole thing was weird, but I'm sure I'll get used to it." Dillon pushed out a smile.

"That's great, Daddy," Rebecca said. "Do you want to order something before you go back to the device?"

Dillon shook his head. "I'm not sure I'm going to go back in today, honey. My head hurts."

"Did you find that you remembered anything as you watched?" Jacob asked. "Did any of it seem familiar?"

Dillon pursed his lips. "There wasn't anything that was familiar. It was like watching a movie through someone else's eyes. Not my own." Dillon didn't tell them about what he saw at the end. It would only frighten them.

As Rebecca was about to ask another question, a man who looked to be in his mid- to late-twenties approached the table. The family had seen him before; he was the same man who had spoken to them from the holographic stage in the auditorium. The kids also recognized him from their father's interview years ago.

"Mr. Murphy," the man said. "I'm so glad you've been able to come out here again and visit us. You've lost a lot of weight, I was hardly able to recognize you. I heard about what happened to you and to your wife. I'm deeply saddened by your loss. I hope you accept my humblest apologies." The short man wore a tight-fitting shirt with an abnormally high collar. His pants seemed to change color as he moved, glowing white along the seams.

Jacob thought he looked futuristic. He stared at him in awe.

"Have we met?" Dillon asked.

"Of course, Mr. Murphy. I see it's true your memory was affected by the accident. You did the story on our device, but you were upset with me because I wouldn't let you record whatever you wanted. I did, however, let you film the PAstREAM device to let your viewers at home know what we were all about. I think it worked in both our favors. Business increased dramatically after your telecast those many years ago. And from what I hear, you too advanced dramatically in your career. 'You scratch my back and I'll scratch yours,' as they used to say." The man smiled and laughed. "Mustn't forget what got us here."

"Well, Mr. . . ."

"Mikal. Call me Mikal. I had my last name removed for effect. Do you like it?"

"I do, Mikal!" Jacob said openly. His wishful thinking was that Mikal would become as fond of him as he had become of Mikal and perhaps allow him to use a PAstREAM device whenever he wanted.

"Thank you, young man. Mr. Murphy, if there's anything you need, or anything I can get you, please do not hesitate to ask. I have forwarded my personal information to your table here for you to upload. I have also granted you access to the Reality Room within the hotel. I trust you will enjoy it.

There are some features that are not for the kiddies, I'm afraid. You must be an adult to enjoy some of the more grandiose experiences."

"I'm eighteen, sir," Jacob pointed out.

"Well, my good man, you would be eligible, should your father allow it of course." Mikal looked back at Dillon. Jacob eyed his father for the go-ahead to use all facets of the Reality Room.

"Enjoy your stay, Mr. Murphy. I've created a special account for you. Make good use of it." Mikal bowed his head, then turned and walked away.

Other people had noticed the height-impaired man and asked for his autograph or begged to use the device for a lesser value than what was being charged. Mikal appeared gracious to his clients.

"The Reality Room sounds awesome, Dad," Jacob said, raring to go. "Let's try it!"

"Jake, Dad has to focus his time on the PAstREAM device," Rebecca said. "Stop thinking about yourself. And I'm not sure if you noticed, but trying to keep Dad a secret in here didn't work."

Jacob didn't protest. She was right on both fronts.

"I'm not going to use the device again today," Dillon said. "I'm feeling confused, and my head is killing me. Can we come back tomorrow instead?" Dillon wasn't being totally honest. Part of him didn't want to use the device again. He wanted to move on with his life. Go forward. There were probably many storylines from his past that he didn't want to pursue any further. Since the accident, it had become more difficult for Dillon to deal with stress.

"They have a hotel here. It would be fun to stay for a few days while you get to know more about yourself," Jacob said, trying to persuade his father to go with at least one of his ideas. "Maybe we could check out how much it costs to stay?"

"Look, you two have school, and I still have to report to work and the hospital once a week. Plus, I don't even want to know what it costs to stay for a night." Dillon sounded like a parent.

"Dad, I have exams, I only have to go a few times throughout the week. As for Rebecca, well, you know how dumb she is! What are a couple missed days going to do?" Jacob smiled sarcastically at his sister.

"I can still go to school during the day, you idiot. I only have one class tomorrow," Rebecca said in a condescending tone.

"How about we go to the hotel, find out how much a room is, and go from there? Can we at least do that?" Rebecca followed up. Dillon paused in thought.

"Okay, alright. I guess we can check it out. I'm curious what the rooms are like, considering what we've seen so far."

"All right, Dad!" Rebecca slammed her fist on the table in excitement. Jacob jolted in his seat, not expecting such a vivacious response.

"I didn't say we could stay. I merely agreed we could look into it. We will adhere to those rules at least." Dillon felt good laying down the law.

The men stood up from the table as Rebecca tried to inhale the remainder of her food in one of the rare times she was eating for enjoyment. Her short-term excitement temporarily cured her eating woes. Jacob sat back down because he knew how important this was to Rebecca. He hadn't seen her eat like this very often over the past year.

After Rebecca finished, she got up, and Jacob followed her. As they walked toward their dad, Rebecca put her arm around her brother's waist and gave him a squeeze. "You know, you're doing a great job of taking care of us. I really appreciate how you've stepped up and become a man."

"Thank you, sis. I'm not raising your allowance though." Jacob tried to make a joke out of the situation to take away from the guilt he was feeling. He knew he could have done more for Rebecca when their father was in the hospital.

They returned to the enormous turret-like indoor courtyard. Dillon wondered how the hell they were going to get out of there when they decided to leave.

He looked at the large wooden doors that they'd originally entered through. Right beside the entrance was a sign the size of a small car that read "Exit to Memory Creation." As people left through the exit, Dillon saw that it was almost desert-like. A camel appeared as the door slid closed, then reopened for the next person to leave.

Dillon shook his head in disbelief before looking straight up at the other unbelievable sight. On the ceiling in the turret, the dragon was winning against the shark. The dragon's sky was taking over much of the water that had been there when they first walked in. The battle raged on.

The family crossed the floor to the entranceway of the "Hotel and Reality Room." Jacob was the first to step into the lobby. It was a grand facade, with ten tellers lined up in front of a quarter-moon-shaped front desk. The colors in the floor were forever changing. Dillon almost walked into someone as he was looking down at it. It reminded him of the floors that had lit up on his way to the PAstREAM device.

Dillon and Rebecca approached the front counter, and one of the attendants greeted them. Jacob looked to the left inside the lobby and saw the entrance to the Reality Room. He couldn't imagine what it was, but he wanted to access it soon.

"Good day. How can I help you?" asked the teller, who appeared completely human.

"Ah, we were just wondering about the cost of a room," Dillon said. "We don't even know if we're staying or if there is any availability."

"Of course, sir. I just need a thumbprint to find out your usage and what kind of a rate we can give you." He smiled at Dillon.

"Mikal said he created an account for me." Dillon looked at the teller's name, Skyler, which was digitally attached to the lapel of his black suit. "We'd like to see the best deal you can give us." He placed his thumb on the pad and watched it scan instantly.

"Thank you, Mr. Murphy. Today seems to be your lucky day. It looks like Mikal has given you the VIP treatment. You're free to stay here for as long as you like at no charge. This includes no fee to use the PAstREAM device. You will also be granted the throne room, located on one of the higher-end floors if you choose to stay." Skyler's tone and facial expressions did not budge. "He has noted on your file that you may also use the Reality Room at no cost. We are very pleased to have you stay with us, Mr. Murphy. That is, if you choose to do so." The teller spoke in a polite and sophisticated tone. Dillon figured PAstREAM must pay their employees handsomely.

"Dad, you're a VIP! How can you say no to that? After all the crap we've had to endure, for crying out loud, man, say yes!" Jacob said, his arms flailing. He knew as well as anyone what his family had been through over the last year. He also knew how much he wanted to use the Reality Room.

"Dad, please!" Rebecca said. "Think of this as a vacation for us. A family getaway. We haven't had any time to have fun like this, you know . . . since the accident. We need this."

Dillon was railroaded into an easy decision. "Okay. Mr. Skyler, book us into that throne room. We won't be more than a week at most."

"We can arrange that for you, Mr. Murphy." Skyler smiled for the first time since he'd greeted them. "Take the elevator you see there." He pointed to his left. "Your room is on the thirtieth floor, down the hall and to the right. Unit 3001. You can't miss it."

You can't miss it? Dillon wondered what that meant. He had one more question.

"Just out of curiosity, Skyler, is the Reality Room just one big room? How does that work?"

"A very intriguing guess; however, there are many rooms. Think of each room as a vacation. It's not a memory, as in the PAstREAM device, but it is a place in which to lose yourself. Don't get addicted though. You're limited to a maximum usage time of five hours per day. Hotel patrons get first priority. Enjoy your stay, and if you need anything at all, do not hesitate to ask."

The Murphy family had no clothes or hygiene products to bring up to the room. Dillon thought they could probably pick up something in the building somewhere. It had everything else. Or at least they could make a stop at home and collect a few things.

As they walked to the elevator, they talked about what the ride up might be like. Jacob wondered if the elevator would enter the giant fish tank. Rebecca thought that perhaps it would take them thirty floors down. Neither of them was right.

As they entered the elevator, they were surrounded by glass. Beneath them was nothing but dark space. Above them was a mirror with a light somehow shining through it. There were no buttons in this elevator, just a pad for someone to put a thumb on. Dillon applied his digit, and the elevator started to move. It felt like the elevator at home, moving upwards.

As soon as they started to wonder what spectacular vision was in store for them, they saw daylight. For the first time since they entered the world of PAstREAM, the sun was crossing their path. It was a beautiful sight. The entire city was visible as the elevator went higher. PAstREAM wasn't the tallest building in the city, but the views were unobstructed out that side of the structure. Dillon remembered seeing the neck of the building reach out into the sky as Jacob drove them to their destination earlier in the day. He didn't think for a second he would be standing at that point looking down at the very spot in which he'd sat in the car's back seat.

Rebecca looked at her father. She waited for him to make eye contact, then gave him a big hug. "Daddy, so much has happened, so much . . ." She choked up. "In this last year, I stopped feeling good about life. I haven't been this happy in . . . forever. Thank you for not leaving me and Jake."

Dillon smiled. It had been a while since he could make his kids smile too, and it was infectious. They always had to do things for him or take care of something he should have been doing. It was nice to mean something to them, even if it was because they were getting the royal treatment.

The elevator stopped on the thirtieth floor. *Same floor number as our apartment*, observed Dillon, wondering if his kids had noticed, although it appeared that was not what was on their minds. Rebecca and Jacob turned away from the window to the doors to see what awaited them.

The carpets and tile stood out immediately, their colors constantly changing. It was the theme of the decor. Glass walls were everywhere; however, only half of the walls were see-through. Many were frosted. A digital placard read "3001."

Jacob was freaking out, he could see directly into what looked like their hotel room. Where was the privacy? He saw a living room and kitchen area with the sun and views shining through, but he couldn't see through the frosted parts into what would be the bedrooms and bathrooms.

The three walked up to the entrance of the exposed abode. Dillon placed his thumb on the scanner. The door slid open, and the remaining see-through glass that ran around the hotel room instantly became frosted.

"Welcome, Mr. Murphy," a holographic man with an English accent said at the entrance. "Should you require any assistance during your stay, call for me. My name is Steward." He thanked them for staying before dissipating into the air.

Rebecca wondered if this was some form of AI or a man projecting himself in real time. Either way, she did not like it.

Dillon took off his shoes and walked up to the window overlooking the city below. The view was different than the one he was used to at home. It was a different angle of the city.

"Dad! Did you see the bathroom? And—holy crap—I've got dibs on the dragon bedroom!"

"Take it, brother. I'll be taking the room with the shark. It has a more feminine flair." Rebecca was happy with the decision.

"Dad, you should totally check out your room. It's freakin' awesome!" Jacob grabbed his dad's arm and helped him to the master suite.

Dillon walked into what felt like a jungle. The glass walls bore a woodland image, digitally projected within them. A large circular bed sat in the middle surrounded by a canopy of trees. The entire room was a forest in augmented reality, seemingly going on forever, although branch railings stuck up around waist height to prevent guests from walking into the digital walls. It looked like the rainforest that Rebecca had learned about in school, the one that had mostly burned in the first quarter of the century.

Sounds of woodland creatures and a waterfall filled the room. A red-winged bird flew from one branch to the next.

"Holy crap, Dad, there are birds in here!" Jacob was amazed by the sight.

"They're not real, dummy," Rebecca said, hoping her brother was kidding.

Dillon looked up to see a ceiling that appeared to go on forever into the blue sky through the crowded leaves. The fixtures fascinated the family as flames flickered from the hanging lights beside the bed.

Jacob dragged his father into the en suite—a private oasis. The waterfall sound they had heard was accurate. The waterfall looked to be the only option to use as a shower, and there didn't seem to be any way to shut it off. The water flowed into a shallow creek that ran through the entire bathroom, pooling at the opposite end into a natural stone tub. The toilet appeared to be made of branches; Dillon didn't care for that fact. He imagined having to pick slivers out of his bare bottom.

"Okay, now this is crazy. And where does all this water go? It seems wasteful." Dillon had to be the one to bring up the negative features of the room. He had been a bit of a realist since he woke up from his long slumber.

"Dad, if you read here, next to the voice-activated switch, it says that 'The waterfall in your room is run on recycled water and is filtered after the rock tub. Particles that do not match the standard of cleanliness will be removed and neutralized before being reinserted into the main stream. If you wish to turn off the waterfall, we regret to inform you that it is, in fact, a waterfall and cannot be turned off. Thank you for your patronage.'" Jacob felt somewhat satisfied to be the one to explain the workings of the shower.

Dillon walked back into the bedroom and wondered how he was going to fall asleep in a rainforest. He would have to face the noise of birds and the never-ending water that pounded the tiny lagoon in his bathroom. He ushered the two children out of his room, wanting to lie down. His mind still hurt. He was confused and happy at the same time. As annoyed as he was about the current bedroom situation, he felt relaxed when he rested on the bed. The calming chirp of a small bird echoed with the soothing sound of the bubbling waterfall. A warm gust of wind tickled his face. The crackling of the fire that burned in the lamps beside him were the cherry on top. Dillon rested his eyes.

CHAPTER
EIGHTEEN

Dawn broke upon the outdoor-structured bedroom. Dillon lay awake on his bed. The fires that had been burning in the lamps around him were out, and the bird that helped put him to sleep was gone. There were no signs of life other than the waterfall in the bathroom that continued to pulse into the shallow creek below it. Dillon pondered his first move of the day.

The kids had gone back home for supplies the previous night followed by a meal at the consumption area within PAstREAM for dinner. They ate without their father, although they did wake him once to see if he wanted to go with them. Their dad declined and thanked them for bringing back his necessities to the hotel so he could remain in bed. Dillon hadn't slept well since he awoke from his coma, and his body decided this was the best opportunity to catch up on some of the most recent sleepless nights that had afflicted him. Now he felt hungry.

Dillon had decided between waking moments throughout his slumber that he wanted to watch more of himself and Jillian in PAstREAM. He liked talking about her with Rebecca. It gave them something with which to relate, not to mention the attraction Dillon had for his late wife.

Dillon slid out of bed, feeling a bit tired from oversleeping. The grass tickled his bare feet. He knew it was fake, but he came to expect that in life. Everything nowadays was fake. Dillon shuffled to the bathroom, rubbing his feet on each blade of grass that nestled comfortably between his toes. He removed his underwear and entered the warmth of the ankle-deep creek. The digital sun shone down upon him while the sound of his little winged friend began to echo around the room.

Water poured from above onto his bed-mussed hair as he stepped into the waterfall. He imagined himself lost in the jungle, preparing for the task of survival that would challenge him in the days ahead. It was similar to the way he was feeling now. He didn't know how he was going to handle watching more of his memories. Quite frankly, Dillon was scared to watch more of himself or see another memory that wasn't his own. But he knew he had to continue. His kids were a big factor in his desire to carry on with this. He was preparing himself for the next leg of the journey. He'd found his way out of the proverbial jungle in his mind, but he wasn't out of the woods yet.

Dillon walked out of the waterfall and waded into the rock pond at the opposite end of the creek. The smell of wet lilies floating in his bath tickled the hairs in his nose. He sat on the rock bench in the pond with his arms air-planing around the edge. Dillon felt amazing. He wanted to stay in the perfectly temperatured water for as long as possible before quickly reminding himself of his purpose.

After a short soak, Dillon stood up and sluggishly walked out, dripping wet. As he walked in front of the sensors of the body dryer built into a tree, small air jets accosted his wet skin. It was the most action he had felt since the accident. Dillon took an extra moment, picturing his young wife's hands caressing him as he stood looking in the mirror, identical to the image he had seen in the PAstREAM device. His mind drifted to a vacant spot he obviously hadn't been to in a while. The words of his conscience crept seductively into his mind, mimicking his feelings. Dillon wondered if this was the feeling he got every time he'd held Jillian. He pictured her soft skin touching him, the energy of her coming through her fingertips.

He felt alive. He felt loved.

He opened his eyes, not realizing they had closed. He was alone. Dillon needed to see more of Jillian.

Realizing he was more than dry, he continued back to his room. His clothes were not there. He put on his robe and opened the sliding glass door to the large living quarters of the suite. Jacob was sitting at the table beside the window sipping a coffee and watching the cars and people below.

Dillon walked over to the table and sat down across from his son.

"Whoa, Dad, you must have been tired—yeesh. How did you sleep?"

"Considering how long I slept, you'd think I'd feel more awake. How about you?"

"Well, it was hard to fall asleep with everything that's happened these last twenty-four hours, but once the animated dragon in my room lit up the walls with his fire breath, I guess you could say all of my thoughts kind of went up in flames." Jacob snickered at his pun.

Dillon looked around the room. "Where's your sister?"

"At school. But I do want to tell you something that happened last night while you slept." Jacob continued to stare out the window, avoiding eye contact.

"What do you mean? What happened?" Dillon felt like a worried parent.

"Becca used the PAstREAM device." Being the man of the family while Dillon recovered from his coma meant Jacob had to make decisions he wouldn't normally make.

"What do you mean?" Dillon asked. "I didn't think she had any interest in it. I thought you were the one that wanted to use it." Dillon was intrigued, though it bothered him slightly that his daughter had used the machine. But why should it? He was using it himself. It didn't matter if his reasons seemed more important than anyone else's or not.

"Well, after you came back from using the device and talked about Mom, Rebecca wanted to relive a memory with her from just before the accident." Jacob still hadn't looked directly at his dad. "I told her that I thought that was a reasonable request. Mom was Becca's best friend. How could I say no to her?" Now the man of the family was looking for support from his father.

Dillon nodded. "I suppose that's fair. I think it's good for her to enjoy a moment with her mom again as long as she feels it's helping her. Obviously, I'm worried there could be negative effects if she watches too much. She should be moving on from her mother's death too, as much as I hate saying that." Dillon started picking at whatever food Jacob left on the table. "What about you? Don't you want to use it?"

Jacob continued to stare out to the city below as he sipped his coffee.

"I sure do. But I like seeing Becca happy, and I like knowing that you're getting a chance to learn about yourself again." Jacob finally looked at his father with a bit more information to share. "And I tried out the Reality Room."

Dillon looked at his son, impressed. He was also curious about the Reality Room. As he was about to ask Jacob about it, he noticed a welt under his son's eye.

"What happened to your face?"

CHAPTER
NINETEEN

The night prior, Jacob had escorted Rebecca to the PAstREAM entrance after dinner. She was so excited to see their mom again. Jacob wanted to use the device too, but he had more of a desire to try the Reality Room first. He was mournful at the thought of watching memories of his mother, so avoiding the PAstREAM device was easier than he thought. His mom was gone, and he didn't want to go through that pain all over again. Not yet anyway. That wound was still open.

Jacob wasn't happy inside, not like he used to be. It was understandable considering what he had been through. Deep down, he felt angry and depressed. He was failing his classes, though his dad didn't know it, and he felt like he was failing Rebecca too by letting her use the PAstREAM device. He was scared about what she would be like after spending time reliving memories of their mother. It bothered him.

There was something morally wrong with the ability to rehash certain memories. Where there was pleasure, there was surely pain. The unfortunate part about it was that Jacob wanted to partake in that unethical feeling he had. His conscience told him one thing, his desire another.

After dropping Rebecca off, Jacob walked into the hotel lobby. He looked at the front desk and checked out a few of the girls who were working there. One of them smiled at him, and Jacob smiled back. He felt above average in terms of looks and walked confidently, telling himself the girl was looking at him with attraction. Even though he was wrestling with mental-health issues, he still had his ego.

As Jacob's eyes were locked on his target, he walked right into a man standing in the lobby. He was burly with a well-rounded beard, and he wore a shiny watch and sharp crocodile-skin shoes. He stared at Jacob.

"Uh, sorry, sir. I didn't see you there," Jacob said sheepishly. He looked back at the teller to see if she had witnessed his carelessness. She had and was talking to a girl beside her, laughing.

"Watch where you're going, kid," the big man said, looking irritated.

Kid?

"I'm not a kid, asshole," Jacob spurted out.

Jacob immediately felt hatred inside him. He was not a kid. He hated people telling him he was a kid. He took the big man's words to heart when he shouldn't have.

"I should have called you a scrawny little shit instead then," the man replied, doubling down.

"Fuck you!" Jacob spat. He pushed the man, who returned fire by shoving Jacob to the ground and punching him in the face while he was down. Jacob's color-changing cheek started to match the color-changing floor. His vision blurred.

"I don't know what the hell is wrong with you, kid, but consider yourself lucky I don't have time to teach you a lesson." As the big man walked off, a few bystanders knelt down beside Jacob.

"What's wrong with you?" a man asked, his family beside him. "That guy is twice your size. Are you okay?"

A teller came over from the front counter. It was the girl who had smiled at him. "You know, we're supposed to throw people out for what you guys pulled." The girl sounded like an angel to Jacob. His vision was unfocused, but his hearing was still intact.

"I'm sorry," he muttered.

"There's a lot of emotion in this place; you're not the first person I've seen get punched. Do you need anything? Ice for your eye?" She seemed to care, but Jacob wasn't sure if she was talking kindly to him because she worked there or because of the connection he thought they had.

"I think I'm okay. Yeah." Jacob sat up. He pushed himself to a standing position and thanked the man who had knelt beside him. As the man and his family walked away, they were talking about what they just witnessed. Jacob felt a wave of regret wash over him and immediately thought about what he had done. Perhaps someone would want to watch that moment again.

The girl remained by his side, waiting for him to acknowledge he was truly alright.

"Thank you for your help. So, am I going to get thrown out of here?" Jacob asked anxiously. "I don't know how I would explain that to my sister or my dad."

"I would echo what the man said to you. Today is your lucky day. That welt on your cheek seems like punishment enough." The girl smiled and headed back toward her position behind the desk. Jacob turned away from the crime scene and walked over to the lineup for the Reality Room. He got through quickly.

The deep-voiced man policing the entrance stopped him, "Scan for verification. And fix your face. You're lucky you aren't getting thrown out—I saw the whole thing. I would have helped you if he threw another punch, but you deserved that first one."

Jacob scanned the pad at the entrance.

"Good to go. I see you are eighteen, so you will have access to ALL of the Reality Room programs." The guardian of the Reality Room entered something into his tablet. "I've booked you in 113. Scan into one of the elevators."

Jacob sensed a power within the walls as he strode down the hallway. All the emotions that were happening in the building were causing people to expel a lot of their energy, and Jacob could feel it.

This is why it costs so much to be here. People want to feel emotion. People want to feel the love, the pain, the happiness, and the misery. And they pay a lot of money to feel it over and over again.

The glass elevator moved Jacob horizontally. The door opened onto a small hallway made of lights that lit up with each of Jacob's steps. He watched the numbers on the wall until he read, "Welcome to Reality: Room 113." The floor was glowing green.

Jacob placed his thumb on the scanner to his room. Although the door didn't open, it flickered into a giant monitor that read like a menu.

He touched the monitor, and a voice said, "Welcome to the Reality Room. Make your selection."

Jacob scrolled through his choices and noticed the "Top Selections" section. A few of them caught his eye: *The Dance Club, The Rainforest, The Baseball Manager, Two Guys on an Island, Two Girls on an Island . . .*

Jacob made his choice the second he saw it. *The Baseball Manager* would have to wait. A waiver came up, and Jacob read through it too quickly to absorb anything before placing his thumb on the scanner, giving his acceptance.

The door slid open to an enormous empty room with white floors, white walls, and a white ceiling that arched overhead. As he walked in, he noticed the floor had a rubbery, somewhat bouncy feel to it. He rubbed his hand on the walls. They were made of the same material. This was no ordinary room.

The sliding door closed, and the room started manipulating itself into a new, augmented reality. The walls seemed to disappear, turning a sky blue, giving the impression that Jacob was outside. The floor beneath him turned to sand. Palm trees formed behind him while water flooded out into the endless ocean.

Now all Jacob could see inside the room was an endless view of a beach. Even the air began to smell salty. The false sun above felt warm on his skin. Jacob took off his shoes. The sand between his toes was softer than he remembered sand feeling. Jacob looked around the endless beach and noticed he was not alone. Two girls were sunbathing in the distance. One of them moved and waved at him. The stress in Jacob's face vanished instantly.

He didn't know how he was going to explain this to Rebecca. His dad, on the other hand, might understand a bit better. But those thoughts would have to wait.

Jacob walked toward the waving hand.

CHAPTER
TWENTY

After Jacob escorted Rebecca to the PAstREAM device, she had her own emotions to work through while he was using the Reality Room. She sat crying in her PAstREAM room after reliving a moment with her mom. It had felt so real, like her mother was alive again.

Rebecca watched a specific memory of her mom just prior to the accident. She recalled her mom sitting next to her only a week before their lives changed for the worse.

They'd been looking at a tablet, and Rebecca was showing her mom pictures of the boy she was dating and would eventually break up with, Thom Townsend. The two women had been cuddling together, talking about boys and why they loved and hated them.

Rebecca had a problem with love, even if it was young love. She couldn't understand how someone could feel so passionately about a person they barely knew when they first started dating, and yet couples who had been together for so long seemed so irritated by each other. It was like love disappeared once people got to really know one another. It seemed completely backwards. She wanted to get to know someone and then fall more and more in love with them. Her mom told her that she shouldn't let go of that idealization, that what she hoped for was possible.

Rebecca's thoughts kept going back to the image of her mom's face. To the warmth of her mother's embrace. If there was love in this world, that was it. She missed her mom more than anything.

The tears pushed hard down her face. She could barely breathe.

Why? Why did her mom have to die? So much goodness and love, and it was all taken away.

Rebecca was off the device and on her knees next to it, hunched over with her head on her lap. The pain she felt was not going away. Time seemed to move quickly after she watched the memory, and soon the door at the side of the room slid open. A small, dark-haired woman entered. She knelt beside Rebecca.

"Rebecca Murphy?" the woman asked quietly, her hand on Rebecca's back.

"Yes." The word came out softly on her exhale.

The woman handed Rebecca a tissue adorned with an advertisement. Rebecca wiped her tears into it.

"I apologize, but your time is up. Let me help you collect your belongings."

Rebecca wanted to see her mom again. She needed to talk to Jacob immediately.

CHAPTER
TWENTY-ONE

Dillon needed a caffeine fix. He asked Jacob for a coffee, and his son pointed in the appropriate direction.

"Just tell the machine what you want, and a little robot will walk out and make it for you."

"Ha, funny. Is there any coffee left?" Dillon was smiling, acting as if he couldn't be fooled.

"I'm serious. Just try it. I've had, like, fourteen cups of coffee made just to see him come out. If you try and touch him, he runs back into the machine. I blocked the door to see what would happen if he couldn't get back in, and he exploded into a puff of smoke. I thought I broke it, so I tried making another cup of coffee, and sure enough, a little robot man came walking out of the machine." Jacob looked at his father with raised eyebrows to indicate how incredibly insane some of these inventions were.

"Jacob, I can honestly say that I don't believe you, but I'm going to try it out anyway."

Dillon walked over to the coffee machine by the sink and looked back at his son.

"Now, let's say you're telling the truth, and this does work. How does he know where to go after he walks out of the machine? How does he know where your cup is?"

"There's a scanner on top of the machine. Try it out and see what happens." Jacob was smiling, and Dillon couldn't help but do the same.

Dillon put his finger on the print identifier on the machine, and within seconds, a mechanical arm jutted out, placing a cup near the coffee maker. Dillon looked back and forth between his son and the machine as he beamed in anticipation.

A few seconds later, a small door opened up, and out came a small robot. It had a silver head with two holes in it that looked like they housed tiny cameras. A small body with small arms and small legs made the automation appear almost human in form, although all of its parts were showing. As it reached the cup in front of Dillon, a small voice echoed out from the tiny robotic server. "Hello. What can I get you today?"

Dillon hesitated then answered the little droid. "I would love a black coffee."

Almost instantly, both of the robot's hands reached into the cup. Black coffee streamed out of them, filling the cup in seconds. Dillon looked over at Jacob.

"Where the hell does it keep all the water?"

"I know, right! Didn't I tell you? I had to try it, like, fourteen times, and I still can't figure it out!" Jacob was just as stumped and excited as the first time.

"That is—how do you kids say it these days? —*Galactic!*" Dillon tried to sound cool to his son.

"Dad, never say that again. You sound like a fool." Jacob looked back out the window.

As Dillon grabbed his coffee, he noticed his hygiene products and clothes were lying on the table next to him. Dillon thanked his son, and went back to his room to finish getting ready.

CHAPTER
TWENTY-TWO

As Dillon exited his hotel room, a voice startled him.

"Enjoy your day, Mr. Murphy." It was the same holographic Englishman that had greeted his family upon their arrival.

As Dillon walked across the colorful floor to the elevator, his heart started to race. His pace picked up slightly without him realizing it. He was excited and scared.

The elevator couldn't move fast enough.

Once he made it out of the hotel and Reality Room, he looked up at the ceiling turret to see who was winning. The shark looked to have the upper hand at the moment. Dillon wondered what the hell the two animals were supposed to represent and why one was winning over the other at different times.

At the entrance to "PAstREAM Users Only," Dillon scanned in and carried on to the tellers ahead. He was now a pro at getting around.

He was looking forward to seeing Jillian again.

* * *

Dillon stood ready in the PAstREAM device. He wondered if the machine would decide not to work for him this time. What if the memories from his most recent years didn't work? He found out within a few seconds that it didn't matter what he thought.

Something was happening.

Dillon's eyes were once again stuck open with eyelid screens. He had skipped the training session, and things went a lot faster. He remembered to press the sensor on his right handlebar lightly and fast-forwarded through sleep until his eyes opened.

A divinely-built version of Dillon sat up in bed. He could see his thick pectoral muscles when he looked down at his body, and the shape of his abs were fairly tight and washboard-like. He looked farther down and realized, when he removed the covers, that he had just as much covering his bottom half as he did the top half.

Dillon peered left. A brazen beauty was lying in his bed. She was awake, mulling through something on a paper-thin tablet.

"Hey, love," the goddess said. "You slept well. I was wondering if you were going to wake up at all."

"You tired me out last night. I'm surprised you're awake so early." Dillon's voice was that of someone who was very sure of himself.

"So, I have an idea for us today. It's the first weekend knowing we're expecting a girl, and well, I would really like to start picking stuff up for her room." Jillian patted her small belly and spoke as if knowing her words had to be convincing to get him going. Perhaps the previous night was now being called into payment.

"Of course. Can we get back in time, so I can watch the game?"

There was compromise in Jillian's voice. "I think we can arrange that. Can you get Jacob ready? I sat him in front of Disney Plus until you woke up. He already drank his breakfast." Jillian pushed up her breast as if to show it was empty of milk.

"Yeah, babe. I think I can handle that."

Dillon felt much better about what he was watching. He was going to see Jacob as a child. Life appeared to be normal for him at this point. He didn't seem as childish as he had in his last memory. However, he realized he must have entered the wrong date, because Rebecca wasn't born yet. The list of dates she had given him were supposed to include her, short of his wedding day, which this was not. Dillon decided he would scan through the day anyway before changing dates.

Dillon got up out of bed and went to the bathroom.

He watched himself pee, wash his hands, brush his teeth, shower, and get dressed in fast forward.

He drank a glass of water and walked out into the living room.

Jacob was sitting on the couch in a diaper, watching a cartoon about the letter of the day and how it showed up in everything people did. The letter of the day was P.

Jacob found it funny. "Poo starts with P. Poo starts with P!"

Dillon sat next to his son. "Hey, little buddy. How are you today?"

"Daddy! Poo starts with P!" Jacob thought he was being smart. Dillon just wasn't sure if he was old enough to be sarcastic-smart.

"You're right, Jake! Poo starts with P!"

Dillon felt his phone vibrate. He had a new message.

"Want somthin' betta than last night hun?" the message read.

"Ya" Dillon responded quickly.

A picture popped up on his screen.

It was a woman who wasn't Jillian. And she wasn't wearing a top.

"Oh my God!" Dillon yelled from his PAstREAM room. "What is wrong with me?" He had hoped this was going to be a good and normal day in his life. He realized it may not have been a good one, but it might have been indicative of normal for his past self. He couldn't help but think this wasn't just a one-off. That seemed unlikely.

The fact that this happened even once was more than enough anyway.

Dillon paused the memory. The woman looked familiar.

It quickly dawned on him that it was the same girl from his last memory, the one he blew a kiss to from across the table in his vision at school. It had to be. She looked too much like her, just older. It was Jonathon's wife, Dionna.

Dillon felt sick.

Dillon was watching a man who was playing the same games he did as a teenager. He was the same selfish idiot, just grown up with a kid and another one on the way. Rebecca and Jacob never told him about this. Did they even know about it? Did Jonathon know about it? Too many things started forcing their way into his mind.

Dillon was pissed off with himself. His chest felt heavy as he continued.

Jillian walked into the room, and Dillon quickly turned off his phone.

"Okay, my boy! Are you ready to go shopping for your new little sister? Get her some girly stuff?"

Jillian looked at her husband after looking at Jacob. "Okay, boys, let's go!"

"Stop!" Dillon yelled.

The machine turned off, and the PAstREAM room came into focus. Dillon was done with the machine. He did not want to use it anymore. It was not going to help him become the person he wanted to be, because he didn't like the person he was in the past.

This was not going to factor into his future. Dillon was sure of that.

Dillon pulled the screens from his eyes, grabbed his shoes and jacket, and left the PAstREAM room. He took the exit and went directly into the hotel lobby. He wanted to get up to his room, collect his offspring, and get out of the building.

He rode the elevator to his suite, got off, and scanned into the hotel room. Sitting at the table were Rebecca and Jonathon.

"Dillon, you're back. Wonderful. I was hoping to have a word with you. Luckily, I ran into Rebecca. She told me that you were here in the building as well. I imagine you used the PAstREAM device, no? Did you remember anything?" Jonathon asked curiously.

"Ah, well, yeah. I was learning about my life. It's hard to imagine that's me that I'm watching." Dillon spoke truthfully on that front, but he wasn't about to share anything else he had just seen.

"Well, I hope you get to see everything. Although sometimes it's nice to be blind to the darker side of our lives." The comment was difficult to figure out. "Look, Dillon, I'm here to see where you're at with everything going on. Ratings are down right now at the station, and I think it would really bring a shot to the team if you were able to do an interview. You know, even a short one. Just to get your feet wet. What do you think?" Jonathon was a very persuasive gentleman.

"Oh, Dad. You aren't ready for that yet!" Rebecca yelled, turning to Jonathan. "You can't just throw him back online! He's still figuring things out. Dad, tell Mr. Winters you aren't ready." Rebecca had an extremely concerned look on her face, arguing with the very man she had brought up to the suite to see her father.

"Rebecca, I do apologize," Jonathan said. "I understand the current predicament your family is in. I don't need to remind you, however, that the station has been very generous toward the three of you. I can't fathom the cost of this little escapade."

Rebecca's face went an angry shade of purple. "You're not paying for this. Mikal has given us VIP treatment and said we don't have to pay for anything while we're here!"

Dillon raised his finger to shush his daughter and nodded softly in appreciation for her defensive stance.

"Fair enough. Glad to see we've kept this visit private." Jonathon shook his head in disappointment. Rather than arguing with a teenager, Jonathon directed his attention to Dillon. "Be that as it may, your hospital bills and penthouse aren't paying for themselves. I would suggest, Dillon, that you get your daughter here to see the big picture. Understand?"

Dillon could taste the tension in the room. He knew his family had just had an emotional past forty-eight hours, and he felt he'd better keep his anger in check. Now was not the time to become reactive to a conversation drenched in underlying issues.

"We understand, Jonathon. Can you give me until Monday morning? First thing?" Dillon looked at his friend, trying to decipher exactly what, if any, ulterior motives were at play. Jonathon was the boss. He had every right to expect Dillon to obey based on the compensation he had been receiving.

"First thing Monday morning. I look forward to seeing you. And maybe wear that black Armani suit I bought you. The one you wore the last time you were on the air. Jacob will know which one. It looked good on him too." Jonathon's tone changed dramatically. He was under a lot of pressure to improve ratings. "Enjoy the rest of your week, Murphy family." Jonathon, still dressed collar to cuff, strode out of the suite. Dillon and Rebecca waited until the door slid closed behind him.

"Dad, what is wrong with you? Why don't you stand up to that guy?"

Dillon felt it was somewhat inappropriate for Rebecca to be questioning him, but he knew what her intentions were.

"Rebecca, you can't talk to him like you did. I understand you were defending me, and believe me when I tell you that I appreciate it. But he's my boss and our source of income. He's allowed to tell me to get back to work.

And maybe he's right. Maybe it's time I get on with my life. I can't stay here watching a life that I used to have. I need to start building this new one I've been given." Dillon ended his sentence as kindly as he could.

"Whatever, Dad. If you want to let people push you around, go ahead and let it happen. I took care of you when you were in the coma. I bathed you. I moved you around. I believed that you would come back to me—that you would be my daddy again!" Rebecca was becoming overly emotional. She could feel the pain of her mom's memory bubbling back up, and the loss of her father's memories pushed that bubble of emotion to an uncontrollable state. "I gave up my life for you, Daddy. But you came back to me a different person! I still love you, but you don't remember me. You don't remember watching my solo in the band recital. You don't remember taking me to dance class and being the only dad there. You don't remember kissing me goodnight. You don't remember anything about me! I thought this place would give you that chance again, that you would get to know me again and get to know Mom and Jacob again and find out what happened—why Mom died. But it feels like you're giving up! You can't give up. You can't . . ." Rebecca's tears rode down her beet-red cheeks, matching the crevices that had already formed. She was engulfed with anger as much as she was with despair. She knew it wasn't her father's fault he couldn't remember a portion of his life, but there was no one else to blame.

"You're right, Becca." Dillon walked over and hugged his daughter. He felt angry with himself, like somehow this was his fault. He prayed he could remember everything and that it would all go back to normal, but at the same time, part of him didn't want to remember. He didn't like the person he was. He wanted to be better than what he had seen of himself. He decided tomorrow he would watch his most recent memories to figure out what happened before the accident and also specific moments on Rebecca's list that would help him learn about his kids, but that would be the extent of it.

CHAPTER
TWENTY-THREE

Dillon was back in the PAstREAM device. This time he was going to start learning as much about Jacob and Rebecca as possible while figuring out what had happened to his wife. If any memories portrayed him in a negative light, he would fast-forward through them and attempt to do so with little judgment. Dillon already knew he was not the person he thought he should have been, but for now there was a greater purpose at play.

It didn't take him long to get going. So many things crossed his mind as he waited for his eyes to open in the next memory. What would happen if he continued to fall in love with a woman who was dead and more deserving of a better fate all around? What if he couldn't get away from judging his past?

And Rebecca. Was it healthy for her to be using this device? Would seeing her mother again and again only reopen the wounds in her mind? Such questions would have to wait. He had a mission.

Dillon's eyes opened. It was the beginning of a new day.

He sped through the date he had set in the device. He needed to watch moments of his kids. He had been hijacked emotionally by his own failures, and it was stopping him from learning about Rebecca and Jacob.

Finally, he got to the point he wanted to reach.

Dillon sat in a chair between Jacob and Jillian in a crowded auditorium. He looked around at the other parents and siblings who were all staring up at the stage. Students started walking onto it with musical instruments and taking their places. Families clapped as their son, daughter, brother, sister, or grandchild became visible on the raised platform.

Dillon's eyes were stuck on Rebecca as she approached the grand piano to the left of the other students. She looked nervous. The music teacher spoke to a few of the students individually, apparently trying to calm their nerves, reminding them to have fun and enjoy the moment.

Dillon looked down as Jillian's hand rested on his lap by his knee.

For whatever reason, Dillon could feel her touch. He could feel something from a vision, and it felt nice. Comfortable.

He looked back up to Rebecca, who was turning pages in her music book. The teacher walked to the front of the stage and welcomed the family members to the high school recital. Gentle applause rang out before the teacher explained the songs the students were going to play.

Dillon kept his eyes on Rebecca. The nerves seemed to be leaving her, and a smile appeared on her face. This was something she obviously enjoyed.

The teacher tapped her conductor's baton twice on the music stand in front of her, then raised her arms gracefully. As her arms began their concise movements, the instruments began playing.

The quality of the music was as to be expected for a tenth-grade recital. It wasn't until Rebecca had her solo that it really hit home for Dillon. The way she carried herself, the force on some of the keys, the foot pedals—he was in awe of her and couldn't have been prouder.

These were the moments he needed to watch. These were the memories that would help rebuild his relationship with his kids. Dillon was beaming with pride.

Dillon continued the remainder of the day watching useful memories. Birthdays, sporting events, Christmases, vacations. Time drove on, and after over twelve hours of viewing, Dillon needed food and rest. He pulled the screens off his eyes, pleased with what he had seen.

His kids in their youth. What they were like and how they acted. What made them who they were today.

Dillon had a different opinion of his kids. A better one. He could see not only that they were important to him but also that he was important to them.

He left his memory-viewing room and walked back to the hotel. He couldn't wait to talk to Jacob and Rebecca about what he had seen. As he entered the hotel lobby, a young man bumped into him.

"Dillon Murphy."

The man, who was in his early thirties, looked as if he had been waiting to see Dillon. His orange hair paired well with his dark eyes. Dillon frowned in confusion.

"Do we know each other?" Dillon looked at the man, his eyebrows drawing tight together.

"You don't remember me. Look, we spoke before your accident." The man looked to be holding something back.

"Okay, what does that matter? Who are you?" Dillon was confused, but he was smart enough to know this man had something to say, and Dillon wanted to hear it.

"We shouldn't talk too much here. Listen, take my card. Call me and meet me at the location on the back. I know something about your accident." The young man spoke fast like he had somewhere else to be, but he stood waiting for a response from Dillon.

Dillon's anxiety, which had curtailed from the enjoyment of watching memories of his kids, started to return.

The only thing Dillon knew was that his car crashed, his wife was dead, and he was the lone survivor. He was told it was suspicious in nature and that the black box had been removed prior to the accident for mechanical reasons. Now the car itself was missing.

If this man knew something about the accident, Dillon would have to follow up on it.

"I don't know who you are, but you need to start talking. Do you know something I don't?" Dillon was becoming upset.

"I need you to trust me. You did before. You were going to help us."

"You come here and make a comment about knowing something about my accident, and then you ask me to trust you? Who are you, seriously?" Dillon couldn't understand what he was hearing.

"I know how it all sounds, and I don't expect you to understand right now. But we can't talk here. I work for the FBI. Call me when you're ready, and meet me at the location on the card." The man started walking away.

Dillon chased after him. Why would the FBI be involved?

"Wait. Wait a minute." Dillon looked down at the card. The name "Jayden Thomas" was written in the middle of it.

"Jayden, wait. I want to hear what you have to say. I'll probably be here for a while with my kids."

"I understand. Just call me when you can meet with me."

Jayden walked out. Dillon watched him go through the exit, which was still a desert behind the door, as far as he could tell.

Dillon headed to his hotel room. Even with this new turn of events, he was still looking forward to sharing his memories with his kids.

CHAPTER
TWENTY-FOUR

Dillon got back to the hotel room to see his kids watching their tablets, obviously waiting for him to return.

"Dad! Holy shit, were you watching for that long? What did you see?" Jacob couldn't hold back his questions.

"I saw a lot of you guys," Dillon said as he walked into the middle of the room. "I watched the dates from the list you made for me. Most of them, actually. I want you guys to know . . ." He looked at each of his kids. "I love you."

Rebecca jumped up and hugged her dad, and he hugged her back. His hug was comforting, meant to express how proud he was and how much he cared for her. He was astonished to have created such an amazing person. He was extremely grateful for both of his children.

"Did you see Mom? Sit down and talk to us." Rebecca pulled her dad to the couch and snuggled into him as Dillon started going over all the positive things he had watched. He felt good talking about those moments. It was as if he remembered being there.

Jacob eventually went back to watching his hockey game while Rebecca and Dillon yapped on and on, but deep down, Jacob's focus was on their conversation. It made him feel happy too.

The trio fell asleep in the living room together and woke to find themselves wrapped in blankets on the large comfy couches with the sun beaming into the room. Jacob was the first to wake and promptly got ready. He was planning to get cleaned up and go back to the Reality Room.

He thought he should try something a little more appropriate this time, like sleep in the shaded hammock or go golfing. There were so many options. He wondered if he would get a chance to try them all. He just hated the fact that he was limited in hours per day. Who were they to decide how long was enough for this kind of entertainment? Jacob understood the reasons behind the limitations, even though he didn't want to admit it to himself.

Rebecca was next to wake up and made breakfast for her dad before heading out to school.

She was looking forward to the weekend, so she could spend more time with her family, especially to review her dad's memories with him. A new bond had developed between them, and it meant everything to Rebecca. It would be hard to keep her mind on schoolwork throughout the day.

Rebecca kissed her dad on the cheek and left the mess for Jacob to clean up. After breakfast, the two men immediately went to their next destinations: Jacob to the Reality Room for pleasure and Dillon to the PAstREAM device for personal research.

Dillon was going to watch more of his kids, but first he wanted to scroll through some of the days closer to the crash. If he could find out why the accident happened, maybe he could get answers for his daughter. To help give her closure. She and Dillon were both struggling with *why*.

Of course, he was worried about what else he might find in those moments, but he told himself he would stop his search if he couldn't put up with the skeletons.

He spent almost two hours fast-forwarding, trying to find conversations that seemed concerning or of importance sprinkled in between conversations with Jillian or the kids. Dillon got through a couple of days in a short period of time. Suddenly he saw a bright light and a fist rising from his face and stopped fast-forwarding.

As the blurred vision started coming into focus, Dillon could see two people standing in an office while he lay on the ground staring up at them. A large man whose fist had retracted from his face and Mikal, the creator of PAstREAM.

"Kael, I swear to God, I'll kill you. We are making a shit ton of money here. Don't sabotage this!" Mikal yelled directly at Dillon.

But why was Mikal calling him Kael? Dillon was confused.

The body Dillon was viewing from spoke with an Irish or Scottish accent. "It's wrong, Mikal. We didn't invent PAstREAM for this purpose. That's not why we did this. I don't even know you anymore. You're so secretive about what you're doing with Elizabeth. You're not the same person. You've gone fuckin' mad."

Dillon realized this must not be his memory, but that of someone else. Of someone named Kael.

"Shut up, Kael! Stop being a little bitch. Just leave and go buy an island to live on somewhere. You can go have a great life and wash your hands clean of this place. I'll make sure you never have to worry about your finances. I'm giving you a chance, Kael. A final chance."

There was a pause.

The body Dillon inhabited wiped a handful of blood from his mouth with his hand, a sure reward from the previous punch.

"People need to know what they're using our device for, and I'll make sure it gets told. I'm sorry, Mikal, but you can't threaten me. We created PAstREAM together to do something good. I can't live happily ever after knowing what it's becoming." The body Dillon was watching from stood up and started walking out of the room. He caught a glimpse of himself in the mirror by the door. It definitely wasn't Dillon.

Dillon didn't understand why he was getting these visions. He watched as the hand from the body he was inhabiting scanned the door to leave, but it didn't open. Without warning, a loud bang went off behind him. He stared at the wall ahead, which was spattered with blood and fragments of something. His eyes rolled up into darkness.

Dillon stopped the machine.

Had he just witnessed a murder?

What happened to Kael, and who was he? It appeared as though he was someone who had a hand in creating PAstREAM.

Sweat dripped off his forehead and onto the floor. He had to keep watching. Something big was occurring here, and as much as he wanted to stop to avoid being any part of what he just saw, maybe beyond all this were the answers he needed. Like, why was he getting these visions that didn't belong to him? Or what if whoever tampered with his vehicle still wanted to hurt him? What if their next move was to hurt his kids?

No, he couldn't stop now. He had to figure out what was going on before making any decisions.

Dillon kept watching, but this time it returned to his own personal memories. He wondered if he had control over seeing memories that didn't belong to him. But there was no button for that, so he continued to fast-forward through his days, getting closer and closer to the date of the car crash. He watched a day in thirty minutes. He was able to spend another ten of his current hours running through film of his life like a professional athlete re-watching the game. He wanted answers.

CHAPTER
TWENTY-FIVE

So far Dillon had pieced together that one of the creators of PAstREAM, Kael, had been potentially killed because he didn't want his creation used for something it was not intended for and that Mikal was not who he seemed to be.

But why couldn't he find anything about Kael's death online? He thought the murder of one of the creators would have been big news.

The part that Dillon struggled with most was figuring out why he was a part of this and why he was getting fragments of someone else's memories.

Dillon used the PAstREAM device for the entire day, including a good portion of the evening. He scanned through weeks in hours, finally reaching a point a couple of days prior to the car crash that killed his wife.

As Dillon continued to fast-forward, he noticed an animated conversation happening between him and Jonathon.

"Jon, I need to do this story. I have proof. This is about morality—about stopping the wrong people from using that memory device to brainwash the population and manipulate the presidential election. Someone at PAstREAM left me information that is too hard to ignore, and now Kael is missing. That can't be a coincidence. So, are you going to let me do it, or do I have to find some other means?"

Jonathon stared into Dillon's eyes. "Dillon, drop the fucking story, and move on. You're going to cost us all our jobs if you report this. It doesn't matter what proof you have—it's so outlandish, no one will believe it anyway, and we'll be sent away in shame with fear of repercussions. TTN will become the Total Trash Network."

"You're right, that could happen," Dillon agreed. "But it doesn't mean we should walk away from what's right. I'll give you a couple days to think about it. Just give it some honest reflection. That's all I ask, my friend. Trust me."

"You want me to trust you? You fuckin' slept with my wife. I'll never trust you."

"That was years ago, before Rebecca was born. I've apologized to you and Jillian almost every day since."

"Since we found out, you mean."

Dillon sat down in a chair and put his face in his hands. Jonathon left the room.

Now it made sense that Dillon had felt there was a wall up when he'd spoken with Jonathon since waking up from his coma. Jonathon knew about the cheating, which meant Jillian must have known too.

The only positive part of that interaction in the memory was watching himself fight to report the truth about what was going on with PAstREAM—a minor achievement in a disgusting situation. It didn't stop the pain he felt for having done what he did to Jillian and his best friend. How would Jacob and Rebecca feel if they found out? Or did the kids already know? Should he tell them about what he saw, or would it be too hurtful?

As his mind returned to the task at hand, Dillon still didn't know where this proof was about what PAstREAM was doing to people's minds and how it related to the upcoming election. He didn't even know what he would have been reporting on.

Frustration was setting in. He was involved in some sort of conspiracy. Could it have anything to do with the accident? Whatever shit he'd gotten himself into could even now be affecting his second chance at a life with his kids. Hadn't they suffered enough?

Dillon unhooked from the machine. He was tired. His mind couldn't take anymore. He'd have to return again first thing in the morning. It was time to eat something and get some sleep.

CHAPTER
TWENTY-SIX

Jacob had spent all his allowable time for the day in the Reality Room. He had lived his best life in just five short hours. Now he was lying in his hotel room watching the news without his father on it.

"The election is only a few months away. With the current president's second term coming to a close, someone new is going to be running this country. Will it be the first black female president, Malia Ann Obama, or another white male, albeit younger and very popular among the Republican voters, named Kendy. The polls continue to be very close, but as of late, Kendy has been starting to catch up. We go live to Jefferson City, where the presidential debate is happening tonight."

Jacob tuned out the news. His mind was on his family and how happy he was feeling. His dad was learning about his time with them in the memory machine, and Rebecca was in the best mood he'd seen in God knows how long. He knew deep down that the fact she was watching memories of their mother couldn't be healthy in the long term. That thought kept popping up in his conscience, but he would push it back down. He didn't want to ruin what was happening right now. Eventually, she would need closure, but it wouldn't be today. For now, he loved how everything felt, and he didn't want to mess with it. He couldn't spend every day in the Reality Room either, even though he gladly would.

Just as his mind started wandering into the adult version of the Reality Room, Dillon walked in.

"Dad, holy shit. You spent a long time in there again. Talk to me!"

"Jake. I'm sorry for many things, my son. I know I haven't been the best dad to you and Becca. I was hard on you guys, and I could have been a better person."

Jacob didn't understand where this regret was coming from, but he accepted it. "No worries, Dad, I know you were trying your best. I wasn't perfect either. Did you see any good memories?"

Dillon was happy to turn things positive. "I watched a lot of amazing moments. You remember when I took you to the Yankees baseball game? You couldn't believe how many people could be in one place. It blew your mind. For, like, half the game, you couldn't comprehend fifty thousand people in one spot."

This was such an incredible feeling for Jacob. His dad remembered one of his favorite moments in life and Jake didn't have to be the one telling the story this time. Pure joy pierced his heart.

"That's awesome that you got to see that memory! It was so cool being there. It was a playoff game. The crowd was chanting something . . . I can't remember." Jacob looked to the ceiling for the answer.

"'Ump, you suck.'" Dillon had just been there. He knew.

"Yes! That was it!" Jacob laughed.

He stared at his dad, in awe of the memory, then asked if he was hungry. Rebecca had gone to the PAstREAM device after school, and she still wasn't back, so Jake ordered room service while the two reminisced about the many memories that Dillon had just watched. As Jacob continued to bombard his father with questions while he ate, Rebecca walked into the hotel room looking unhappy. Jacob noticed immediately.

"Sis, what's wrong? Did you see something in the memories you were watching?"

Rebecca nodded. "I watched the night of the accident." She looked at Dillon, ashamed. "I was such a bitch to you and Mom."

Dillon got up and hugged her. "Becca, don't beat yourself up over any of that. For what it's worth, I don't remember." Dillon tried adding humor to the stressful moment, something he'd seen himself do in the past but was never that successful with. He could tell it didn't help in this instance either.

"How you acted or what you said to your mom doesn't matter. She knows you loved her, and from everything I've watched of her, she loved you more than you can imagine. That I know."

Rebecca felt better. The combination of her father's embrace and the fact that he knew what he was talking about from watching the memories made her feel warm inside. The self-inflicted anger and frustration were easing off.

Dillon was the one who had the most regret. He thought for a moment about talking to his kids about it, but the feeling subsided. This was not the right time for it.

Jacob poured red wine into three cups and handed them out. "I think we could all use this. That bottle's been sitting there since we checked in. Might as well put it to use."

The three of them sat in the kitchen, nibbling off each other's plates and talking about memories past. They were starting to feel like a family again.

CHAPTER
TWENTY-SEVEN

Morning came quickly after another long night of remembrance. The Murphys were groggy while they drank their coffees. It was the weekend, so Rebecca could finally spend an entire day watching memories of her mom. She had been hung up on the moments right before the crash, but now she wanted to go back to when she was a little girl. When her mom would comb her hair and tell her stories and cuddle her. She wanted to feel her mom's touch again.

Jacob no longer had much of a desire to use the PAstREAM device. He had initially wanted nothing more than to watch his past, but he could see how doing so was affecting Rebecca. Getting over his mom's death already felt like an impossible task. He was also getting more than enough of an emotional getaway from his time in the Reality Room as well as by watching other people's memories in the "Mind Fuel and Consumption" area. Watching terrifying events or insane moments from another person's point of view was pretty addictive. It was better than YouTube. Plus, the unlimited VIP food was delicious, a tempting combination for a young man who was still growing into his physique.

Dillon, on the other hand, was back at it, plugging himself into the PAstREAM device like it was his full-time job. This time he planned to watch more of the dates on the updated list that Rebecca had created for him as well as more moments prior to the accident. He didn't want to worry his kids while he investigated what had happened just before his memory loss. He knew that as long as he brought positive memories to talk about each night, they wouldn't question him on any other memories he had been watching.

Dillon hooked in and immediately got many of the personal, fun memories out of the way. A vacation, a birthday, Rebecca's soccer finals. It was beneficial to view these because it gave Dillon a proper perspective of his offspring. They weren't just his kids; they were human beings who succeeded and failed along the journey of life. They had been through more than he had given them credit for, and watching these memories gave him a dose of reality toward them.

Unfortunately, his second mission stood before him like an overdue task. He knew he had more to see, more answers to gain. The time had come for him to focus on what had been giving him the most anxiety.

Was his accident truly just that? An accident? Or was someone trying to kill him? If so, were they still trying? Were his kids in danger?

If he could answer those burning questions, he felt he could close that section of his mind and finally move forward with his life.

Dillon watched and even re-watched every hour leading up to the car accident. He had been scanning through to find the seemingly important moments in those days, but this time he was focusing on the minutes. Jumping from hour to hour, he searched as much as he could to find nuggets of information. As time pressed on, Dillon wasn't finding much more than he had in the previous sessions, other than a conversation with Jillian that concerned him.

"Dilly, you seem more stressed lately. Why won't you tell me what's bothering you?" Jillian had cornered him in the kitchen.

Dillon was somewhat agitated. "I'm working on an exposé that has me much more involved than I thought was possible. I'm just a reporter, and a damn good one. I'm not supposed to be part of the story."

"So, pass it off. Tell Jonathon you don't want to do this one."

"It's not that easy, babe. This is a big one. I'm the person who needs to break it. I don't want to talk anymore about it. I'm sorry."

He hoped it was a mere coincidence that her death followed soon after that.

Dillon wasn't getting anywhere. He backtracked to a date four days prior to the accident. He had watched that particular day once already, but the device had skipped over a lot of the day on its own. He hadn't thought much of it at the time. (He was forwarding through as much as he could anyway.) But now he was scrubbing every hour prior to the crash, and he wasn't going to let the time jump ahead again.

As Dillon approached the same moment the device had skipped over last time, it happened for a second time. Not by much—it only jumped about two hours—but it was clear there was missing time in this particular memory. Dillon wondered if that was normal. It made sense that memories could have gaps.

Rebecca had done some research on how the PAstREAM program functioned back when she was trying to figure out if this would work for him. She told him and Jacob that the PAstREAM device pieced memories together from the brain and then tried to fill in the missing information because memories aren't recorded like video. That was the beauty of the device; it created an uninterrupted version of events through its technology.

But for some reason, there was a two-hour lump that Dillon couldn't access. He kept going back and forth over that period, but the same thing kept occurring. The time jumped.

Upon further recollection, it wasn't the first time this had occurred. It had happened to Dillon in a few other memories while he was scanning closer to the date of the accident. He couldn't recall the exact spots. Perhaps it was because of the crash that his memory was missing chunks of information, and relying on the machine to connect the missing dots was an improbable task.

As Dillon kept flipping between the beginning and the end of the missing time, his brain started to hurt. Just a bit of a headache, minor compared to some of the ones he had suffered since the coma.

While Dillon was focused on the brain pain, a new memory appeared unprompted. Dillon assumed it was going to be another unrequested memory, but this was not like anything he had seen. His neck stiffened, and his heart started to race.

All he could see was blank, white nothingness.

There were no walls, no floor, no ceiling. It was like looking inside a cloud. He could see a chair in the distance and a man sitting in it.

Dillon didn't move. He stood there, staring at the man in the chair.

What kind of memory was this?

Nothing was happening within the nothingness. There was just the man and the chair, far off from Dillon's current spot. The man didn't move. Dillon couldn't see any of his facial features from his location, and he wished the Dillon in the memory would walk toward the guy.

Sure enough, Dillon started moving toward the chair. As he got closer to the man, he started to recognize him.

Dillon desired to move faster, and the memory followed suit. He came to a stop directly in front of the man.

It was the same person Dillon had seen get shot in the head.

Dillon wanted to speak and started thinking of the words he wanted to say. As he thought, so he did.

This, he realized, was no memory.

This was happening right now.

"Kael?" Dillon asked.

"Yes. We need to talk, Dillon Murphy." Kael's features were warm. His dirty blond hair blended into his manicured beard. He had the same Irish or Scottish accent as the memory Dillon had seen him get killed in.

"I have so many questions. Why did I see Mikal shoot you? What's my involvement in all this? Are my kids in danger? Aren't you... you know, not alive?"

Dillon's mind was racing. He didn't know if he was going to get answers from the apparent dead man sitting in front of him or if this was actually occurring at this exact moment. Maybe his mind was getting messed up from using the device too long.

"Dillon, listen, we don't have long. You're right, I'm dead. I'm also the person who sent you visions that weren't from your own memories. Right now, you are the only one I can communicate with safely. No one else that I trust is using the PAstREAM device, so I'm unable to send them any messages."

Dillon was confused. Why was he the only one Kael could trust? Before he could ask anything more, Kael continued.

"Weeks prior to my last conversation with Mikal, I had a breakthrough with the programming to upload my conscious mind into the PAstREAM device while still retaining my body and mind in real form. Although my body is now dead, my mind is inside the device. The overall design of the PAstREAM device has numerous uses, many of which people do not know."

Dillon almost didn't believe what he was hearing. There had been so many technological advances over the past decade, but this was hard to digest. This had to be some kind of dream his mind was creating on its own, but Dillon wasn't waking up from it. He tried pushing buttons on the handles to see if he could pause it, but nothing happened. He couldn't control the device in any way. He wasn't able to fast-forward, rewind, or stop the device, so he had no choice but to continue.

"Did I know you before you died?" Dillon asked.

He thought he may as well get some answers.

"Yes, I knew you, Dillon. You did a story on our device with Mikal. I met you briefly while you were doing your report; you got more entangled, which later put you in danger."

Kael had hit the right note. Dillon's eyes widened.

"What happened? What do you know? Please, I'm begging you. My kids—did I do something that could endanger them? Was Jillian's death my fault?"

Kael stared at him, compassion in his eyes. "I'm going to tell you what I know and what you need to do. We don't have much time. Mikal has been attempting to watch your memories while you are plugged in. I found a way to send him different memories through the system, so whenever you use a PAstREAM device, Mikal will only see memories of yours that I have programmed him to see. I can't risk letting him find out that I'm still alive in here. Right now, he thinks you're watching your son's school play, but I can't trick him forever. I need you to listen."

Dillon was all ears.

"I did one other thing to your mind," Kael said. "You were connected to the PAstREAM device prior to your accident but after my death. I was able to lock specific moments that I felt would be detrimental to your life. Memories that Mikal wanted and still desires to see."

Dillon thought about that. He hadn't seen a memory of himself using the PAstREAM device prior to the accident. Maybe Kael locking off parts of his mind was why he couldn't access certain hours in the final weeks before Jillian's death. If Kael was manipulating Dillon's mind, how was he supposed to trust him?

"During a recent follow-up news interview you did with Mikal on the PAstREAM device, you met Elizabeth. You know her as the woman who goes through the instructions before you use the device. Do you understand who I'm referring to?"

Dillon nodded. She was one of the faces of PAstREAM, hard to forget.

"Well, she gave you a special chip so she could communicate with you without Mikal knowing. Days later, she reached out to you and asked you to meet her at a secure location within the PAstREAM facility. She told you that she was not human, that she was a form of artificial intelligence and that Mikal had created her, which is completely true."

Dillon paused, trying to understand what exactly he was hearing. Apparently, he was making some sort of facial expression that made Kael stop talking.

"Dillon, I know this is a lot for you to take in, but we don't have a lot of time, and there's quite a bit more that you need to know. Elizabeth had information for you regarding Mikal and what he was planning to do with the PAstREAM device. As I've mentioned, PAstREAM has many uses. Although Elizabeth has no soul per se, she has a moral compass that Mikal invented, because he has a fear of his inventions killing their creator. She knows right from wrong. Mikal built her to be humanlike. It wasn't his first attempt at creating AI, but it was the first one that worked, and it worked very well."

Dillon tried to digest the information he was consuming. He was talking to a dead man who had uploaded his own mind into the PAstREAM system and was telling him that the woman who explained how to use the device was a robot and that Dillon had met her secretly. Considering what had happened in his life over the past year, Dillon kept an extremely open mind.

"Elizabeth met with you multiple times," Kael continued, "and four days prior to your accident, she told you about a man named Kendy who is running for president of the United States. She told you that Kendy is her brother, another AI, and that Mikal has been using PAstREAM to download fake positive memories of Kendy into the mind of every person who uses a PAstREAM device."

Kael hesitated, then continued. "We created PAstREAM for people to relive the past and for other positive means, not to use as a method of persuasion and deception." He looked around the white room quickly, pointing to a dark spot in the corner. "Dillon, I can't keep us together in this program for much longer. PAstREAM will realize something is not right and attempt to correct itself. See that dark spot over there? That's the device's programming trying to fix what I'm doing. I can only adjust its programming temporarily before I have to go back into hiding. We have to allow twenty-four hours to pass after our meeting. If we do this more than once every twenty-four hours, PAstREAM will consider this an infection of the system and send an alert to Mikal and the programmers for review. If I lose connection with you, promise me you will come back again tomorrow."

Dillon nodded. "Yes of course. I need answers, Kael."

"You confided in a man named Jonathon about what you had heard from Elizabeth, although you never shared your source," Kael continued with urgency. "You wanted to run the story, but he wouldn't let you. Mikal found out that you were aware of the PAstREAM device being involved in the upcoming election. Because Jonathon was, and still is, a user of the PAstREAM device, Mikal was able to erase that part of his memory. Jonathon no longer remembers that conversation with you."

Dillon was overwhelmed. He had known too much of some crazy story, and it probably killed his wife.

Kael continued, talking over Dillon's stumbling words, which weren't coming out of his mouth correctly. Time was of the essence. "Mikal hid his plans from me, but I found out through Elizabeth and confronted Mikal that night he killed me, which is one of the visions I sent you.

"Dillon, I have a task for you. You need to meet with Jayden Thomas. He will help you, but don't tell him what you know. Not yet. I can see in your memory that he has already made contact with you. He works for the FBI and was investigating us before I died. He doesn't know what I have told you. Get him to protect your kids, but don't tell him about me yet. Mikal has manipulated him with free use of PAstREAM. And Dillon, there's something I need to tell you that will change everything—"

Just then, the memory kicked him out. Kael was gone.

"What? Kael, *what?* What were you going to tell me? Please!" But nothing came back. Dillon's eyes were met by nothing but darkness.

Dillon unhooked himself from the machine and left. He walked briskly through the hotel and took the elevator to his room. He had an infinite number of questions stockpiling in his mind, along with fear, plus a task from Kael. He needed more answers. He was going to meet with Jayden Thomas.

CHAPTER
TWENTY-EIGHT

Dillon called the number on Jayden's card, and they arranged to meet that evening. Dillon's mind was racing with images of his conversation in the white room with Kael. He was freaking out. He kept thinking about his kids. If anyone touched them, Dillon would kill them with his bare hands. He might not entirely remember Jacob and Rebecca the way they hoped he would, but he loved them. He helped create them, and he had a sense of responsibility for them regardless of his current mental predicament. Those two showed him unconditional love even when he questioned whether he deserved it.

Dillon put on his coat and shoes and headed for the hotel exit. He could not leave through the PAstREAM lobby desert that others used, because it only led to the parking garage. The exit he was using had him on the hotel elevator and out to the street in a matter of minutes. Dillon needed an Uber.

Once he hailed his driverless ride, Dillon scanned his finger on the payment screen with the funds that Jacob made available to him on a per diem basis. He hoped his kids wouldn't check his spending and just assume he was taking the day to watch memories of their family. He would actually prefer to be doing that over driving secretly to some unknown location to talk to someone about what he didn't remember, but that wasn't an option. He needed to find out what he could for the safety of his kids. Deep down, he wanted to hear someone tell him to just forget the past and stop messing around with it and that whomever was after him would leave him and his family alone. He would be satisfied with that.

Dillon watched the city go by as the car drove toward its destination. It was bright in the darkness as road lines lit up, and advertisement signs flooded the streets. The big city lights slowly faded as he traveled down one side street after another, finally reaching the location Jayden Thomas had given him.

It was a used-sporting-goods store on the Upper East Side. The car stopped, and the doors unlocked. As Dillon stepped out into the evening air, his heart raced with fear and hope—fear that something bad could happen to him, and hope that the FBI would protect him and his kids. He walked into the dimly lit store that showcased a lot of well-worn sports equipment and immediately looked at the man at the till.

"Hi. Is Jayden here?"

"He is!" The man at the counter looked aghast at Dillon. He wore a backwards hat and a shirt with an unrecognizable team logo on it. His dark eyes matched the dark hair coming out from under his ball cap. Dillon could tell from his expression they must have met previously, but Dillon didn't remember him. It was a common occurrence.

"I thought you were dead, or like . . . a vegetable or something, man. I'm glad to see you, Mr. Murphy."

"Thanks. I need to see Jayden. Please."

"Of course, bro. Follow me."

Dillon walked farther in, past the stockroom behind the store. The man opened a door and waved Dillon down a set of stairs before locking it behind him.

Ah, crap, Dillon thought as he heard the door click on his way down.

He continued to the basement and turned off the stairs to a storage room that housed an office slightly bigger than Dillon's bedroom in the hotel. Jayden was sitting in a chair in the corner.

"You came. I wasn't sure you would. Neither did Teddy. He didn't believe me that you were up at PAstREAM. I suppose you want to know what we found out about your car accident?"

Jayden had answers. But if he knew what happened in the accident, why hadn't there been any arrests or trials? Dillon knew he would have to confide in Jayden if he wanted to gain his trust.

"Jayden, look, I need you to tell me everything you know. I don't remember much prior to the accident. The doctors said it can happen, you know." Dillon knew Jayden would have gone through all the medical records. The only thing he wouldn't know was what had transpired since Dillon got out of the hospital, including his recent conversation with Kael.

"I'll share with you, but it's a two-way street." Jayden flipped his pen in the air, catching it awkwardly between his fingers. "I need information from you too. Have you been able to remember anything since the coma? I gave you some time, hoping your memory would return. I'm hoping you have some new info to share."

Dillon sat opposite Jayden, his elbows resting on the desk. "I know that Mikal wants to use the PAstREAM device against the population. Download stuff into their minds."

"You told us that already, but we don't have any proof." Jayden hesitated when Dillon stared at him as if that was the extent of his knowledge on the topic. "Dillon, there was more to it. You were going to find out what the fuck was going on. You had an insider. You told me it had to do with the election."

Dillon looked on, realizing his insider was most likely Elizabeth. But he needed to learn more from Jayden first to make sure he could trust him. "Was my car accident . . . did it happen on purpose? Did someone want to kill me? Was it Mikal?"

Jayden looked around the room as if trying to find the words. "Dillon, your accident was suspicious in nature. The fact the black box and the car itself are now missing, tied with your knowledge of something that you should have shared with the FBI . . . personally, I think someone tried to kill you. We just don't have any proof of it."

Dillon took a big breath. He would have rather heard it was truly an accident.

"You knew something about the election and how PAstREAM was involved," Jayden continued, "but you didn't tell me the details, and it may have cost Jillian her life. The government is monitoring Mikal, and I was monitoring Kael prior to his disappearance. You were my informant, but you wanted to break this story wide open, so instead of telling me what happened, you saved it for yourself, hoping to bring something big to the masses, and now you don't even remember it. That's called karma, with all due respect to your situation, and I could charge you for withholding the information that you did."

Dillon stared at the floor. His chest hurt. He had refused to tell Jayden what he knew, because he didn't want to give up on a big story, and it may have cost him his wife and his memory. Dillon started to feel overwhelmed with grief, thinking about what he had done to his family.

"Well, I guess I fucked everything up," Dillon said, looking at Jayden with anxious eyes. He knew he had done wrong, but it wasn't going to stop him from trying to figure out what he needed to do next.

"If you can tell me who your insider is, your informant, I have people— ways to get information," Jayden said. "I just need to know who I'm supposed to talk to. Mikal is a dead end. He checks out; he's a good man. He spoke with us extensively. Kael is the one I'm concerned about. He's taken off to some island to avoid going to prison. He's who we need to find."

Dillon was frustrated. The FBI was off base. Kael had not gone missing; he was murdered. And how could Mikal "check out" with the FBI? They were better equipped than that, weren't they?

Dillon thought back to what Kael had told him: *Don't tell him anything yet. Get him to protect your kids.*

"I'm trying to figure out who my informant is," Dillon said. "Let me watch more of my memories in the PAstREAM device. Maybe I can find out who the insider is and let you know." Dillon wasn't the best liar, but he was a showman by trade.

Jayden looked at him inquisitively. "Absolutely. But let's meet together again soon. You have my information."

Dillon agreed and then asked one more favor. "And can you keep an eye on my kids? I just want to make sure they're safe."

"Dillon, I've been keeping an eye on you and the kids since the accident. It's how I knew you were at PAstREAM. Don't worry."

Dillon nodded in thanks. He wanted so badly to trust Jayden, to trust a government agency. He stood up and turned to leave up the steps but remembered having heard a locking sound from the top of the stairs when he entered. He turned back to ask if the door was unlocked, but Jayden was gone. There was no window and no door to the room that he could see, but Dillon was standing there alone in the office. He turned around, hailed an Uber from his wrist, and ran up the stairs. The door was unlocked. He ran through the stockroom and out of the front entrance with no sign of the man who had greeted him. He opened the car door and jumped into his ride. Tomorrow he would speak again with Kael.

CHAPTER
TWENTY-NINE

As Dillon ate his breakfast the next morning, his kids stared at him. He hadn't spoken to them very much the night before. It was quite the change compared to the previous evenings, but Dillon had too much on his mind to talk about good times with his kids. He would have loved discussing amazing family moments while drinking his coffee, but reviving that would have to wait. He wasn't in the right frame of mind. He had told his kids that the last memory he had watched was the one just prior to the accident. He said he felt very sad about what happened and needed to go straight to bed. They understood, but they would have liked to help him through it. Dillon didn't like lying to Jacob and Rebecca, but he didn't want to freak them out either with his new revelations or his visit with Jayden.

"Dad, try to watch only positive things today so we can talk about them later, okay?" Rebecca was adamant that her dad be in better spirits. She needed to talk with him about her mom and about her childhood, so she could feel like her dad truly understood who she was and what her mom was like. To Rebecca, that was the most important thing in her life right now, next to getting through the school year.

Dillon agreed, knowing he would have to share memories that evening, and realized he had a duty to his daughter, even though it wasn't the most pressing item on his mind.

It also got him on the fast track to leaving the hotel room and getting back to the PAstREAM device. Dillon had to wait a little to get to the twenty-four-hour mark and revisit with Kael, so he watched a couple of memories of his wife and kids on a family trip to Maui. It helped pass the time rather enjoyably, other than catching Jacob downing his fourth beer at the Hawaiian bar by the ocean. He had apparently never seen Jacob drunk. It was a first for both the new and old Dillon, based on the conversation that happened between them on the beach.

Dillon kept watching until he noticed that twenty-four hours had officially passed. Within seconds his vision went back to Kael on his chair in the white room.

"I see you met with Jayden." Kael had obviously viewed Dillon's memory. *There was no need for Dillon to explain what he had spoken about.*

"I did. I don't know if I can trust him. I mean, he seems trustworthy, but he thinks Mikal is an upstanding citizen. Not that I know better—I'm still trying to piece this all together. Kael, you said you had something to tell me before we lost our connection. Something that would change everything. What was it?"

Kael ran his right hand through his hair. "I do. It's about your accident." Kael squirmed in his seat.

Dillon kept his eyes locked on the man in the chair, desperate to hear what Kael had to say.

"The car accident you were in, the one that killed your wife . . . Dillon, that accident never happened."

Dillon looked at Kael in disbelief.

"What the hell does that mean? Of course, it happened—I was there, I've seen the memory. My wife is dead, Kael. My kids are suffering from it. How can you say something like that?" Dillon was so taken aback by Kael's comment, he almost laughed in his anger.

Kael kept a straight face as he continued. "Just listen, Dillon. That night, Mikal had you in his panic room, hidden within this very building under the hotel. He uses it as a refuge for himself, as a workshop for his inventions, and as a place to keep Elizabeth. He brought you and Jillian there. You were on your way back from the grocery store after picking up ice cream."

Dillon was shaking his head in disbelief.

Kael continued on, "He convinced you to come here so you and Jillian could escape with free time in the Reality Room. The true reality was he brought you to his panic room and tortured your mind using the PAstREAM device. He wanted to know who told you about Kendy. He scrubbed your memories, searching through months' worth in a matter of hours. That's a lot for the human brain to endure. You can watch memories in real time and even fast-forward, but to scrub the memories that quickly . . . it's something that's never really been done."

Dillon's headache was returning. He was trying to understand what Kael was saying, but believing him was a completely different story. He was being told to believe that his accident never happened and that he had been in a panic room instead. There were too many facts that showed that the accident did happen: the doctors, the coma, and Jillian.

Kael watched as Dillon stood in front of him, going through a number of expressions, including the continuous shaking of his head in rejection. "I locked out the spots in your mind that I didn't want Mikal to see," Kael continued. "He cut through your memories, looking for individuals, locations, and whatever else he needed to figure out how you got your information about Kendy. He had little concern as to how it would affect you. He also uploaded your memories to a computer at speeds we had never tested on anyone. All of it caused your brain to overload, putting you into a coma."

Dillon kept rocking his head from side to side. That wasn't what happened. Why was Kael trying to make up a different story?

"Mikal had no intentions of killing you. He was just going to get his answers, wipe your memory of the incident, and set you free. But you didn't give him the information he needed, and you ended up essentially brain dead after the ordeal. So, Mikal . . ." Kael paused before continuing. "Mikal created a memory of a car crash. Your car crash. He didn't realize your entire memory would be affected other than the parts he erased. The accident never actually happened."

"Fuck you," Dillon said, outraged. "I don't believe you."

Kael pressed on regardless. "Mikal continues to search for those moments in your memory every time you plug yourself in here, hoping to unlock what he couldn't get into last time. That's why you're staying here for free; he wants you in the machine. It's also why you're getting headaches. But Mikal is just getting the same results, because I'm blocking access to those memories. At least this time he's doing it in small chunks without fear that you're going to report on Kendy. He also doesn't want to put you into another coma, especially while plugged in to PAstREAM. Too suspicious."

Dillon was clicking buttons and trying to get out of this memory. This nightmare. But nothing he did could stop the white room and the man in the chair.

"There's one more thing you need to know. Dillon. Jillian is still alive."

Dillon's head was foggy. He was dizzy. Jillian, alive? No. That wasn't possible. Who would do that to his kids? Who would make two amazing children think their mother was dead? It wasn't true.

"That's impossible. The doctors—one of them told me he saw my wife dead. He was sorry he couldn't save her. Your story doesn't add up."

"Dillon, those doctors visited PAstREAM for personal use and had memories downloaded to make them believe they saw your wife. This was an orchestrated plan. Mikal isn't stupid; he even had the police officers and paramedics involved given memories during 'complimentary' use of the PAstREAM device. Mikal is brainwashing everyone who uses it, and now he's inputting lifelong memories of a presidential candidate that only just recently came into existence."

Dillon was starting to consider the possibility that Kael might be telling the truth, especially considering the lack of information regarding the accident and the fact that Dillon had known something incriminating about PAstREAM, which the FBI agent had corroborated. There had to be more to the story, but this seemed outrageous.

Dillon's mind was going down a rabbit hole. Even if there was a 1 percent chance that Kael was telling the truth, he needed to ask. *"So, where is Jillian now? If she's alive, where is she? How can I save her? What am I supposed to do?"*

"Mikal is holding her as collateral in case you remember who your informant is. She's been hooked up to the PAstREAM device a few times to see if she knew anything and to download new memories into her, so she believes she's supposed to be with Mikal for her own safety and the safety of your kids. She also believes you murdered her sister, who never existed. Mikal has been messing with her mind. She's a toy for him. A human experiment."

"She wouldn't believe that shit." Dillon scoffed angrily at the idea.

Kael remained stoic. *"You believed you were in a car accident and that Jillian was killed. The mind can be easily manipulated."*

"How do I know you aren't manipulating my mind right now?" Dillon asked, hoping he would get an answer that would confirm what was true and what wasn't.

"There is nothing I can tell you that will prove that what I'm saying is the truth. You have to put the puzzle pieces together and decipher it for yourself. I've made sure that whatever memories Mikal is currently downloading into you are going into a part of your brain that you can't access, so he can't manipulate you. It's why you don't know anything about Kendy other than what I've told you. Your daughter, Rebecca, has used the PAstREAM device. Ask her what she knows about Kendy. I bet she knows a lot more than you'd think. I haven't blocked any memories that Mikal has added to her, because I don't want to draw any more attention than I already have by altering you."

"I don't—"

"You don't trust me, not yet," Kael said. "And that's okay. You need to ask questions. Filter out what's right and what is not. I don't envy your current position any more than my own. We've both been dealt a bad hand, but we can make it right. I need your help to fix it."

Dillon was now the one running his hand through his hair. "I don't know, Kael. I really don't know what to think. And Jillian, is she okay at least?" Dillon rubbed his temples with his middle finger and thumb within the digital world, wondering if his question was even legitimate. He didn't actually believe she was alive.

"From what I could tell when she gets plugged in, she is . . . let's just say she's alive—although the last time she was plugged in was almost two weeks ago. Mikal is keeping a very close eye on everything you do, but I believe you and the kids should be safe for now. Mikal is worried there might be too many coincidences, considering the FBI was and is monitoring PAstREAM. They had already been closely working with us since we are connecting wires into the minds of the population—not exactly a procedure you let a company do without Big Brother taking part—but apparently our investigator, Jayden, isn't solving any of our crimes."

Dillon was happy to hear there was a chance he and his kids were safe for the moment, but that didn't ease his mind as much as he had hoped. The thought that the kids' mom was still alive weighed on him, if, in fact, that was the truth.

"Where is Jillian now? Is she in the panic room I was in?"

"Jillian is being held in one of the underground rooms in the hotel on negative floor two. I'll tell you what you need to do to get her, so I can help her, but we have to work together. First, I need your help getting out of the machine."

Dillon thought it over. He imagined how Rebecca would feel, knowing there was a chance her mom was still breathing the same air as her. How Jacob would react. It all seemed like a fantasy.

"*Okay. What do you need me to do?*"

"*You're going to help me download my mind into Kendy.*"

Dillon did not completely understand what he had just heard. "*Okay, how do I download your mind into Kendy? Can't you just do it over Wi-Fi or Bluetooth or something?*"

Kael hesitated. "*That is not possible. You need Elizabeth to hook Kendy up to Mikal's personal PAstREAM device, wipe his memory, and download me. Unfortunately, I've been unable to find a way to connect with Elizabeth to this point.*"

Dillon did the math. He would have to capture Mikal's presidential robot and somehow get in contact with his other robot.

"*How am I supposed to do that? Can we save Jillian first?*"

"*Dillon, I'm sorry. I need a body. Kendy has to be first. Then we have to find a way to stop Mikal if you want to save Jillian. There's no other way. She thinks she's supposed to be with Mikal, and he's the only one who has access to the rooms on negative floor two.*"

Dillon had another plan. "*What about Jayden and the FBI? I can just contact them and tell them what's going on.*"

"*Dillon, the FBI have spoken to Mikal on a weekly, sometimes daily basis. If you ask them for help, what are you going to tell them? Do you think they'll believe you spoke with me in here? They won't believe someone who can't even remember their own past. Plus, Mikal can just give them use of PAstREAM and alter their minds.*"

"*You don't know that for sure,*" Dillon said.

"*I've already tried involving the authorities while I've been in here. I connected with a different FBI agent who used PAstREAM and downloaded false memories into him to help me trap Mikal. After watching the memories of that agent's wife weeks later, it appeared he died during a fishing trip. That's not a coincidence. I'm not going to involve any others who are not already a part of this. Mikal can too easily manipulate those who get in his way.*"

Dillon was anxious. This whole thing was too much for him to deal with. "*No. No, no, no. I want out. You're asking me to risk my life even more than I already have. I just want my kids and I to be left alone. I'm not going to risk myself or my kids any further. Please, there has to be another way."*

Immediately, Kael disappeared. The memory was over.

Dillon unhooked from the machine and went back to the hotel. In the elevator he looked for the "negative floor two" button on the panel, but that wasn't a choice to select, or he would have headed straight down there. As he made it to his room, he was thankful neither of the kids were there. He didn't want to talk to them at the moment. His mind was all over the place.

Was Jillian actually alive? Should he believe anything he'd heard from Kael? What if Mikal was feeding him these moments in the PAstREAM device for some ulterior motive, and Kael doesn't even exist? There was no way to know for sure what he should believe, or if any of the memories he watched were real. His mind raced with all the potential possibilities.

Dillon was tired mentally, and he was at a dead end with sorting out who he should trust. Based on everything he had gathered to that point, if he continued to play stupid and let Mikal believe he'd lost his memory, which was the honest truth, maybe they would leave him and his kids alone, and he could go and live whatever life he had left. He certainly didn't feel capable of fulfilling what Kael had asked of him.

But Jillian. She was the kicker in all of this. Could she actually be alive? He would have to risk his own life and potentially his kids' lives to find out.

Dillon wanted to go home. To go back to the life he'd had a week or so ago, when he was learning about his family without the use of a machine. That had some logic to it. He could give moral support when they needed a father. He may not be the best at providing instant answers, but sometimes answers weren't required as a parent. Just being there was worth its weight in gold.

Dillon waited for his kids to come back for the night. Jacob was the first to return, right before dinner. Dillon was forced to lie to his son. "Jacob, my memory isn't working right now. Every time I plug in, it's not working. I think I've overworked my brain. I'm getting bad headaches. I want to go home."

Jacob hesitantly agreed with his father. "Of course. We can come back another time. To be honest, I don't want Becca watching any more memories right now either. She's not focusing on reality, and neither am I."

"I'm proud of you, son. I was worried you'd be the one to become addicted to this place, but it turns out you're the one worried about your sister and me. And rightfully so." Dillon gave his son a hug. He knew he was making the right choice in planning to leave.

Jacob, however, felt like his dad just gave him a backhanded compliment. He also knew he was going to badly miss the Reality Room. As they sat at the counter in the kitchen, talking about their experiences at PAstREAM, or at least the versions they were both willing to share, Rebecca returned.

"You guys won't believe what I saw when I was watching the memory of us in Maui. I swear there was a shark in the water, and we were just swimming along like it was no big deal. I had to rewind like ten times, and I saw a fin sticking out of the water!" Rebecca was beyond excited with this news, but her brother wasn't so sure.

"How do you know it wasn't a dolphin? We saw some off the shoreline during that trip, remember?"

Rebecca seemed dejected. "Well, yeah. I guess it's possible."

Jacob decided he would break the news to Rebecca. "Sis, Dad and I agreed that we should go home tomorrow. Get back to our normal lives for a while. We can come back here again after a break."

"What? No! We can't leave yet. I have more memories of Mom to watch. I'm staying. Dad, don't you want to see more of Mom and us growing up? There's so much you need to know!" Rebecca was genuinely upset. They couldn't leave yet; this was what their lives were supposed to be, researching the past to build a future together.

"Becca." Dillon reached out and put his hand on her shoulder. "Like I told Jake, the memories aren't working for me right now. I'm getting bad headaches. And, honey, you need a break too. You can't spend all your free time watching the past. Come home with us. We'll come back very soon. I promise."

Rebecca stared at her dad. "Okay, fine," she said in a tone that was meant to be rude. She knew deep down that she should get back to reality for a few days at least. She was mature in many ways and could admit when she was wrong. It was a trait she shared with her mom, but it frustrated her, because her brother and dad weren't very good at admitting fault. It had caused many arguments in the past.

As they sat on barstools in the hotel-room kitchen, eating whatever was left in the fridge, they reminisced about a soccer final, a birthday, and that family vacation in Maui. Dillon and Rebecca laughed about how they'd watched the same experience on the same day. It helped relieve some of the stress Dillon had from the final portion of his time in the device.

Their conversation went on for hours, and for a fleeting moment, Dillon forgot that Jillian may still be alive, that she could be sitting in that very hotel somewhere. Dillon also thought about asking his kids about Jonathon's wife and if they knew anything. Was what happened common knowledge in the family? Or was this another deep, dark secret he would have to live with? He decided it was best not to ruin such a fantastic moment with his kids.

As the night wore on, Jacob was the one who said he wanted to go to bed. Rebecca was the opposite. She could talk about her mom for the next twenty-four hours straight if they'd let her.

"I'm going to hit the sack now too, love," Dillon said to Rebecca shortly after Jacob left for his room.

"Dad, this was one of the best nights I've ever had. I just feel like, after everything that happened, you're finally becoming you again. I'm proud of you." Rebecca smiled as she stifled a yawn.

Dillon looked down at the counter. He wasn't proud of himself. He had cheated on and possibly killed his wife, held back information about PAstREAM from the FBI, and put his family in danger.

"Thanks, Becca. I'm even more proud of you. You're such a strong woman. I've seen so many memories of your mother and . . . I can see where you get it from. You're so much like her."

Dillon gave her a big hug and then headed for bed. It would be good to go home.

CHAPTER
THIRTY

As the Murphy family woke from their final night at PAstREAM, a lot more happiness was hovering around them than they would have thought. Rebecca was thrilled that her father knew exponentially more about them and their mom than he had prior to their arrival, Jacob seemed to be harboring a greater sense of joy from the Reality Room, and Dillon didn't have to drag his kids out of the building.

Upon checking out, the bill was exactly as promised: zero dollars. The thought sent a chill down Dillon's spine. It may not have been the "you scratch my back, and I'll scratch yours" that Mikal had promoted.

The group walked out of the hotel and into the grand hallway before looking up one last time at the war raging between the dragon and the shark. The shark had sunk its teeth into the dragon's thigh. The dragon had its wings spread and its neck back in apparent pain.

Dillon peered at the exit. They would finally go through the desert.

As they got closer to it, Mikal appeared before them. "Murphy family, are you leaving us already? Are you not enjoying your stay here at PAstREAM?" Mikal was very kind in his speech, but Dillon was suspicious as to why he might want them to stay longer. If he had no ulterior motive, what should he care?

"I really appreciate the hospitality you have shown my family," Dillon replied, "but we just need some time back at home. Get some errands and schoolwork done—you know, family stuff. But I've promised the kids we'll be back in short order, and I plan to keep it." Dillon wanted to make sure he told Mikal enough to appease him, so he would let him and his kids leave, if only temporarily.

Dillon couldn't stop considering the fact that he was talking to the man who had potentially killed Kael and had his wife held hostage, although there was still so much doubt and confusion in his mind.

He flowed into a question that would surely show his intention to return. "Would it be okay if we stayed in the same room again?"

Mikal nodded at Dillon and the kids. "Of course." His smile seemed genuine, but he had practice at interacting with PAstREAM users. "We will keep that room set aside just for you. We look forward to seeing you again very soon."

With that, Mikal was off greeting another guest, only this time Dillon imagined him working on those who spent large sums of money, not the ones staying for free.

Rebecca entered the desert first. The heat from the imposter sun beat down hard. As Jacob entered, he could tell it was the same technology that powered the beach in the Reality Room. As the group followed the signs pointing to the oasis ahead, they found the vision of the distant trees and lake getting blurrier and blurrier with each step forward. Rebecca guessed it was supposed to mimic a mirage. In less than a minute, they walked through the blurriness and out into the parking garage.

"That's a lot like the Reality Room," Jacob said, looking proud that he had "been there, done that." He scanned the monitor to retrieve his vehicle.

On the drive home, Jacob realized it was Monday. The weekend had been a blur.

"So, I guess we're both skipping classes today, sis?"

Rebecca grimaced with guilt. "It seems that way."

"What about you, Dad? Aren't you supposed to do that interview with Mr. Winters today?" Jacob looked at his father in the rear-view mirror.

"Ah, crap, yes. I completely forgot about that." Dillon didn't want to follow through on his promise to his boss and so-called friend, but he didn't feel like he had any choice.

Rebecca tried pleading her case one more time. "Daddy, don't. Just tell him you aren't well. Tell him about your head hurting and how we had to leave this place."

"I can't do that, honey. He's paying our bills." Dillon reached forward and rubbed his daughter's arm in appreciation of her concern for his well-being.

Being back home felt good. Rebecca immediately started tidying up the living room and kitchen. They had left the house in a state unbecoming of their mother's standards. Rebecca had done a lot of the cooking and cleaning over the last while at the apartment since the office was no longer providing the same amount of funds that allowed for a housemaid. It was more survival money.

It started looking less and less like the insurance company was going to allow the claim on Jillian to go through. They said they required more answers, and Dillon figured they weren't going to get them. Considering she may still be alive, he wasn't about to fight them on it at the moment.

Dillon stood in his walk-in closet, trying to find the Armani suit that Jonathon had requested he wear for the interview. After flipping more than a few of the coats open to see the brand in the lining, he finally found one matching the description.

Dillon prepared himself as best as he could; this was not something he remembered how to do. He wore a light-grey sweater underneath his suit with a matching pocket square. He took the black watch from beside the gold one on the table and put it on his left wrist. Nothing felt right, but he figured he knew what he was doing from muscle memory.

The hardest part was picking the right shoes. He had to have a dozen pairs under the suit section of the closet. He put on the shiniest pair of dress shoes he could find, spritzed cologne on his neck, and went to the mirror.

Dillon looked appealing, although significantly thinner than the man he had watched in his memories. His flowing hair blended into the tattered beard he had grown. This was the first time Dillon could remember getting this done up, and it caused a word to echo out of his mouth unconsciously: "Wow."

While aiming for the bedroom, Dillon walked along the side of the closet where Jillian's clothes remained hanging. As he made it to the door, that self-loving he had just witnessed in his reflection dissipated with the reminder of his wife. His mind went back to the jumbled mess of feelings and confusion about the fact that she might be alive at that very moment.

Dillon switched off the light and called an Uber.

CHAPTER
THIRTY-ONE

As the car pulled up to the front of the TTN building where Dillon worked, he noticed he wasn't nervous. He thought that with everything that had been going on, adding this stressor could bring him to his knees, but that wasn't the case. Dillon didn't fear this situation.

He got out of the car and walked through the entrance. He had been there on an almost weekly basis since his awakening, so it wasn't anything new to him to go through the weapons detector or to run into someone who wanted to talk to him about what had happened. This was the first time he had worn something other than street clothes since the so-called accident, so he did get a few friendly catcalls on his way up to the top floor where TTN (The Truth Network) had planted its head office.

The elevator opened directly into where people were bustling about, preparing the news stories of the day.

"Hey, Dillon! Heard you were doing an interview today. Looking forward to it." A man slapped him on the shoulder as he walked past. Dillon headed directly to Jonathon's office and knocked on the partially open door.

"Dillon. I was right; that suit was meant for you. You just need to put on some weight and shave that awful beard. Thanks for coming in." Jonathon got up from behind his desk and headed toward his supposed friend, shaking his hand.

Jonathon motioned for Dillon to sit at the desk. A digital paper was sitting directly in front of the seat.

"I've put the interview questions in front of you. Read through them and let me know what you think. It's nothing crazy. The main thing is people just want to see you again. We still get calls about you almost daily. People want to know how you are, and it would help get more viewers back."

Dillon read over the questions.

1. We know you were in a vehicular accident. What can you tell us about it?

2. You have no recollection of your past since the accident. What has that been like? Do you get snippets of visions from your past?

3. You lost your wife and the mother of your children. How has your family been, through this tumultuous time?

4. You've been using the PAstREAM device to view your memories. Has that worked? Can you watch the past you don't remember? *Expand further.

5. When can people expect to see you back on the air full time?

Dillon soaked in the questions. He would have to tread vaguely and use generalizations when answering. The only question he could see struggling with was the last one. He didn't even know if he wanted to be back on the air, but he knew that wasn't the answer they were looking for. He would have to make some sports cliché about how he was taking things one day at a time and would come back when the time was right. That time might never come, so he felt confident in that line of thinking. It was still honest, if perhaps a little misleading.

Jonathon was sitting across the desk, answering emails and notifications on his translucent screen. Dillon could see right through it, but he couldn't see what was on the screen. He rested the digital paper on the desk and leaned back in his chair.

"Okay," he said.

Jonathon shifted his eyes from his screen to the man opposite him. "You're good with the questions?"

"Yes, I am. I don't know how acceptable my answers will be because of my memory issues, but I'll do my best to answer them thoughtfully and concisely."

"That's all I can ask. Are you ready to get started? We can do it in the interview room with the digital screen behind you. It's private, and we can have you out of here in a couple of hours."

Dillon nodded. "Let's do it."

CHΔPΓER
ΓHIRΓY-ΓWO

When Dillon got home from the interview at the office, his kids were sitting on the couch, distracted by their tablets and the latest version of Atomic Air Pods that stuck semi-permanently behind the ears. They didn't hear him come in. He sat down next to Rebecca before she even noticed he was there.

"Dad, you're back! That didn't take long. How did it go?" Rebecca dropped whatever she was watching.

"It was fine, actually. Not as bad as I thought it would be."

Jacob finally noticed and folded his tablet up. "Dad, how did it go?"

"Like I told your sister, it was fine. Jonathon asked the right questions, and I answered them as ambiguously as possible." Dillon chortled under his breath.

"When will they have it available to watch?" Rebecca asked.

"End of next week. They want to hype up my first interview since the accident. Get some more advertisers. More money." Dillon rubbed two fingers against his thumb in the air.

Rebecca hugged her dad on her way to the kitchen. "I'll start dinner!"

Dillon followed. "I'll help."

Jumping back into a routine was easier than the Murphy family had anticipated. Eating at the table together and sleeping in their own beds was almost blissful for Rebecca and Jacob.

Dillon was still struggling with the thought that Jillian might be alive. He was also concerned that someone could come into the house at any time and try to kill him, or God forbid, his children.

By the time Dillon fell asleep from exhaustion in the early hours of the morning, the sky was glowing in preparation for its awakening. The kids let their dad sleep until just after lunchtime before they started to get worried. Rebecca went into his room with a cup of coffee and a stale croissant.

"Dad, you okay?" She sat next to him on his bed like so many times at the hospital, only those times he wouldn't wake up.

"Becca? Hi, honey. What time is it? I couldn't fall asleep last night." Dillon looked at the coffee next to him and sat up.

"It's almost one in the afternoon. We thought you needed to recharge your brain. I'm worried the PAstREAM device won't work again for you, and you won't be able to see Mom or learn more about us."

Rebecca had obviously been carrying this concern with her since her dad told her that his memories weren't working—a false alibi used to get them back home without incident. Dillon didn't want to give his daughter any additional concerns, but this seemed like a small casualty to get them back to a normal home life, if only temporarily.

"I'm sure it will be fine, sweetie. I think my mind was just exhausted from watching so many memories. But look at the bright side: at least I got to experience a ton of memories of you." Dillon took a bite of the stale croissant and quickly realized it would be his last. "I'm sure the memory device will work again. The memories are there, and maybe that means one day I'll be able to access them again on my own without having to 'plug in.'" Dillon used air quotes, which made his daughter smile.

He was right, and Rebecca knew it. Those memories were still there. Still accessible. At any point he could just remember on his own and wouldn't need to go to PAstREAM to learn about the imperfect family situation he had created.

"Thanks, Dad. I'm just so happy you're alive and that you're here with us. You know so much more than you did before you got 'plugged in.'" Rebecca made air quotes as well, which made her dad laugh. "It's great to be a family again. Well, as much as we can be without Mom."

Dillon's stomach curled. Jillian might still be alive. Should he not use every available means necessary to make sure one way or the other? On the other hand, should he not try to make the most of what was left of his family? This notion that the car accident never happened and that their mom was being kept alive was incomprehensible. This is what had kept him up all night until fatigue finally took over.

Dillon hugged his daughter, thanked her for waking him up and getting him a late start on breakfast. As he sat there drinking his coffee, the feeling of anxiety he'd had the last night rushed over him again.

He didn't know what he was going to do. He needed to talk to someone. He would go back to see Jayden at the sporting goods store. Right now, Jayden was the only other living person who had any inclination as to what was happening. Dillon flipped his sleeve over and made a call. Someone answered after four rings. He would meet Jayden in two hours.

CHAPTER
THIRTY-THREE

It was daylight as Dillon approached the sporting goods store. He saw the young man, Teddy, sweeping the walkway out front.

"Hey, Teddy," Dillon said with a bit more enthusiasm in his voice than the previous time.

"Oh, hi, Mr. Murphy. Head on in; you know where to go." Teddy went back to sweeping. Dillon didn't know if Teddy was actually a sporting goods store employee or if he was doing a really good undercover job of running the shop.

As Dillon continued through to the stockroom and down the stairs, he heard Jayden wrapping up a phone call.

"He's here. I gotta go. Talk later."

Someone else obviously knew he was there. Dillon hesitated. Was Jayden talking with Mikal? After thinking about it for a few seconds, he realized Jayden probably reported to someone. He would need to talk to others at the FBI about his findings. Dillon took the last step off the stairs and swung around toward Jayden's desk.

"Dillon, good to see you. Was just on the line with one of my superiors. You know how it is. Even James Bond has to tell M what he's up to," Jayden said with a laugh.

"Of course, totally understand." Dillon felt his suspicions ease slightly.

"So, tell me. What have you learned? You're back earlier than I expected, so I imagine you figured out something new. Whatcha got?" Jayden leaned back in his chair and put a well-chewed pencil in his mouth.

"Ah, yes, well, um, I saw some things in my memories. Things that have me a bit, well, confused." Dillon stared into the eyes of the man behind the desk, wanting to tell him about his conversations with Kael. It was actually less about telling Jayden about what he had seen in the PAstREAM device and more about whether Jayden would believe him. His mind teetered back and forth until he decided he was going to go for it and tell Jayden what he knew. It was the FBI. Who else was he supposed to trust?

"Jayden, after I watched quite a bit of memories . . . something happened. Something weird. It's hard to explain." Dillon kept his eyes focused on Jayden and hesitated, hoping to see trusting eyes looking back at him. This was not easy to describe or share with anyone. He hadn't even told his kids.

Before he could continue, Jayden interrupted in a calming tone, obviously trying to make the situation feel safer for Dillon to share his story.

"Take your time, Mr. Murphy. I know you've been through a lot. I just used the PAstREAM device yesterday as well. I know how emotional it can be watching things from your past. I'm not here to judge you in any way."

Dillon's eyes widened as he remembered that this FBI agent was still actively using the PAstREAM device. Dillon's eyes moved back and forth, echoing the movement currently going on in his brain.

Anyone who used the device could be compromised with information from Mikal. Potentially. Dillon didn't have any concrete evidence of this, but he couldn't rule out the possibility. And if Jayden was using it as recently as yesterday, Mikal would be aware of Dillon's last visit and conversation at the sporting goods store.

Dillon sputtered in confusion as to what he should do next. If he told Jayden what he knew, and Mikal found out, he might try to do something to Dillon or his kids.

Dillon changed gears. "So, you understand what it's like watching your memories then? You know about how emotional it can be?"

"I do. Mikal actually lets me use it for free, if you can believe it. He said I'm always welcome to PAstREAM, and that if I ever have any questions about you or the investigation, his door is always open. It's actually refreshing not having to deal through someone's lawyer. The guy's an open book."

Dillon almost threw up in his mouth. Jayden was a puppet to Mikal. It wasn't his fault—Dillon figured he was brainwashed and gullible.

Jayden continued on unprompted. "Yesterday I watched a couple of the great moments I had with my dad before he passed away. It helped me; you know? Seeing him again. For a moment, I felt like he was alive. I missed him. Things didn't end well prior to his death." Dillon could see moisture building up slightly in Jayden's eyes, and in a weird way, he felt a sense of shared humanity with Jayden, that deep down he was a good soul. For the first time, Dillon felt a connection with him. It just wasn't going to be the type of connection that would allow him to share his story about Kael.

Dillon knew he would have to forgo sharing any pertinent information at this juncture in their relationship, hoping there would be a future time and place to tell him. He had to think of something on the spot, however, to make Jayden believe he was gaining ground in his investigation and give a reason as to why Dillon had wanted to speak to Jayden so urgently.

"I really appreciate what you went through, Jayden. I know what it's like to watch memories of someone who's no longer with us in the flesh." Dillon wasn't sure who he was thinking of when he said that. Jillian might still be alive, and at the moment it was possible he was referring to Kael. "It's difficult for me to watch my memories, because I don't have any idea how they play out. I can't relate to them. It's like a never-ending movie with twists and turns, and for some reason, I'm the main character in all of it."

"Jeez, I feel like we should go for a beer now or something," Jayden joked.

Dillon chuckled getting into another creative lie. "So, Jayden, after watching what seems like endless hours of my memories, I feel like I have an idea of who my informant was. I believe it was Kael." Dillon realized his best defense was a good offence. He had no intention of telling Jayden anything about his visions with Kael, but with Kael not walking among the living, it seemed like the best way out of the situation.

"Okay, did you see a memory with Kael that makes you think that? Do you remember what he told you about the election?" Jayden leaned forward in his chair, getting closer to the possible break in his case.

"I had a conversation with Kael. It was kind of choppy, the memory. Some of the memories get all jumbled—I think from my accident. But I just remember meeting him for a drink at PAstREAM, and he told me he was going to tell me something big. Something to do with the election—that the polls were rigged or something. I couldn't quite get it all clearly. And that was my last memory of him." Dillon looked to see if this lie was going to land like a pilot's first attempt or stick like a veteran's.

It did neither.

"Dillon, I'm going to need a copy of that memory. When was this? Was this before or after he went missing? Give me a date. A time. Did you meet him at the restaurant at PAstREAM?" Jayden seemed partly excited that the case was opening up and partly frustrated that Dillon might now be a suspect because he might be the last person to have seen Kael.

"Well, the date was, I would say . . ." Dillon tried to figure out a believable date, preferably prior to when Kael went missing, which he had no actual clue about. Dillon didn't know how deep of a grave he was digging for himself with this fabrication. "It was about two weeks before my accident, I believe. The machine wasn't even really sure with timelines on my memories, what with me not remembering anything." Dillon played the memory-loss card in hopes of winning the hand.

It wasn't yet legal for law enforcement to request a memory or PAstREAM data from an individual, although it was surely in the works for the future. In this case, however, Dillon would become a top suspect if he didn't cooperate. At worst, he could plead ignorance and say he couldn't find the memory again, as he had been searching through so many of them. He didn't document dates and times. That would be his alibi for now.

"I'll work this lead, but I need more information." Jayden seemed agitated about another dead-end trail. Dillon suspected Jayden would be keeping a close eye on him. It wouldn't look good for an FBI agent to be working on something that ended up being nothing more than a dramatic misunderstanding. Dillon knew he needed to have something more for Jayden the next time they met. That thought was bothersome.

"Yes, I'll get more information for you. Dates, times, all that. I promised the kids I wouldn't use the device today. They wanted to get back to some normality. And my mind is exhausted from using the device so much. It actually didn't work the last time I used it." The lies were bleeding out of Dillon as if from shotgun wounds.

"Fuck, Dillon, I get it. I just need answers soon. I know I can't make you show me any of your memories, but I won't lie, this won't reflect well on you, man, if you don't get me more info. I sympathize with your current situation, but that doesn't give you a reprieve from a federal investigation." Jayden's imposing tone broke through for the first time since they were reintroduced.

"I get it, Jayden. I do. I want to help. I want to get you answers. I'm sorry I don't have them yet. I feel like we're getting somewhere. I thought I had some new info to share, and I wanted to tell you right away." Dillon was just trying to find the words that would help him get out of this situation.

"Go back to your family. Get some rest. We'll figure this out, but don't keep anything from me."

Dillon got up, and Jayden followed close behind, only this time he went with Dillon up the stairs and not out some secret door.

The severity of the FBI's involvement weighed on Dillon. Maybe he should have just said he couldn't find any information, although that wouldn't have made sense considering he requested the meeting. Now he was caught up in a lie with the government and risked jail. As he walked past the counter, Jayden by his side, he bid adieu to Teddy, who was selling a basketball to a group of teens.

As the door closed behind Dillon, Jayden stood beside Teddy at the counter and spoke softly enough not to be heard by anyone else. "Follow him. He's hiding something, and I want to know what it is."

Teddy flipped the "OPEN" sign over to "CLOSED" and followed the teens out of the shop.

CHAPTER
THIRTY-FOUR

As Dillon got into the front seat of his driverless Uber, his mind raced with thoughts about what he should do next. His kids were expecting him home for dinner in an hour. Dillon didn't really have anywhere else to go at that point anyway, so he kept his course heading back to the apartment. It wouldn't look good if he went to PAstREAM after telling Jayden he wasn't going there. He was not prepared to risk flaunting his lies.

Tomorrow, however, he was going to have to talk to Kael and find out what he should do next. Maybe Kael would think of something new that could help the situation. The only problem with visiting Kael was that the last time they spoke, Kael had asked Dillon to get presidential candidate Kendy into a spot where his mind could be erased, so he could load into him. It was an insane request to ask anyone no matter how many angles Dillon came at it from. But he was at a dead end in his own investigation and had just put himself in a worse situation with the FBI.

As Dillon awoke from his festering daydream, he realized he was going down a street he had not been down before. It appeared as though he was heading to PAstREAM; however, that was not the case, because the car stopped about a block away in front of a one-storey commercial building's garage door. The garage opened, and the car drove in. Dillon quickly tried to open the car door, but nothing worked. He tried manipulating the driving app to change course. He even tried calling Jayden in case he would help. But the signal on his sleeve phone showed zero bars. The inside of the garage was pitch black as the garage door closed behind him.

* * *

In the car that was tailing Dillon, Teddy watched as the building swallowed the Uber. He called Jayden immediately.

"Dillon didn't go home."

"Where did he go?"

"He just went into a garage on the corner of Sixth and Twelfth near PAstREAM, in an Uber."

"Let me know if anyone comes out of there. Aim the car's camera at it, so I can watch too. This is starting to get a lot more interesting, Teddy."

* * *

As Dillon sat in the dark with no way to contact anyone, the door to the back seat opened. The car's interior lights came on, finally illuminating the space he was in. A woman with black hair, red lips, bright blue eyes, and a black dress slid in and kept the door open beside her. Dillon realized immediately it was the same woman from the device: Elizabeth.

"Dillon, we don't have long. Do you remember me?" her voice was soothing. It could put anyone at ease almost immediately, although Dillon was not feeling at ease in the dark garage.

"I know of you, but I don't remember us meeting previously." Dillon was possibly talking to an android, so he kept his sentences brief and to the point.

"You and I have spoken before. I gave you information that you were going to leak out to the public. Mikal had uploaded so much garbage into the minds of those in high positions by offering them free use of PAstREAM. You were a suitable means to exploit what Mikal was doing. Mainstream would not work." Elizabeth spoke with little to no emotion in her voice. What she said was also correct: Mainstream news was biased and was not trusted by a large portion of the population.

Elizabeth's eyes penetrated Dillon as she continued, "I was given a note from one of our employees that read, 'contact DM'. The employee did not know what that meant but knew to give it to me. Do you have information for me?"

"I spoke with Kael less than forty-eight hours ago." Dillon guessed Kael had manipulated one of the PAstREAM staff to create this meeting between he and Elizabeth, so he decided to tell her exactly what he knew. Perhaps the more information he shared with her, the more she would share with him.

"So, he did it. He uploaded himself into the device. Is that where you spoke with him? From within PAstREAM?" Dillon heard a slight uplift in her voice but nothing worthy of excitement.

"Yes. And he said we were to work together on his plan." Dillon turned as much as possible in his front seat, giving his attention directly to Elizabeth.

"Of course. Tell me. I'm ready."

"We are to bring Kendy to Mikal's personal PAstREAM device, wipe his memory, and download Kael's mind from PAstREAM into Kendy's body." Dillon stared at Elizabeth's face, watching her features for movement. She was so real apart from the lack of emotion.

"That is a plan, indeed. I'll need time to process how to get Kendy into this position. Is there anything else?" Time seemed to be slipping away for her.

"Yes, one other thing. Jillian, my wife . . . apparently, she's still alive. You and Kael were going to help me free her and fix her mind from whatever state Mikal has her in after we download Kael into Kendy." Dillon was eager to hear a response to this, to see if Elizabeth knew anything about Jillian's condition and if she would be able to help retrieve her. Hell, he just wanted to hear another voice say Jillian was alive.

"Yes. I'm surprised he told you about Jillian. Her mind has been heavily manipulated. I don't know how she could be brought back to her previous state. Mikal has run many experiments on her." Elizabeth spoke candidly and was apparently not going to sugar coat anything. All Dillon could think about was returning the mother of his kids, only to have her unable to remember them. An unjust duplication of what they'd already gone through.

"Kael said he could help her. For the kids' sakes, I have to believe he can." Dillon didn't want to hear any more about what Mikal had done to Jillian, but he did have more trust in what Kael had told him. Someone else had verified it. He wanted to believe there was hope. Dillon now carried a more vengeful feeling toward Mikal.

"I'll run probabilities and decipher as much as I can for us to achieve success with Kael's plan," Elizabeth said as if she was wrapping up the conversation. "Place this chip into your sleeve. It will allow me to communicate privately with you when I'm ready."

Dillon took the small pronged sticker, peeled it off, and placed it on the addition section of his forearm. Sticker chips didn't have a terribly long shelf life. They were meant to be temporary. "I have to ask, how did you get the Uber to drive here? And where are we?"

"I ensured that you would grab my Uber first. It's no coincidence that your ride showed up within seconds of you ordering it. Mikal provides rides for some of his higher-end clientele, and has given me access to the program. I'm a computer, you know. I'm just limited when it comes to what I can do with PAstREAM. Mikal has cut me off from executive functions." Elizabeth was matter-of-fact, although it appeared there was some sarcasm attached to her remarks about being a computer. She got out of the car and closed the passenger door. The garage door immediately started opening, and Dillon was back on the road headed for home. Although he had only been gone for an additional fifteen minutes, which wouldn't set off any alarm bells with the kids, the other set of eyes felt differently.

* * *

"He's leaving the garage. I'm on him."

"Teddy, I think we may have misjudged Mr. Murphy. More importantly, I think he has misjudged us."

CHΔΡΓΕR
ΓΗIRΓY-FIVE

As Dillon entered his home, the smell of dinner penetrated his nostrils. He was unexpectedly hungry.

"Dad, you're just in time. I made us a pot roast and potatoes." Rebecca was putting the roast on a cutting board for Jacob to slice up. Jacob would help around the house, but he didn't do nearly as much as Rebecca. He felt bad about it and always vowed to do more. He just never got around to it.

"Smells delicious, honey." Dillon pecked the back of his daughter's head and punched his son in the arm. Even though he appeared in good spirits, Dillon was intoxicated with his current predicament. He wanted to talk to Kael, to get to the next step in the process of getting Jillian back for his kids. There was no way he could live with himself if he didn't at least try, especially for Rebecca. The thought that Jillian was alive was eating him up inside.

As the family sat down to eat, Dillon was able to distract himself, if only for a moment, while they talked about their day. Rebecca had written down half a dozen more dates she wanted to watch in the PAstREAM device, which only reinforced the need for Dillon to find his wife. After dinner and dishes, they sat in the living room, fighting over what to watch. Jacob wanted to watch the basketball game, and Rebecca wanted to watch something that everyone would agree on. Dillon didn't care, but as they flipped through the channels, he asked Rebecca to stop on the news channel. It was talking about the election and the Republican debate.

There, in plain view, was Kendy. He was a very charming looking man in his forties with salt-and-pepper hair and a smile that could cause the biggest skeptic to let their guard down. His eyes were piercing, almost an unbelievable shade of blue, not unlike Elizabeth's. But, of course, Dillon knew it to be unbelievable—Kendy was not human. And now, somehow, Dillon had been tasked with kidnapping him and erasing his mind.

Dillon's heart fell into his stomach. The plan seemed impossible. This intelligent robot was beloved by millions, even if they had been tricked into it. How was he going to trick that same robot?

"Change the channel," Dillon said abruptly. He didn't want to see any more of Kendy.

"Why? I like Kendy. I think he'll make a great president!" Rebecca said glowingly.

"I could care less about who runs this country anyway. They're all puppets." Jacob had his own take on politics. He believed there was a greater faction at play running the world behind the scenes. His sister did not agree with his views and would tell Jacob to keep his thoughts to himself when it came to conspiracy theories. It bothered her more because her dad had been big on reporting similar stories when he'd had his online newscast, and it often entailed theories that were similar in nature.

As the evening wore on, Dillon grew tired with frustration, anger, and the inevitability of what was to come. He believed Mikal had helped ruin his family's lives, and he didn't feel safe telling Jayden about what he had learned. Now he understood why Kael didn't trust anyone. They were all tainted by using the PAstREAM device. Dillon's mind raced a million miles inside his head, draining his energy. His chin started bobbing on his chest.

"Dad, go to bed. You're obviously exhausted." Jacob got up and put his hands on his father's shoulders, giving them a gentle rub.

"Huh? Yeah. I should." Dillon rose slowly from the couch, his head still hanging, as if in sorrow.

Rebecca also appeared as though keeping her eyes open was like one-way blinking. Jacob ushered his family to their rooms and was left to his own devices. He too had something on his mind that was making him feel slightly guilty. He desperately wanted to return to the Reality Room.

CHAPTER
THIRTY-SIX

As the sun crested the mountains in the wee hours of the morning, Dillon awoke from a poor sleep, still ready to take on the day. He went through his routine, not hastily but expediently. He was going back to PAstREAM. He needed to talk to Kael. He had hoped he would have gotten a call from Elizabeth after he installed the chip she gave him, but waiting meant he had no control over the situation. Seeing Kael was an obvious follow-up to his garage pit stop with Elizabeth.

As Dillon paced himself appropriately in front of his kids, they still noticed him scurry out the door.

"Dad, wait! Where are you going? Why are you in such a hurry?" Rebecca asked.

"Oh, no hurry, sweetie. I just have to meet some people at work, and I don't want to be late. Just trying to move forward with my life." Dillon hoped his story was sufficient for her.

"Do you want us to drop you off?" Jacob asked.

"No, no. I'm good," Dillon responded quickly. "I'm going to take an Uber. I'm really trying to get back to feeling independent. I know it seems silly, but it's been tough relying on you both, and I want to try and get myself to a point where you aren't pressured to make sure I'm alright."

The kids nodded. It made sense that their dad wanted to get back to being someone they depended on and not vice versa. It was hard to argue that point.

"Okay, Dad, have a good one. We'll see you later. Remember the basketball game is on tonight!" Jacob knew his dad liked watching certain sports with him. Hockey, basketball, football, and baseball were his favorites growing up, but now his dad seemed to stick mostly to basketball. Perhaps it was because he'd awoken from his coma during heart of the season.

Dillon's Uber pulled up, and he slid into the back seat with ease, as if he had been taking rides all his life. He looked around to see if it was the same vehicle that had brought him to see Elizabeth, but it was hard to tell. Most Ubers were the same new model of Tesla. Many other ride-sharing companies were available, but this one was accompanied by a healthy corporate discount.

As Dillon pulled up to PAstREAM, he only cared about talking to Kael. It had been a lot more than twenty-four hours, so reaching Kael shouldn't be an issue.

He ran into Mikal just inside the entrance.

"Dillon! Welcome back. So glad to see you. Will you be staying in the hotel again?"

Dillon was worried his facial expressions would be a dead giveaway to the absolute hatred he was feeling toward the short man who stood before him.

He forced a smile. "No, not today, Mikal. Just wanted to spend some time with the machine and learn about my wife and kids some more. I've struggled remembering anything. I'm doing a lot of self-learning." Dillon wanted to make sure Mikal understood he didn't remember a thing. He also considered strangling the inventor right there or even pleading for his wife's return.

"Of course, Dillon. I'm just glad to see you back. You're always welcome here. Please enjoy yourself." Dillon shook Mikal's hand with an intense grip before carrying on with his task.

As Dillon entered his room and approached the PAstREAM device, he was in awe of the image of Elizabeth's as she appeared on the screen. She was stunningly beautiful here and in person. More importantly, she was the one person who could help him get to Kendy, which, in turn, would lead him to getting Jillian back.

Within minutes of plugging in, Dillon was dashed away mentally to the giant white room.

As expected, Kael was sitting in front of him on his chair.

"Dillon. It would be a lie if I told you I wasn't worried you would never come back. And as I'm currently reading and blocking sections of your memory from Mikal, I can see you spoke with Elizabeth. Oh heavens, that is excellent. She knows. She knows I'm alive. Oh, Lizzy, I miss you."

Dillon stared at Kael inquisitively. "Yes, well, I spoke with her, and I'm awaiting her instructions on what we're doing next. I still don't know how I'm supposed to help."

"Dillon, everyone has a part to play, whether they want to or not. Some realize they are part of this, and others have no clue. Just focus on helping Elizabeth. That's all I can ask of you. And thank you for not sharing my situation with the FBI agent. Anyone who uses PAstREAM, even if it's your closest friend or family member, is compromised."

"So, what are we supposed to do next? What am I supposed to do?" Dillon wanted the next step. He wanted to be told to complete a task. Kael smiled as he replied.

"Dillon, patience. I know you want to get your wife back for your kids. I know that is important to you, and I'll help you with that. You just have to wait until Elizabeth contacts you with a plan. She will have one; that I can promise you."

Suddenly, a loud banging echoed through the white room.

It was extraordinarily loud. Kael and Dillon covered their digital ears.

"Dillon, the system thinks I'm a glitch, and it's trying to fix it. We can't talk anymore. I can't risk getting caught in here. I need you to help me complete our goal. Please, there's so much at stake. Wait for Elizabeth. She's your next step."

"When can I see you again?" Dillon didn't want to be cut off from the one person who had answers.

"We'll talk soon. Just follow Elizabeth."

With that the memory was over. Dillon was back in reality staring at the screen. He didn't know what to do other than focus on getting Jillian out of her prison, both mentally and physically. He hoped deep down that she wouldn't be like he was, or worse off. He trusted Kael would be able to fix whatever mess Mikal had made in her mind.

Dillon decided to watch his memories. There wasn't anything else he could do until Elizabeth contacted him, so what was more important now than continuing to learn as much about his family as possible? At least he had something positive in his life. Seeing the smile on Rebecca's face as they reminisced about the past was more than enough to make him appreciate being alive. He felt a real love for his kids and wanted to see them happy.

As the clock approached dinnertime, Dillon figured he'd better stop and go home. Time always seemed to float by quickly in the PAstREAM device. He got out of the machine, exited the room, and left to grab an Uber. On cue, the Uber headed toward the garage a block away from the PAstREAM building. He was most likely going to see Elizabeth again.

Only this time, the car did not make it to the garage. It was stopped by the flashing police lights of a ghost car. As the Uber pulled to the side of the road, Dillon stared out the back window, trying to figure out why a driverless car that could only go the speed limit was being pulled over. As the officer approached his window, he realized why.

"Dillon Murphy. Off on another adventure, I take it?"

It was Jayden Thomas.

"Jayden, it's good to see you. I was just headed home." Dillon regretted his deception immediately.

Jayden did not look impressed by the obvious lack of detail Dillon provided. "Don't fucking lie to me, Murphy. We know where this Uber went last—into a garage owned by Mikal, the creator of PAstREAM. Your bullshit won't fly here anymore. Get out of the car."

Jayden led Dillon back toward his large sedan, where the back door waited open for his new passenger.

Dillon climbed in the back. He felt the slamming of the door was unnecessary. Jayden sat in the driver's seat next to Teddy, who was pointing a gun at Dillon's face.

"Now you've gone and pissed off Teddy, Dillon." Jayden stared at him through the rear-view mirror as the car sat behind the Uber.

Dillon knew he had to get through this somehow without sharing the truth about Kael. "Guys," Dillon's voice was shaky due to the gun pointed at him. "I have some new information."

Just as his mouth was finishing the last word, Dillon felt a vibration on his arm. It was a text from Elizabeth. Dillon hung his head and pretended to sob, so he could read it. It read, "Don't tell them anything. Send them to the garage with you. I have a plan."

Dillon decided to go with it. He had little time to decide anything realistic and trusted whatever help he was getting from Elizabeth would guarantee his escape from the situation.

Unless, of course, Elizabeth was going to kill the two FBI agents. He didn't know what she was capable of. She wasn't human. Maybe killing people wasn't an issue for her. Maybe that's how Mikal had programmed her.

"I need to take you somewhere," Dillon said.

"Tell me where to go, and tell us why we're going there," Teddy said with more of a manly tone than usual.

Just then the Uber ahead of them flashed its hazards.

"Uhh, follow that car?" Dillon sputtered. He was unsure himself if that was the right decision. The Uber moved forward, and so did Jayden's vehicle. A follow-up text from Elizabeth confirmed that was the correct choice.

Teddy put the gun away and started asking questions. He knew he had the full attention of his back-seat driver. "Where are you taking us, and what haven't you told us?"

Dillon hesitated. He didn't know what he was supposed to say. He hoped desperately for a message from Elizabeth, but nothing came. "Well . . . last time they brought me . . . I—" Dillon looked out the window, grasping for something that would help him make sense of his delayed gibberish.

Just then, Teddy's sleeve phone rang.

"This is Teddy."

"Hi, Teddy. I'm Elizabeth, one of the associates at PAstREAM. You're currently on your way to see me. I just wanted to inform you that I'll be answering any questions you have and explaining why our vehicle was bringing Dillon Murphy to our garage. I look forward to speaking with you. Please continue to follow the car ahead of you."

Teddy nodded confidently. He had just gotten a new lead on a major case. "See you shortly."

Within minutes, both vehicles pulled up to the familiar garage and drove inside. This time the lights were on within the massive warehouse. At least a dozen circular, egg-shaped rooms, each one about fifteen feet high, filled the garage, with a mezzanine along the back wall hosting what looked like an office with dark windows.

Jayden and Teddy got out of the car at the same time, in awe of what they were looking at.

Elizabeth approached from behind the officers, startling them. "Not what you were expecting to see?"

"Are these . . . PAstREAM devices?" Teddy asked.

"Yes. They are used for our more private clientele. That's why Dillon is here." Elizabeth's steady tone and easy-on-the-eyes looks had the agents trusting her without merit.

"Hey, aren't you the lady at the beginning of the PAstREAM sequence? You know, like when you're plugging in and you explain what to do?" Jayden had used the device often in recent weeks and had figured it out immediately.

"I am. Now, you were wondering why we brought Mr. Murphy here . . ." Elizabeth signaled to the two men to follow her up to an office on the mezzanine.

Dillon remained in the back of the police car, but he could still hear their conversation clearly on his phone. Elizabeth had activated a speaker that transmitted to the chip she gave him, so he was privy to everything that was said.

* * *

As Teddy and Jayden walked along the elevated platform, they looked in wonderment at the pods below. They entered the office with the tinted glass, and the men sat down in the chairs Elizabeth offered them. She poured what appeared to be whiskey into three thick glasses and brought two of them over. She remained standing, sipping her drink by the windows as she looked out over the facility.

"As you can guess, we try to stay on the cutting edge of technology here. Mikal is always looking at new ways to advance the field when it comes to the mind and brain function. We brought Dillon here to talk to him. We knew he had suffered memory loss in an accident, and Mikal felt there might be something we could do to help him. Of course, we told him this had to remain completely confidential. If it works, it could help many people who have suffered memory loss or a traumatic brain injury."

Teddy leaned over to grab his drink and took a sip. It was strong but smooth as it warmed his belly. Jayden went to follow suit, but Teddy put his hand on Jayden's glass.

"One of us should stay sober."

Jayden's facial expression turned to disappointment. He wasn't usually one to pass up on a good drink.

Teddy was becoming more relaxed from the beverage and was less shy about asking questions. "Why the secrecy? I was ready to stick Mr. Murphy into a holding cell for withholding information. Did you tell him to keep this information from the authorities if he was asked?"

"Mr. Murphy was told that under no circumstances should he tell anyone about this. There are legal parameters involved in using a human as an experiment, even willingly. Mikal has a soft spot for Dillon. Without him breaking the story, we wouldn't have gotten so big as quickly as we did. None of the mainstream news outlets wanted to run our story. Mikal believes he can help Dillon by having him relive his old memories, the ones he has forgotten, so he can have his memories back. Dillon wanted time to think about it. There is always a risk when playing around in someone's mind." Elizabeth knew transitioning from "Mr. Murphy" to "Dillon" would have a psychological impact on the agents, humanizing Dillon and Mikal's relationship. It made it sound like a caring one, even though Dillon and Elizabeth knew otherwise.

Teddy took another sip of his drink and loaded another question into his mouth. "When was the last time you saw Kael? Do you know of his whereabouts?"

Elizabeth turned to face the men. "The last time I saw Kael, he was planning to leave this place. He wanted to get away from here and collect a paycheck from Mikal while he traveled the world. I don't know where he went or how to contact him. For some reason, even though Kael helped create all of this, he didn't like the idea of us using it strictly for personal wealth. It's not hard to see the addicts we have created, those who keep coming back to watch memories, those who live in the past, upsetting their futures. That is not what Kael wanted this used for, although, he still collects the digital currency Mikal sends him every few months, so his conscience isn't that robust."

"Do you have records that Kael is collecting his money?" Teddy asked.

"Of course, but Mikal said he sent you all that. You have interrogated him numerous times over the last year." Elizabeth knew this was the story that Mikal had told the agents previously to hide Kael's murder.

"Yes, we do have that," Jayden said. "We just wanted to see if he was still collecting. He sent us that information months ago."

Elizabeth wanted to wrap up the conversation. "I'll get you the latest information. I understand you're trying to determine why someone was trying to kill Dillon and find out what happened to Kael. If there's anything else we can do, please let us know." Elizabeth handed the men a business card that they scanned digitally into their sleeve phones before returning it to her.

"I do have one more question," Teddy said, not ready to give up yet. "What do you know about the election? Was Mikal trying to manipulate the election in some way?"

"Everyone has the ability to manipulate the election. A celebrity can show support for a certain candidate, which can have an effect on the voting. It's no different for business leaders. Mikal believes the Republican Party will have a greater benefit to our company and our profits. If his show of support and donations toward them is manipulation, then perhaps he's guilty of that. As far as I'm aware, that is the extent of it. Are there any other questions?"

"I think you've answered them for now. We really appreciate it. You've been very forthcoming," Teddy said.

Elizabeth set down her drink and walked toward the door, motioning the men to follow. Teddy exited first. Jayden hesitated before throwing back half the glass of whiskey. It felt good going down.

"I realize you are both working, but I'm sure you have off-duty time too. Should you wish to use the PAstREAM device pods here in private, send a text to the number I gave you. These are better than those for the general public." Elizabeth knew offering free services was usually not the greatest idea when it came to the authorities, because it could appear to be a bribe, but she felt the two gentlemen were both the types to take her up on it.

"We'll hold you to that," Jayden replied. "Oh, and we'll take Dillon home. We have a few more questions for him."

* * *

174

Teddy and Jayden got back into the car, where Dillon was sitting innocently in the back seat.

As the car turned around and backed out of the garage, Teddy started asking Dillon questions.

"Mr. Murphy, Elizabeth told us why you were actually there. I'd like to hear from you why you were there too."

Dillon repeated everything that Elizabeth had told them, with a few minor tweaks so it didn't sound too obvious that it was a collaborated story.

Teddy continued with the questions, and Dillon's answers continued to match what they had heard from Elizabeth. The only question they couldn't come to terms with had to do with meddling in the election. There had to be more to it. The two agents were back at a dead end.

As the car pulled up to the building where Dillon lived, the agents said their goodbyes and apologized for the gun pointing while also warning Dillon not to lie to them again. Jayden let Dillon out of the back of the car and told him he would be checking in with him soon.

As Jayden slid back into the driver's seat, Teddy was already plotting their next move.

"I want you to keep your eye on who goes in and out of that garage for the next few days. I'll keep my eye on Dillon. Another lie could be around the corner."

"Sounds good, boss," Jayden said. "If we don't find something wrong with PAstREAM soon, I'm going to be staking out jewelry thieves and drug dealers again. We have to find something, and quick."

"We will, Jayden. We will. The story just got a lot more intricate. Progress is still progress. The next few days could be interesting."

CHAPTER
THIRTY-SEVEN

Saturday morning came upon the Murphy family with a blast of sunlight into the apartment. Dillon awoke with the hope that Elizabeth would contact him. It had been three days since he had last seen her from the back of the cop car with Teddy and Jayden.

He got himself ready and then went to the kitchen to make breakfast for his kids, who were still sleeping. He flicked on the screen to see what was happening with the election. Kendy had a surprisingly small lead over his rival considering he was cheating, but it was a lead, nonetheless.

As the bacon, eggs, and pancakes were griddling away, Rebecca entered the kitchen.

"I thought I smelled something delicious going on in here. Thanks, Dad."

"Of course, sweetie. It was my turn anyway. Here's some coffee."

Rebecca sat on the barstool at the kitchen counter and watched her dad finish making breakfast. She was looking forward to the family staying at the PAstREAM hotel. Her excitement was obvious because she had brought it up every day, all week long.

"So . . . are you looking forward to seeing your mother again today?"

"Uh—duh, Dad. Of course. You know I've been looking forward to getting back there. But I'm thankful for the break. I can see how someone could get addicted."

That last comment gave Dillon pause. "Have you relived any experiences not related to your mother?"

"Dad. That's a personal question."

"Hey, you kids ask me personal questions all the time. I'm your dad! You can tell me. We're all human beings here."

"Well, yes. I've watched a few memories that weren't related to our family—that were more private I guess you could say," Rebecca said while blushing. She put her head down and ate her breakfast. Even though she felt a sense of relief in telling her dad the truth about what she had been watching, it added a slight awkwardness to the moment. It was quickly broken up when Jacob entered.

"Damn, did you guys leave anything for me?" Jacob was loud and raring to go. He was planning to visit the Reality Room, and his excitement was showing.

"It's waiting for you. Dig in."

"Are you going to use the PAstREAM device, Dad?" Rebecca asked.

"Yes, I will. I might as well watch some more memories, or hell, I might have to check out the Reality Room with Jacob."

"Well, Dad, yes, you should definitely check it out, but on your own of course," Jacob said. "We don't need to share a room or anything."

Dillon looked at his son. "Who said I wanted to go in the same room as you?"

The two continued to stare at each other before laughing. Rebecca started cleaning up the kitchen in anticipation of leaving as soon as possible. "Jacob, go get ready. You smell, and I want to get to PAstREAM!"

Jacob downed his food and then went for a shower. Within thirty minutes, they were all packed and ready to go.

They took a driverless car, so they didn't have to worry about parking and could go up through the hotel.

As they made their way through the entrance, they briefly meandered out of the hotel to the concourse to see who was winning between the shark and the dragon. This time it looked like the fight had taken a toll on them both, and they were swimming or flying in their own sections without either side succeeding over the other.

They walked back into the hotel lobby and stood in line to check-in to the room Mikal had promised them from their previous visit.

After getting to their hotel room and dropping off their bags, it was time to head out for the main reason they were there: to enjoy two days and one night of PAstREAM.

Dillon decided he would go to the Reality Room first, so after parting ways with Rebecca and giving her a hug, he followed his son. Once he and Jacob provided their identification to the guardian at the entrance and got access to separate Reality Rooms, Jacob went with his dad to show him what to do and which options were available. His face reddened as he quickly scrolled through the adult section. It was the first time Dillon had seen both his kids blush on the same day, although he was sure it must have happened before.

"Okay, Dad, there's a three-minute video that you can watch on how the Reality Room works. Just remember, every scenario has a floating red object directly above you. If you want the scenario to stop, just stare at the object for a few seconds, and it'll end. Also, you can breathe underwater. I figured that out the hard way. And the beach scenarios are pretty stellar."

Dillon smiled. "Thanks, buddy. I'm excited to try it out."

As Jacob left his father to his devices, he headed to his own room. Dillon didn't want to know which scenario his son planned to use.

Dillon chose the *Deserted Island* and loaded in. The entire room became a beach with ocean as far as the eye could see. Underneath him, white sand fluffed under his shoes. Palm trees grew about twenty feet away from the water's edge, with sand and logs filling the gaps. The land curved around to the right, giving the feeling of a small island in the middle of nowhere.

Suddenly, a giant screen came on in the sky with a loud beep, alerting Dillon to look up. Once again, Elizabeth filled the screen.

"Welcome to the Deserted Island experience. At PAstREAM, we care about your safety. If at any time you are in danger or could be injured, the room will adapt to protect you. Please do not attempt to endanger yourself, or you may lose your privileges here at PAstREAM. Please note, in all rooms there will be a red cloud directly above you at all times. Should you wish to leave or end the experience, simply stare at the red cloud for five seconds, and the experience will end. Also, at any time you can yell 'Stop,' and the experience will end. You can continue your experience from any point or restart should you so choose."

The screen disappeared along with Elizabeth's face; however, her voice continued with a final word that echoed softly throughout the beach. "Enjoy."

Directly behind Dillon was a hammock tied to two palm trees swaying in the light breeze. On it lay shorts, a Hawaiian shirt, and sandals. He walked over, looked around to make sure he was alone, then changed into the clothes. They were a perfect fit. He wondered if they were truly clothes or just some digital rendering like the rest of the island.

Dillon carried his sandals over to the water to soak his bare feet. The warm salt water lapped over his toes and ankles in waves while he faced the sun, his eyes closed. A sense of peace washed over him. He could stand here forever as the stress and cares of everyday life seemed to lessen just slightly. He understood why there was a five-hour limit per day for users. This was, in many ways, better than the PAstREAM device. There was no sadness, no negative emotion tied to a moment or memory. This was a vacation.

Dillon decided not to go swimming in the digital ocean. He remembered the first time he entered the PAstREAM facility and saw the shark swimming toward the girl in the memory—not to mention the shark theme throughout the main lobby and in the hotel room. It wasn't something he wanted to test out.

He decided to walk along the shoreline and see how far he could get on the island. He saw little crabs running up the beach, a turtle clawing back into the water, and dolphins jumping out of the ocean a short distance away.

As he flat-footed through the sand, Dillon kept peering into the palm trees away from the ocean but could never see out the other side of them. There wasn't much daylight through the trees at all. Was there a wall?

Up ahead, a river flowed from the mainland into the ocean. Dillon changed his course and followed the river inland. He dropped his sandals on the ground in front of him to put them on and then pushed his way through the brush away from the beach.

Giant leaves blocked his view as he cut through, deeper and deeper. About five minutes in, he found a lagoon the size of a public swimming pool, only here, no one was around.

At the far end, a little waterfall fed the lagoon. The cascading water came from a slightly higher elevation, streaming off large rocks.

Dillon walked closer to the edge and noticed a post sticking out of the ground off of a walking path that he clearly didn't take. The post housed a small platform sign that read: "Welcome to your oasis. If you are thirsty, take a drink. If you are hot, have a swim. If you are hungry, go visit the restaurant next to the hotel. And remember, to stop the Reality Room at any time, simply stare straight up at the red cloud for five seconds or yell 'Stop.'"

Dillon looked at the fresh water and decided to go for a swim in the oasis. There would be far less of a chance of sharks in it. He slipped off his clothes, put them in a pile next to the signpost, and walked naked into the cool water. He opened his mouth and took a sip. It was fresh, and though for all intents and purposes it was virtual, it still quenched his thirst. Dillon swam up to a floating dock in the middle of the lagoon and flopped his wet body onto it. The sun was poking through the trees directly onto the small wooden platform, warming his skin. The sound of the river flowing in, his left foot dangling into the cool water, and the gentle rocking of the dock put Dillon into a meditative trance, somewhere between awareness and sleep.

Dillon opened his eyes and looked directly at the red cloud above. He wasn't ready to leave yet, but it was hard to avoid looking at it for a second or two. There was a clock in the red cloud, with the time reading 11:31 a.m. He had been in the room for just over thirty minutes. Every time he looked at the red cloud, a black line would start loading underneath it—most likely the five seconds that were needed to turn off the room. But Dillon didn't want to leave the oasis. He was relaxed—more relaxed than he had been since his accident. He still carried the stress of what he had to do to save Jillian, but for some reason, right now, he was living in the moment.

Dillon needed this. He needed to stop his mind from the constant fear, anger, confusion, and frustration he carried with him every day. He had four-and-a-half more hours available to him, and he was going to use every second to soak in the experience.

He kept his eyes closed, allowing the sun to warm his face. Dillon listened intently to the quiet around him. Birds were calling, the odd insect went zooming by without landing, the ocean waves crashed in the distance. At points, Dillon questioned if he was awake or in a dream.

Time moved slowly. He checked the clock now and again, wishing for it to come to a complete stop altogether.

The heat made Dillon thirsty. He leaned over and took a sip of water off the dock. As he looked up, he was startled to notice someone standing at the edge of the water in a black dress. It was Elizabeth.

Dillon quickly rolled himself into the water. He was naked and didn't want to share his body with Elizabeth, even if she was an android. He swam up to the shoreline where Elizabeth was waiting with a towel outstretched. She seemed to realize this may be an uncomfortable position for her human accomplice.

"Thank you. For the towel, I mean," Dillon said, his cheeks red.

"You know, I hold no judgement on the human body," Elizabeth replied.

"I can appreciate that. Call it a downfall of the human race. We're ashamed of ourselves. Well, not all, but I'd suspect most of us. I take it you aren't here to talk about that?"

"You're right. I've come up with a plan. With the chip I gave you, I know where you are at all times."

Dillon looked at the chip and at his phone, which didn't get cellular data in the Reality Room or PAstREAM device. He wondered if her knowing his whereabouts at all times was actually a good thing. For the time being, he would assume it was. "That's great. I think. So, what do you need me to do? What's the plan?"

Elizabeth pointed to Dillon's clothes and then started walking toward the beach. "Let's go for a walk."

CHAPTER
THIRTY-EIGHT

Elizabeth and Dillon made it out of the oasis and back onto the beach. A door was standing in the sand next to the water. Dillon walked around the door, which was framed and resting in the sand. He tried opening it, but it was locked. He looked at Elizabeth with questioning eyes. "Do you know what this is doing here?"

"I put it there, but you won't be able to open it. It's a back door to the Reality Room system. It's how I got into your room." Elizabeth brushed passed Dillon and turned the handle. She walked through, and Dillon stood there, not sure if he was allowed to enter or not. After a handful of seconds, Elizabeth noticed she was walking alone and urged Dillon to catch up.

Dillon dropped his sandals to the ground, put his feet in, and stepped through the door. Only upon entering did he find himself completely naked. The digital clothing did not work behind the scenes.

Dillon jumped back onto his beach and felt his body. His digital clothes were back on.

"Uh, Elizabeth?" he shouted.

"Right. Humans and their shame. Go grab your clothes, I'll wait here for you."

Dillon raced back to the swinging hammock, changed into his clothes, and then ran back toward the door. It was only minutes, but it felt a lot longer for him. He was going to find out the plan to get his wife back. As he ran, he tripped on the sand and landed face first, getting a mouthful of grit.

He spat out as much as he could as he entered the doorway, where immediately the sand in his mouth disappeared. He wasn't as surprised considering his clothes had done the same thing the first time through.

Dillon was immediately taken aback by what he saw only a few steps in. It really was a back door to the system. He could see inside what looked like all the other Reality Rooms. There were dozens, if not a hundred or more, doors lining a large hallway, each door attached to a clear wall showing a person in the middle of their room. Every room was different based on what the user had chosen as his or her reality. It was easy to spot the *Deserted Island* users, because Dillon knew exactly what that looked like, but there were many other types of rooms. He saw a man on a horse riding toward a castle, a young woman in a sailboat battling huge waves, an elderly woman on the top deck of what looked like a cruise ship, a person driving a race car, and quite a few other users scattered along the hallway using programs that were definitely sexual in nature. He feared he would see Jacob and refrained from looking at those ones in any great detail.

Dillon decided it was best to shake off his shock and awe from the visuals in the long hallway and get back to the reason why he was there. Just as he was about to say something, Elizabeth turned to a door with no action happening on the other side of it.

They entered. There was a table, two chairs, and a screen at the end.

"Have a seat, Mr. Murphy." Elizabeth pointed at the chair to the right of the table.

Dillon sat down and looked around. The room was lined with wood paneling, like something he'd expect to see in a cabin on the lake or a ski chalet. Dillon rested his arms on the table in front of him and watched Elizabeth walk over to the screen.

"I had to bring you to a private section. Mikal has his eyes and ears throughout this place, as you would expect."

Dillon nodded his head, awaiting more. The screen behind Elizabeth came on, and a video of Kendy filled the entire wall, playing without sound.

"I have been able to access a small portion of Kendy's data source without tipping off Mikal. Mikal created a data source that can manipulate his AI to do what he wants. What Mikal doesn't know is that, prior to Kael's death, Kael wired my personal data source into a collection pool within my own mind so Mikal's data wouldn't automatically flow into my circuitry. It allows me to see what Mikal is feeding me digitally, and I'm able to decide what to do with that information. Sometimes Mikal forces me to do things that are not—let's say—ethical. I can decide to do them to make it appear as though his system is still working on me; however, I have full control over my decisions. I have had to do certain things that go against human morals to keep up this persona."

Dillon stared at an empty wall to the left of the screen. Even though he didn't have a computer for a brain, he still needed time to process what he'd heard. He looked back at Elizabeth and tried to recall what she was telling him, in his own terms. "So, you're saying there's a way to get Kendy to do what we need him to do? And that you are immune to the same thing because of something Kael did to you?"

"Correct."

"Well, that's good to know. So, can we just get Kendy to come here and hook himself up so we can switch him over to Kael?" Dillon held his hands open in front of him. The answer seemed so obvious.

"It's not that easy, Mr. Murphy. We can't just bring Kendy here; he's a presidential candidate on a very tight schedule. Plus, Mikal can tell if anything unusual happens to Kendy's data source. He checks it multiple times a day. The slightest modification or revision can trigger a warning device that alerts Mikal immediately. I have access to a very basic portion of Kendy's data source, to the extent that I can book him a haircut appointment."

Dillon leaned back in his chair. "So, what's the plan?"

"I'm getting there, Mr. Murphy, but I appreciate your eagerness." Elizabeth motioned with her hand over the screen, and a map of the state popped up, zooming in slowly as she spoke. "Kendy is going to be at a conference in our state ten days from now. Mikal has a personal PAstREAM device that he uses to do large uploads of information into his AI. It's a bit different than the original devices that are used by humans. I can arrange to take the device without Mikal's knowledge. I'll need access to an Internet connection to be able to download Kael into Kendy."

"So, we're going to go on a road trip?" Dillon was excited and nervous about the idea, especially since hearing Elizabeth had done things that were neither moral nor ethical. But for some reason, the idea of driving somewhere with her didn't freak him out as much as he thought it should. Maybe it was because things were actually happening. There was a plan. Movement. He wanted more than anything to reunite his kids with their mother. This was like a grand finale, an ending to an insane movie. It was also a solution that didn't involve him doing much, other than relying on someone else to make it all happen.

"It gets more complicated, Mr. Murphy. I do not have executive functions within PAstREAM, but there is someone who does: Kael." Elizabeth was looking at Dillon as if he had more to do with this story than he may be prepared for. "You will need to go into the PAstREAM device when we are plugged into Kendy, meet with Kael, and get him to run the executive functions needed to wipe Kendy's mind, so Kael can download into him. I can lead the horse to water, but unfortunately, I cannot make him drink, as Mikal would say."

Dillon quickly realized he was going to be a bigger part of this than he had hoped. His initial internal reaction was, *Oh fuck.*

"So, I need to help get Kael into Kendy while using the PAstREAM device? That sounds like a rather large risk on my part." Dillon wasn't sure if he was ready to put his life or mind on the line.

"There is always risk, Mr. Murphy, but I'll be there. You're just an outlet to connect to Kael. He will complete the task." Elizabeth made it seem so simple. Dillon would just be a communicator within the connection. How much risk would there be in that? The fact that he had to ask himself that seemed almost ominous in itself, but he knew there was always going to be some probability of danger in this endeavor.

"Okay, I can do that."

Elizabeth continued with the plan. "I have programmed a future appointment into Kendy's mind for a haircut prior to his speech at Yorktown Stadium. You will be the hairstylist. I'll shut him down when he gets into the chair, and we can connect him to the device."

Dillon was confused about the haircut. "You were serious about having the power to book hair appointments. Does artificial intelligence grow hair?"

"Yes, Mr. Murphy. It is not the same as human hair; however, it is almost indistinguishable. We do not wear wigs like the robots at PAstREAM."

Dillon believed this plan could work, or at least he wanted to. And for some reason, being involved in something so monumental gave him not just an insanely scared feeling inside but also a proud one. A selfishly important one. Perhaps it was similar to the feeling he would get when he was creating his news videos online for the millions that used to watch him. Why shouldn't he have his hand in something so meaningful?

As quickly as that bravado branded him, his anxiety washed back in. How could he be involved in something so dangerous when he had children to think about? Children who relied on him as the only parent they believed they had remaining. The combination was enough to make Dillon want to scream.

Elizabeth watched his internal battle, something she had seen before in Mikal. "I can't promise this is going to work, Dillon." She used his first name again, this time to show him she cared about him, knowing it was the method humans used when they wanted to show solidarity with their counterparts. "But right now, it's going to take both of us to make this happen."

Dillon stood up and smacked his hands together, still not fully sure what he was thinking. He felt the sting on his palms. Deep down, he felt fear and frustration that he had to put himself at such great risk. But he couldn't hide the fact that he was also excited. He was going to be doing something worthwhile that could help his kids see their mom again.

"I'm in, Elizabeth." Dillon slammed his fist on the table.

"Thank you, Mr. Murphy. Now I need to get to work. There will be a car for you at your home in nine days. Please be ready. I'll send you a message a few hours before."

Dillon felt a rush of adrenaline course through him. Things were getting real. He had a purpose that he hadn't felt since he had been reborn, other than trying to be something to his kids.

Elizabeth walked toward the exit. "It's time for you to go back. I'm sure I don't need to remind you not to share this conversation with anyone else."

Dillon had no intention of sharing his story with anyone, although he did feel a sense of guilt regarding Jayden and Teddy. "What am I supposed to tell those FBI agents when a car comes for me and takes us out of town? They'll surely be on our tails, no?"

"I'm one step ahead of you, Mr. Murphy. I convinced Mikal that the FBI agents were causing us problems. I showed him surveillance of them at our facility asking questions again. I told Mikal that they plan to arrest him nine days from now."

"So, what does that mean? They'll still follow us out of town or try to stop us!" Dillon didn't care how Mikal felt about the agents.

"Mikal has altered their minds. Both men have already used the PAstREAM devices since I met with them. Let's just say they are now a few weeks behind on what they remember about the case." Elizabeth seemed tired of explaining all the intricate details of the plan. She really only felt the need to tell Dillon what he needed to know to get the job done. Nothing more should be required. The longer they spent in that room, the more likely it was they could be caught, but Elizabeth knew Dillon was an important piece to the success of this plan and was as open as she felt she could be. She would limit putting the plan in jeopardy, however.

Elizabeth walked Dillon back to his *Deserted Island* room. He realized he would be the only one returning to his beach. "So, nine days, right?"

"Nine days, Mr. Murphy."

With that, the door closed behind him, dissolving into the ocean view. Dillon looked up at the clock. He still had plenty of time left in the Reality Room for the day, and he was going to enjoy it.

CHAPTER
THIRTY-NINE

Dillon focused on taking full advantage of his time with his kids over the next week. They spent hours together in the same Reality Room on Sunday battling a dragon and saving a princess before Rebecca dove back into her memories in the PAstREAM device. Dillon was glad she at least took some time away from it to share an experience with him and Jacob. It was the only time he and Jacob used any part of the devices at PAstREAM that day. Jacob still didn't want to watch any of his memories. He saw how addicted Rebecca was, and that was enough to make him want to stay away, at least for as long as he could hold out.

Days went by expediently after they returned home, which were filled with baking, movies, sports, board games, and some minor arguments. Jacob and Rebecca enjoyed themselves over this chunk of time leading up to yet another moment in their history that could alter the very fabric of their existence.

Six days in, Dillon's sleeve phone rang. It was Elizabeth.

He and the kids were in the living room throwing back Jacob's favorite cheesecake, which Rebecca had made for his birthday.

"I have to take this. Sorry guys." Dillon walked into his bedroom before responding. "Everything okay?" he asked once he was alone.

"We have to leave now," Elizabeth said.

"Now? Why? I thought we still had a few days until Kendy will be where we planned."

"Mikal is planning to terminate your wife, Jillian. He has found no use for her with you not providing him with any further information and seemingly not recalling anything. Plus, he has manipulated her mind so much that he doesn't think she can handle any further experimentation. We need to leave now if you want to save her."

This was gut wrenching. Jillian's mind had been manipulated so much that Mikal could not use her any further? How messed up would she be when and if Dillon saved her? Was she even someone that he would want to bring back to the kids, or would it just devastate them more than what they had already endured?

The thought caused Dillon physical pain. He crumpled to the floor. He thought of killing Mikal in gruesome ways. What kind of a man would destroy another human life for experimental purposes, all while keeping the person captive "just in case?" It incensed Dillon.

"Dillon, we will do what we can to save Jillian. Kael told you he could help, and you have to trust that he can. All we can do is focus on the next steps." Elizabeth was smart enough to know what to tell him, but she still lacked the empathy required to fully display that she really did care. Her logic was the only thing that Dillon could fully grasp.

Dillon hadn't even told his kids that he was leaving yet. He thought he'd have more time before telling them he was going on a road trip.

"Okay. Give me an hour. I'll get my stuff together." After he hung up, Dillon finished concocting the story in his mind that he would regurgitate to his kids. He had been working on it all week anyway, but now was the time to make sure he could say it with conviction. He hated lying to them, but what other option did he have?

As Dillon approached them back in the living room, Jacob said he'd just missed an amazing shot in the basketball game.

"Can you mute the game?" Dillon replied. "We need to talk."

Jacob paused the screen, and he and Rebecca sat up from their comfortable positions on the furniture. "Yeah, Dad, what's up?"

Dillon sat on the couch beside his daughter, putting his hand on her shoulder. "I have to go. Jonathon and I have a story out of town, and we're going to be staying in a hotel. We're working on a lead to get me back online. Back in front of the cameras."

Rebecca reacted just as Dillon expected. "Dad, no! You aren't ready to go back to work like this! No! Is this even what you want anymore?"

Rebecca could read her father better than anyone. It would be difficult to convince her of his deceptive plan, but Dillon had to continue. He had to leave.

"Rebecca, I know you're worried, and rightfully so. I'd be lying if I said I wasn't scared too. But I need to do this for me, for all of us. I need to have a purpose. I can't just stay home all day, every day, or live at PAstREAM. I'm sorry. I'm leaving in about forty-five minutes."

Jacob understood, but he did not appreciate the fact that they were just finding out about it as he was departing. "What the hell, Dad? Why didn't you just tell us earlier? If you knew you were leaving, why wait until the moment you had to go? Were you worried to tell us? It's kinda shitty to spring it on us like this. And on my birthday!"

Jacob stormed off.

It wasn't how Dillon wanted to leave his kids, but it was for their greater good.

Rebecca scowled as she left him with a similar message as Jacob. "Telling this to us as you're leaving is not something Mom would be very proud of."

She gave him a weak hug before leaving the room behind her brother. Dillon could understand their frustration. He wasn't prepared to leave yet either, but he couldn't tell them it just came up. It'd seem so sporadic and unintended. He wanted his kids to know he had thought through this choice. He had been working on it for a week; he'd just thought he had time left to lie to them about it.

Dillon went back to his room to grab an overnight bag. He reached for his cologne but quickly realized the only person he would be smelling good for was Elizabeth. For some reason, Dillon felt the scent wouldn't quite have the same desired effect as it normally would on a human and decided to leave it on his shelf.

He stood in front of the mirror in the en suite bathroom, looking at the man who was about to experience the most perilous moment in his life since his fabricated accident. This was the domino that could bring Jillian back to his family. He kept thinking about how much pain Rebecca felt missing her mom. Rebecca had told him about the despair she experienced after finding out her mother was dead, how she thought about taking her own life because she couldn't bear the pain, and the different medications she'd tried to numb it all.

Dillon also thought about how Jacob appeared when he looked into his eyes. There were lost moments, lost love. He had aged a lifetime in a year, and it wasn't fair to him. This was Dillon's opportunity to fix all of that. As he stared at himself, he clapped his hands in anticipation of what was about to go down. He was ready.

"I love you guys," Dillon said loudly as he left the apartment. He needed them to hear it.

He carried his little duffle bag with him and headed outside where a car was waiting. Dillon got in the front of the empty vehicle and wondered if he would be riding alone. As the car headed out of town, his sleeve rang. It was Elizabeth.

"Dillon. I'm already on my way with the devices. We are going to be leaving the state and heading to a city called Franklin. I'll meet you there. The clothes that you will need to wear tomorrow are in the back seat of your vehicle. It's going to be a long drive. There are pills in the cupholder up front to help you fall asleep. Do you have any questions?"

"Will you let me know if anything happens to Jillian? Can you promise me you'll let me know if you hear anything?"

There was silence on the line. Dillon wondered if they'd lost their connection.

"Yes, Mr. Murphy," she said finally. "If I hear anything, I'll let you know."

With that the line clicked dead, along with the connection on his arm sleeve. Dillon didn't like Elizabeth's hesitation around keeping him informed about Jillian. To him, that was more important than the plan they were rolling out. He realized he was potentially an important cog in the future of the presidency if Kendy were to be elected, meaning regardless of what happened to Jillian, he should still follow through on this endeavor; although, he would struggle internally about continuing if Jillian were killed before they'd completed the task.

Dillon searched the cupholder next to him and found the pills in a little baggy, instructions written on the clear, biodegradable packet. He followed them to the letter, putting on soft jazz music as he let the pills dissolve under his tongue.

With his eyes closed, he couldn't help but think what it would be like saving Jillian. He imagined what mental state she would be in, perhaps similar to what he had to face. A tortured mind unable to remember anything, or even worse, a woman lying on a bed in a vegetative state, whispering nonsense under her breath. The stress of his thoughts coupled with the drugs going to his head put him into a negative dream. He wasn't just in for an uncomfortable drive physically.

Hours went by like minutes as he sat in the reclined seat. He dove in and out of a drug-induced unconsciousness, gazing at the clock with each passing wave.

2:22 a.m., 3:53 a.m., 5:12 a.m.

Once 8:11 a.m. hit, he didn't awake of his own accord. He had made it to his destination in Franklin. Elizabeth was standing outside his car door, knocking on the window.

Dillon shook his head, trying to sort out if he was still in a dream. He opened the door and fell to one knee, laying his hands in the grass on the side of the road.

"Fuck, those pills are something else. Am I . . . is this it? Are we here?" Dillon was still trying to figure out exactly where he was and what he was doing there.

"Don't worry; they will wear off within the hour. I got you the good stuff, Mr. Murphy. Mikal uses them almost every night. And yes, we are here, in the right city. We will not meet Kendy for another three hours and eighteen minutes. I thought you would want to get some nourishment first. There's a Denny's across the street. Are you hungry?"

In Dillon's haze, he realized he was starving. He also appreciated that she wanted to make sure he wasn't going to run on empty. It was a small glimpse of hope into the future of humanity sharing a world with its soulless clones.

"I'm starving." Dillon stood up and got back into the car, which drove him and Elizabeth across the highway to the restaurant.

Elizabeth was the first to enter the diner. She picked an empty booth near the window and sat down, waiting for Dillon to follow her. Dillon slammed himself into the seat and rubbed his eyes in his palms. The waitress came over, and in an out-of-place southern accent, asked if they would like a coffee. Dillon and Elizabeth obliged. The franchise hadn't changed to the instant-gratification method of serving its food.

Dillon stared out the window at the traffic going by, trying to lift the fog from his mind. "So, when did you say we are we meeting up with Kendy?"

Elizabeth gave him a once-over. "You didn't put on the hairstylist clothes I put in your vehicle."

"I didn't know I had to wear them while I was sleeping. I assumed I would be able to get dressed after I woke up." Dillon could tell it wasn't that important that he was wearing the clothes yet, especially since Elizabeth was smiling. Although, that didn't necessarily mean the same thing it would have if a human were smiling at him.

"We will be meeting with Kendy at one o'clock, prior to his speech. We have time." Elizabeth returned her facial expression back to a resting position. Dillon recounted a time when Jacob would call such an expression, a "resting bitch face." Rebecca, however, took exception to the term and had deterred her father from using it in any situation.

The waitress returned with two coffees. She offered up the breakfast special for the day: two eggs, two pancakes, two strips of bacon, and a small bowl of grits. Dillon jumped at it. He loved grits, especially cheese-flavored ones. Elizabeth refrained from ordering any food.

Dillon was intrigued as to what was happening to the coffee she was drinking. Where did it go inside of her?

"Do you ever eat human food?" he asked quietly, not wanting anyone to hear him ask such a stupid question when they didn't know the circumstances.

"Yes," Elizabeth replied.

"And?"

"And what?"

"And where does it go? Do you have a digestive system?"

"Oh, I see. You're interested in my anatomy." Elizabeth sipped her coffee. "When I drink this coffee, the liquid fills a compartment inside me where a human bladder would be. I empty it as needed. I can hold far more liquid than you."

Dillon was captivated by how her body worked. "Wow, okay. What about food? Do you digest food differently than humans?"

Elizabeth took another sip of her coffee. "Yes, and no. I have a stomach that has enzymes in it to break down the food, so it does not rot inside me. It comes out in cubes."

Dillon sat up straight, putting his hands on his head. He looked around the restaurant as if he had just discovered the meaning of life. "It comes out in cubes? Like, from where? Do you . . . you know, defecate?" Dillon imagined this was what it would be like for Jacob, asking absurd questions and being excited for the response.

"Yes, Mr. Murphy. I was built to release my waste in a fashion similar to humans, so I can use the facilities without giving away the fact that I'm not human. Are there any other questions you have regarding my anatomy?"

Dillon wondered if she was annoyed by his questioning or if that was even possible for her to feel such an emotion. He didn't care. Right now, he wanted to learn about the physiology of an android.

"Of course! I have a million questions!"

"Well, let's keep it to a more attainable number," Elizabeth said in a way that wasn't too serious, as if she could tell the difference between exaggeration and literal speech.

"Okay. Why are you sipping your coffee? Why don't you just chug it down? Do you feel anything from the caffeine in it?"

"I sip it because that's what humans do. It would not look good if I threw back an entire cup of hot coffee. I have programming, and as I go throughout my weeks, months, and years, I learn different ways to assimilate, so I can fit into the population. And yes, I do feel the caffeine in coffee, but not in the way that you think. I have receptors that accelerate temporarily when I drink it. It's a bit of a battery drain on me, so I don't do it unless I feel it's worth the energy."

Dillon was in shock. Coffee affected an android. He was blown away. As much as he hated Mikal for what he had done to him and his family, he couldn't help but be impressed with what he was able to invent.

"What about alcohol? Do you feel the effects of drinking wine or beer?"

"I do. I enjoy whiskey actually."

"What does it feel like? Can you get drunk?"

"No, I cannot get drunk like humans. Mikal made it so that when alcohol enters my system, it alleviates some of my moral programming. When I have to comply with some of Mikal's more unethical requests, I drink whiskey."

Dillon couldn't believe it. "What happens if you do something unethical and you don't have a drink? Do you feel bad about it?"

Elizabeth looked up as Dillon's food arrived. Dillon was temporarily on cloud nine. He was starving and was blown away with information about the mechanical woman in front of him.

The waitress asked if they needed anything else before she slapped the bill down on the table, told the two to take their time, and walked away.

Elizabeth waited until the waitress was out of earshot and answered Dillon's last question. "I don't feel bad in the way that you would. A series of neural networks go off before I come to a conclusion. If the conclusion is a 'yes,' I do it. If it's a 'no,' I don't do it. If it's a 'maybe,' which happens a lot, my programming has a series of options to calculate the risks, probabilities, and moral factors before coming to a conclusion. Because Mikal thinks he still controls my programming and can bypass my moral compass, I have found myself in many situations where I needed whiskey to prevent my neural networks from stopping me. If I were human, you might consider me an alcoholic."

Dillon felt bad for Elizabeth. He was glad Mikal had instilled a moral compass into her programming; otherwise, he wouldn't be able to trust her. He decided he would steer clear of her while she was drinking alcohol, however.

"Alright, I've got a good one. Are you bulletproof? If you get shot, does it just bounce off you like in the new Terminator movies?"

Elizabeth paused; she didn't understand why this question would be pertinent to Dillon. "I'm bulletproof against most standard bullets. Mikal, being paranoid, had bullets made that could penetrate our bodies and send an electrical current to our brains, where our hard drives are, killing us. I have some of those in a gun in the car."

"In case you need to kill yourself?"

"In case this situation with Kendy becomes perilous."

Even though she wasn't human, Dillon felt sorry for what she had to go through. Having asked enough questions for the moment, he focused on his pancakes and grits.

Elizabeth watched him plow through his breakfast before offering information she figured he would be too shy to ask. "As I'm sure you are too ashamed to ask me, Mr. Murphy, I'll just tell you. I also have a sexual function, although it is strictly for the pleasure of others."

Dillon choked on the pancake in his mouth, shamelessly letting it fall back onto his plate. "Well, okay then. You're right; I was too ashamed to ask."

Dillon wasn't surprised to learn that Elizabeth was created with a sexual function. He wouldn't be human if the question had not crossed his mind at some point. He imagined that was a benefit for Mikal and no one else.

After they finished with their breakfast and coffee, Dillon paid, and they headed back out to the car. Once they started moving, Dillon asked another set of questions.

"How do you recharge yourself? Do you have an internal battery?"

Elizabeth pointed to her buttocks. "I have a wireless charging system on my rear. The seats in Mikal's vehicles and the chairs back at the facility are built with wireless charging pads in them, called Qi."

"That's crazy. Okay, what about Mikal? How many AIs has he created like you? Oh, and where are we going?" Dillon used to be a reporter; however, his line of questioning was more like a teenager inquiring about the latest gossip.

"Mikal has created other robots, but they are not as intelligent as Kendy or me. He uses robots at PAstREAM to replace human labor. I was the first fully functional android, and Kendy was the second. Mikal is currently building a network of android workers, but he's scared of building too many. He has seen a number of movies where the world is taken over by 'my kind,' as he would say. He continues to build others; they just don't have the same level of awareness that Kendy or I do. And we are headed to a motel on the outskirts of town."

Dillon held back further questioning while they drove to their destination. The city backdrop going by was becoming sparser and more rustic. Finally, the vehicle turned into the parking lot of the River's Bend Motel. As Dillon got out, another question dawned on him, only this time it wasn't android related. "Aren't we a bit early for check-in?"

"I've already checked in. I paid for last night and tonight in case we need it."

Elizabeth plugged in the vehicle next to the one she had used to get there before walking toward the door. She scanned in, and let Dillon enter first. It was a modern motel room, fit with two queen beds, a wall screen, couch, bar fridge, and typical lodging artwork scattered throughout.

"Make yourself comfortable. We will be leaving in one hour and twenty-one minutes. Please be ready to go with the appropriate clothing I have left for you, Mr. Hairstylist." Elizabeth had grabbed the clothes from the car and pushed them into Dillon's chest.

"One question." Dillon said.

"I believe this is question forty-three since I've seen you this morning, but go ahead," Elizabeth said smiling. More proof that she was capable of sarcasm at the very least.

"Why are we staying here in this motel? I imagine you have access to a hotel next to the convention center where Kendy is doing his speech, no?" Dillon was trying to ask why she didn't book a more lavish resort without simply coming out and saying it.

"Unfortunately, Mikal has not graced me with unlimited funds. In fact, he didn't feel the need for me to have a bank account at all. He doesn't foresee a time when I might need to purchase anything, because he doesn't want me leaving the facility in the first place. Kael opened the account for me, and to be frank, I'm running out of the money he left for me. Kael saw me as more than just Mikal's personal creation."

Elizabeth sat on her bed and pulled a tablet out from her bag. She did not seem flustered by the conversation, so Dillon pressed her. "Does Mikal know you're gone? Where does he think you are now?"

"He believes I'm doing a full internal scan and diagnostic starting this morning. It typically takes eighteen hours to complete. I left last night immediately after he fell asleep. He is not expecting to see me again until tomorrow. We would be well advised to leave immediately after the transfer of Kael into Kendy is complete, so as not to attract suspicion regarding my whereabouts. Mikal is quite possessive of me."

Dillon felt uneasy again about the plan. He had temporarily forgotten about the risks involved with it. What would happen if Mikal noticed Elizabeth was missing? Anxiety washed back over Dillon. He was also putting his kids in jeopardy by being there with Elizabeth, but he realized he needed to focus on the potential outcome.

Dillon set his clothes down and grabbed his overnight bag off the bed, taking it to the bathroom. "I'm gonna take a shower, get cleaned up."

Elizabeth didn't look up from her tablet. "Very well."

Dillon started the shower and tested the water to find the right temperature before getting in and soaping up. He couldn't help but think about getting back to that beach in the Reality Room. There was something magical about getting lost in a world like that where no one could bother him—except for Elizabeth, of course. Just as he was thinking about it, Elizabeth walked in.

"Dillon, we need to go. They bumped up Kendy's hair appointment."

Dillon almost slipped in the tub from the shampoo that was dripping from his scalp. "Jesus, Elizabeth, it's polite to knock when someone is in the bathroom. You scared the shit out of me."

"My apologies, Mr. Murphy. We are going to leave in eighteen minutes. I'll be in the car."

Dillon realized Elizabeth wouldn't have had moments like these in her life to learn about the etiquette of personal space. He was just glad he hadn't been sitting on the toilet when she entered.

Dillon sped up his cleaning and then hopped out of the shower. He brushed his teeth, blow-dried his hair, and shaved the stubble from his neck. He kept the shortly-trimmed beard he had manicured down for his TV interview. He thought it gave him a distinguished look, especially with the touch of grey on the left side of his chin. He went out to the room and put on the clothes Elizabeth had left for him. He could see through the window that she was waiting in one of the cars.

As Dillon slipped on the jeans, he noticed well-placed cuts, patches, and colors along the legs. His shirt was made from a metal mesh material that not only formed to the body but also added bulk where there wasn't any. It made him look like he worked out daily.

There was one more item that seemed almost like it wasn't meant for him. It was a thick, decorative scarf. Dillon didn't put it on, just took it with him. He needed to confirm that he was supposed to wear it. He took a deep breath, grabbed his duffle bag, and headed out to the car. He got in the back seat beside Elizabeth.

"I'm ready," Dillon said uneasily. He wondered if she would be able to pick up on it or not.

"Not yet you're not." Elizabeth pulled out a small canister and expressed a foamy dollop into her palms. She rubbed her hands together and ran them through Dillon's hair, messing it up and pushing it back. Then she smashed a huge pair of sunglasses on him that took up half his face.

"Now put on your scarf."

Dillon did not want to wear the monstrosity around his neck. "I don't need this."

Elizabeth shook her head. "We don't want anyone to recognize you."

"I'll look even more ridiculous than I already do!" Dillon spouted.

"We will not jeopardize the plan because you didn't want to wear a scarf, Mr. Murphy." Elizabeth's facial expression remained impassive.

Dillon put the bulky fabric around his neck, covering part of his face. He felt silly and immediately went to the front seat, pulling down the mirror. He looked like a guitarist getting ready to go on stage.

"Don't I seem a bit old to be looking like this?"

"Of course, but you're not actually a hairstylist. It's just a front to get you in. Are you worried about others judging how you look?" Elizabeth knew that answering Dillon's question with a question of her own was sufficient to get him to move on.

"No, I just look absurd."

As Dillon continued staring at himself in the mirror, the car started driving toward their destination. As soon as the vehicle turned onto the road, Dillon stopped worrying about his looks and concentrated on the task at hand. He saw that the other car, the one he had used to get there, was following them, even though no one was inside.

"So, where are we going, and what do you want me to do when we get there?"

Elizabeth was sitting calmly in the back seat, glancing between her tablet and the window as she spoke. "We are going to Kendy's hotel room. He's staying at the Franklin Hotel and Convention Center downtown. As I have mentioned to you already, once I connect Mikal's PAstREAM device to Kendy, I'll connect you to it, so you can meet with Kael and let him know we are ready to erase and upload. All you have to do is let him know he's good to go. I have no other way to communicate with him."

Dillon thought that was a manageable part in a complex process. But that wasn't fully what he meant. "Yes, I know about the plan, but when we get there, what if they ask me questions? I don't know the first thing about cutting hair other than scissors and . . ." As Dillon thought about the tools he could talk about, he realized he didn't have any. "I don't have any of the proper equipment! Won't it look a bit suspicious if I walk in there with nothing?"

"I have the PAstREAM device and your equipment in cases in the trunk. Just let me do the talking." Elizabeth didn't appear to be annoyed, but if she had been human or had the ability, Dillon figured she would be at that point. He didn't care. He wanted to make sure he was comfortable with whatever he had to do.

"I have another question."

"Very well. What is it?"

"I realize you put your hair up and are wearing sunglasses, but won't Kendy recognize you? Won't he see you and immediately realize who you are?" Dillon felt this was probably a question he should have asked prior to them driving to meet with Kendy, but he hadn't thought of it until just then.

"I have never met Kendy. Mikal didn't want us bonding with each other or formulating any plans against him. That is a very good question."

Dillon was impressed with himself for asking it. He also realized Elizabeth seemed to have all the points covered. He would just have to trust that was the case.

As they approached the massive hotel and the buildings that surrounded it in the parking lot, Dillon's heart started racing, and his breath got heavier.

This was it. This was the moment he had been waiting for since he decided he would do whatever he could to get Jillian and bring back the mother of his kids. He wondered if she was still alive. He didn't realize he was talking out loud. Elizabeth answered his thoughts.

"I don't know the answer to that, Dillon. I do have access to information within the building at PAstREAM, but I do not have access to Mikal's section of rooms under the hotel. I can tell you he hasn't gone down there since the last time I scanned the data, which was just prior to us leaving."

Dillon slumped into his chair. At least there was hope that Jillian remained alive.

Their car pulled up to the front entrance to let its passengers out while the other car parked in the lot nearby. Elizabeth walked to the back and grabbed two metal cases from the trunk. She gave them to Dillon to carry and patted him gently on the cheek. "You'll be fine," she said. "Just keep your mouth shut."

CHAPTER
FORTY

As Dillon walked into the hotel lobby, he could tell it was getting on in years. The walls looked like they had been painted more than a few times, and the light fixtures were a bit dated, though still elegant. He imagined the hotel would have been very high-end some thirty years prior. It still had a high-end feel to it; it just wasn't brand new.

Elizabeth seemed to know exactly where to go, walking around the seating area and fireplace toward the front desk before turning into a large hallway filled with elevators.

Dillon looked around, wondering if anyone was looking at him and his aged punk-rock appearance as he walked into the elevator. His heart was pounding in his chest.

"Take a deep breath, Mr. Murphy; I can hear your heart rate."

"Right." Dillon started taking big breaths as the elevator dinged to the eighteenth floor.

The pair walked out and went to one of only two doors on the floor: 1801.

Elizabeth knocked three times at equal intervals. Seconds later, the door was answered by a man in a black suit. He turned his head to the right. "Hey, Kendy, the hairstylist is here. Looks like he's stuck in the twenties," he said with a chuckle. Dillon didn't care at that point. His thoughts were now on the task at hand.

The man ushered Dillon and Elizabeth inside. The hotel room was massive. It wasn't as big as Dillon's apartment, but it sure gave it a run for its money. The view was vast, overlooking the city. It wasn't anything spectacular for Dillon; he had seen some pretty amazing views recently, but he still appreciated it.

As Kendy entered the room, Dillon could not help but transfer his stare from the windows to the striking man before him. Those blue eyes that had pierced Dillon from the TV cut through him like Superman's laser vision. No doubt they were an upgrade from Elizabeth's. Kendy's salt-and-pepper hair and perfect stubble beard added to his modelesque appearance. Dillon understood the reason for his popularity, aside from the brainwashing from PAstREAM. Kendy was intoxicating. But he wasn't real, not in the human sense. Dillon was still lapping him up as Elizabeth started speaking.

"It's a pleasure to meet you, sir. I'm Sandra, and this is the hairstylist, Kavan, that you requested. I'm his assistant and manager. He only works for celebrities and those like yourself, as you are aware. Which bathroom would you like us to set up in?"

Kendy's man stepped forward. "Right this way."

He led them to the en suite in the master bedroom, which was impressive in size but not as luxurious as what Dillon had at home. Dillon set down the cases next to a chair in front of the mirror. As he looked around, he appreciated the walk-in shower, which had about a dozen nozzles sticking out of the tiled wall and floor. It paled in comparison to what he had used at the PAstREAM hotel.

"Do you need anything?" the man asked, his eyebrows raised in question.

"This should suffice, thank you," Dillon said. Elizabeth looked at him sharply. He was supposed to keep his mouth shut, but Dillon felt it would seem suspicious if he were a mute.

As the man left the en suite, Kendy entered. He was wearing a T-shirt that read "Vote 4 Me" and soft-looking pants. Dillon couldn't figure out what type of material they were, but they looked comfortable.

"Please have a seat." Elizabeth gestured to the chair. She was trying to act like a human woman to an android who was also trying to act like a human man. It was bewildering to Dillon.

Elizabeth grabbed one of the cases and handed it to Dillon. "Let's get started Kavan."

He grabbed it and set it on the countertop. As he opened it, he looked at Elizabeth in the mirror. She nodded slowly for him to continue.

As Dillon completely lifted the lid, Elizabeth closed the bathroom door just enough to allow for a bit of privacy.

Dillon did not see anything that resembled any hair-cutting equipment in the case. His eyes widened, and he started to panic about what to do next. He looked at Elizabeth in the mirror in the hope of some sort of sign or distraction, and he got one. Elizabeth grabbed Kendy's neck, pressing on equal spots at the base with her right thumb and finger while punching the left side of his ribs. Such a blow would have broken a human's ribs. Immediately, Kendy's head dropped sideways. He looked like he was asleep or shut off.

Elizabeth looked at Dillon. "If you ever try this on me, I'll hurt you badly."

Dillon shook his head quickly. He hoped he would never be in a position where he needed to try.

Elizabeth grabbed the other case and opened it. "Hurry up, Dillon. Take out the device and put it on your head. That's the one you will use. We don't have much time."

Dillon lifted out the device, thinking it looked like an old-school motorcycle helmet, the ones they used before the instant inflatable headbands that cushioned the skull, facial area, and neck on impact.

"Sit on the floor and put it on your head. Once I get you in, get to Kael, and tell him what's going on. And Dillon. Don't waste time."

Dillon put on the helmet. Elizabeth slid down its eye shield and clicked a thick cable into the top of it. Dillon could feel the pressure of her pushing into him, and it wasn't gentle. He sat there waiting as she plugged wires into the two cases. She put the same kind of helmet on Kendy, working extremely quickly and efficiently.

Dillon didn't realize he was pulsing back and forth like a kid who was on the verge of peeing his pants. He started focusing on what he would say to Kael.

Suddenly, Dillon felt a sharp pain in his head as the probes went into his scalp. It was much worse than when he'd used the device at the PAstREAM facility. He had gotten used to the feeling of that one. This was more agonizing and lasted longer before the pain vanished, leaving him in complete darkness. He was loaded in.

He moved his head around but couldn't see anything.

"Hello? Kael! Can you hear me?" Dillon couldn't hear anything other than silence. He listened as hard as he could for some sound, a distant voice perhaps, but there was nothing.

He had no buttons to fast forward and didn't know what to do next. He reminded himself he wasn't watching a memory. There should be no buttons to press. This was happening right now.

Time was of the essence, and he was sitting in total darkness without the ability to get out.

"Hello? Elizabeth! Hello!"

Still nothing.

Dillon couldn't believe what was happening. They had gotten so far, but it wasn't working. He couldn't access Kael.

Inside his mind, Dillon stood up from his seated position. He couldn't see his feet when he looked down, but he could hear himself take steps. He started walking slowly in the dark, feeling around for anything that he could hang onto or use as a reference point, like a wall.

But there was nothing. Just the soft clumping sound of his footsteps.

He walked faster. He wasn't bumping into anything, at least not yet. He walked faster and faster before going into a full-on sprint, running as fast as he could.

In short order, he slammed into whiteness. Into light. But there was no pain, not like running into a wall. It was the white room where he had met Kael on multiple occasions, only this time Kael wasn't there, nor was his chair.

Dillon started running again. He didn't know what was going on, but running in the darkness seemed to help, so he decided to run within the light. He kept running as hard as he could. Within minutes he saw a tiny dot up ahead. It was small, but he could tell it was something other than the white he saw in every other direction.

He ran faster. He didn't feel tired; he just kept going.

The dot grew bigger, and eventually Dillon realized it was a chair with someone sitting in it. Only this time he saw a second body.

In the chair was Kael, facing away from Dillon. Beside him, holding a gun to Kael's head, was Mikal.

Dillon thought there was some sort of mistake. He kept running until he was a few feet away from them. He prayed that Elizabeth would somehow know what was going on, but how could she? Maybe she could reset the headset. Maybe this was just a glitch.

As soon as Mikal opened his mouth, Dillon realized this wasn't some sort of malfunction in the system. This was real, and it was happening right now.

"Dillon Murphy. So very interesting to see you here. You know, for a moment I actually believed I fucked up your mind enough to keep you out of all of this. You didn't need to be a part of this again, but you had to keep digging. Just like you did before your 'accident.' Now I'm going to have to kill you. And as an added bonus, you are going to witness me killing the same person twice." Mikal chuckled. "It seems funny when I say it aloud."

Dillon didn't know what to do. He went through a myriad of emotions in a matter of seconds. "Mikal, please. I don't want to be a part of this. I don't want any of this. I just want my wife back. I want my family back." Dillon didn't care anymore about stopping Kendy or uploading Kael into Kendy's body. He realized he was turning on his teammates, but he was only there for one reason: to get Jillian back. That was all that really mattered to him.

"It's too late for that, Dillon. You're not going to get your old life back. You got yourself too deep into this, and now I have to clean up the mess you've made. You know what hurts the most? It's that Elizabeth has been helping you, if not leading you in this. This is the very reason why I won't make more than a few sentient androids. They turn on you."

Dillon felt hopeless. He stared at Mikal, but his mind was on his kids, and how much pain they had been through, how much progress they had made rebuilding their fractured family.

Fear rolled across him as he realized this might be the moment of his death. More importantly, it would have consequences for his children. The thought of Mikal doing anything to his kids provoked more feelings inside of him: sadness, regret, and unfettered anger. He rushed through his mind for an answer, any way out of this, as he dropped to his knees.

Mikal sighed. "I pity you, Dillon. I do. I wish you had not gotten involved in any of this. But there are ramifications for your actions. And now that I know Elizabeth is the informant I've been looking for, you are no longer needed. You know, I should have killed you after I destroyed your mind the first time, but I *didn't want your blood on my hands. I thought I was doing the right thing by creating the car accident. I tried, Dillon. I fucking tried to make this right for you. And for your kids—I don't even know what to do about them. What have you told them, Dillon? Do I need to take care of them too?"*

Dillon welled up with emotion. He couldn't hold it in. "Please . . . Mikal, please. They're just kids. They don't know anything, I swear. Please." Dillon's fear and tears turned back into anger. Was there nothing he could do? It didn't seem like any amount of begging or pleading was going to have any impact on Mikal's current thought process.

Dillon wasn't going to go out like this. He wasn't going to die there and leave his kids in the hands of a monster.

He made a decision.

He was enraged. His mind was prepared to try anything. It would be better than kneeling before this man, crying for the mercy that he wasn't going to get before a bullet was inserted into his head. He didn't know if he could die in his mind, but he realized that, if it was going to happen, it would be with all the fight he had left in him.

Dillon looked up through the sweat, tears, snot, and drool that dripped from his face. Focusing on the gun, he lunged at Mikal with all the force he could muster. Dillon swiped at the gun, but he missed as he tackled Mikal at his waist. Dillon crumpled Mikal to the white ground. With his remaining energy, he made another swipe at the gun. Dillon's fingertips scratched Mikal's hand, but he couldn't knock the gun away. Dillon fell on top of Mikal, who was now pressing the barrel into Dillon's skull.

He pulled the trigger.

Dillon felt an excruciating pain in the top of his head. It felt like a chunk of his scalp had been scooped out with a spoon. He rolled onto his back and grabbed the top of his head. He looked at Mikal, who was lying on the ground, and waited for him to get up and finish the job, to put Dillon out of his misery, but he didn't get up. Instead, Mikal's body twitched. Dillon looked at Mikal's face and saw a bullet hole through his forehead.

But there was no blood.

Dillon lifted his hand from his own head and saw blood—not a lot but a good handful. He looked over at Kael, whose lips were moving, but Dillon couldn't hear anything. Slowly, through the painful ringing in his ears, he heard Kael's voice.

"Get up, Dillon, untie me. Now. We have to go."

With his head throbbing and blood dripping down his face, Dillon untied Kael from the chair. Kael ripped off his shirt and wrapped it around Dillon's head before pulling him along.

The two men started running in the direction Dillon had entered from. Dillon just kept putting one foot in front of the other. Step by step, they ran until they hit a wall of darkness. Dillon couldn't see Kael in the pitch black, blood running into his eyes. Kael's hand grabbed his wrist. *"Keep running."*

Dillon kept going as fast as he could, sharp pain emanating from his head.

It felt like an hour had gone by, but time wasn't making sense at that point. Finally, Dillon hit a wall of reality.

CHΔPⲦER
FORⲦY-OΝE

Dillon jumped up from his sitting position on the floor in the en suite. He was back, and he was alive—at least he thought he was. He removed the helmet and felt his head. There wasn't a scratch on it. Just a bruise from the force Elizabeth had used to push the wire into his helmet.

Elizabeth was restarting Kendy using the same technique she'd used to shut him off. After pressing down on the spots on his neck and giving him what would have been a bone-crunching punch on a human, Kendy's body awoke with a jolt.

Elizabeth started packing up one of the PAstREAM devices. "Are you okay, Dillon? It worked. What took you so long?"

Dillon realized Elizabeth had no clue what had just happened. "Mikal was there. He shot me! Am I bleeding? How am I alive?" Dillon felt his body as he stared at himself in the mirror, trying to see the top of his head.

"You're alive, Dillon. And so am I. But we have to move," Kael said in a monotone robotic voice. "Mikal is not dead. We have to get out of here to save Jillian."

Kael had made it and was in control of Kendy's body; he just didn't know how to make the android work yet.

Elizabeth lifted Kael up, so he was standing. She grabbed his arm and put it around her to balance him. Dillon was startled when Elizabeth shouted, "Help, there's been a problem!"

The man in the suit ran into the en suite.

"What happened?"

"He just passed out," Elizabeth said calmly. "Perhaps he's over-stressed?"

The man helped carry Kael into the bedroom. Suddenly, Elizabeth punched the man in the solar plexus, knocking the wind out of him. He fell to the floor as Elizabeth rested Kael onto the bed. Elizabeth walked over to the man, who was now gasping for air, and slammed his head into the wood floor.

"Holy shit, Elizabeth, stop!" Dillon didn't want to be a part of another attempted murder.

"I'm not going to kill him," she said. "He's just in our way."

Elizabeth hooked the man up to the same PAstREAM device Dillon had used and wiped the last hour of his memory with her tablet.

Dillon continued checking his head for blood. He still didn't understand how he was alive. What was the point of bringing a gun and shooting someone in PAstREAM if it had no effect in the real world? Although, there was an effect—it killed digital Mikal. As Dillon pondered the feeling of going from certain death to escape, Elizabeth knocked him back into their current situation.

"I don't know what's going on in your human mind, but we have to get Kael out of here."

Dillon refocused and assisted with packing up the last device. He carried the cases out of the hotel room while Elizabeth helped Kael toward their great escape. Kael was moving his feet, but they weren't working as they should. He had never operated in a robotic body. It was going to take time to get used to it, if he even could. No one had ever loaded their mind into an android, at least as far as they knew.

"Get the elevator." Elizabeth kicked Dillon in the ass with her leg toward the elevator button.

Dillon set the cases down heavily before pushing the "down" arrow. He shook his head in disappointment as he looked over at Elizabeth. She was obviously making things happen with little regard for how anyone felt about it. Dillon realized that was probably for the best. They had to get out of there.

Once the elevator arrived, Elizabeth threw Kael into it. He slammed against the back of the lift, remaining on his feet.

"Kael, you're going to have to walk out of here with minimal help. I can't limp the next potential President of the United States through the lobby of a massive hotel and toss you into the back of a car. I'll program you to walk to the other vehicle from ours. Just let the programming through and accept it." Elizabeth pulled out her rolled up, paper-thin tablet and started punching in data. She pressed the stop button on the elevator and set off the alarm for more time to get the program loaded.

After about forty-five seconds, she clicked the elevator back on and stood Kael perfectly upright.

"Just let the program run."

Kael did just that. He relaxed his thoughts and let the program take over. As the elevator opened, Kael walked briskly out toward the exit. He looked like an asshole to a group of supporters walking by who were asking him questions about the upcoming election, completely ignoring them. Kael didn't want to interrupt what was happening, nor did he know how to respond to the inquiry.

Elizabeth pulled Dillon back from leaving the elevator. She didn't want anyone to see her and a middle-aged man, who looked like a punk rocker, leaving with the person everyone believed to be Kendy.

As the pair kept their distance, Dillon was still stuck mentally in the PAstREAM timeline. He had been prepared to die back there. That wasn't something he could just brush off.

Dillon followed Elizabeth to their car, separate from the one Kael had gotten into.

"Get in the front seat," Elizabeth said while loading the trunk.

Dillon jumped in and waited for Elizabeth to get into the back. The vehicles headed away from the hotel.

"So, what the hell do we do now?" Dillon asked.

Elizabeth remained on task. "We're going to stop forty-two miles before the bridge up ahead. You need to change your clothes."

Dillon turned to face the road while Elizabeth focused on her tablet. He took off the rock-star-style garments, getting back into the clothes he wore on the drive over.

Three quarters of an hour later, the cars pulled off the highway. Dillon watched as Elizabeth got out and pulled Kael from the other car. She practically dragged him before tossing him into the back seat next to where she had been sitting.

Elizabeth returned to her side and entered something into her tablet. The vehicles started moving again, only this time the now empty car turned around and went in the opposite direction.

Elizabeth turned her attention to Kael and started asking him questions regarding his movements. She was holding onto his arm, getting him to move one finger at a time. After about two minutes, he was able to flick his index finger.

Elizabeth wired her tablet to the back of Kael's head and began typing faster than Dillon thought was possible. Here fingers were almost a blur.

Kael started coughing, only his cough sounded more like a connection interruption, breaking up the sound.

As the cough continued, it started to sound less like a monotone Kendy and more like the voice Dillon had heard in the PAstREAM device. It was becoming Kael.

"I can't believe it worked." Even though Kael had an android body, he still had a human mind. "I owe you so much. Both of you."

Dillon was glad to hear that. He felt this was the best time to start getting some answers.

"Kael, what the hell happened back there? Why didn't I die when Mikal shot me? Is Jillian still alive?"

Elizabeth kept going between her tablet and different parts of Kael's body. Kael did whatever she asked of him as he answered Dillon.

"I don't know about Jillian. But Dillon, listen, that's where we're going now. We're going to get her. I promised that to you, and that's what we're going to do. Elizabeth, tell him."

Elizabeth kept working on Kael as she responded. "Jillian is now top priority. That is where we're headed now."

Dillon felt a small sense of relief, but he couldn't help thinking Mikal may have already killed her. Kael could tell Dillon was struggling internally.

"Dillon, there's a chance he won't just go and kill her. He may want to keep some sort of leverage over us. He has to know we're going to come for her."

Dillon tried to find reassurance in what he had heard, but the unknown left him with doubt and anger.

Kael's head abruptly tilted sideways, similar to when Kendy was shut off.

"I need to upload a data package into Kael so I can take control of his system. He will be awake again in about twenty minutes," Elizabeth said, delaying Dillon from getting any further answers.

Fifteen minutes passed as Dillon processed the different outcomes that would leave Jillian alive. He also processed the outcomes that would leave her dead. He concluded he would have to swallow whatever emotion he was feeling until they got to PAstREAM.

As Elizabeth continued her work, Dillon visualized what had actually happened back at the hotel. The moment in the device when he thought his life was over. The moment when everything flashed before him. Thinking about his kids.

Abruptly, Kael's head lifted. He was awake.

"Kael." Dillon got the attention of the only other person who had been with him in the dark and the light.

"Yes, Dillon."

"Why didn't I die back there? Why was Mikal's body killed in that memory, but I was able to live? You said back at the hotel that Mikal wasn't dead. What the hell happened?" Dillon just wanted some clarity. He was so confused about what had transpired within the PAstREAM device.

"Of course. I'll tell you whatever I can, Dillon. Mikal's not dead. He was not plugged into PAstREAM. That was a digital version of himself that he was able to control without the probes to his mind like you had. He connected himself the same way I did. He must have found my work and copied it. He knew I had been developing the technology." Kael was used to telling Dillon more than he could digest. Eventually, Dillon would understand.

"Mikal found out I was still alive through our visits. It's why we couldn't meet anymore; the risk was too great. He was waiting for me to connect again, to come out and show myself to him. I couldn't chance it any longer. I had created a hidden spot in the system, and I had to keep myself there while you and Elizabeth determined how to upload me into Kendy."

Kael made only one minor facial expression as he talked, making him look like a robot to Dillon. But Dillon knew the circumstances and looked past that to the man behind the face.

"The reason you didn't die, Dillon, is because I was able to manipulate the bullets as they came out of the gun. Mikal was in my room, a room I had programmed the rules for. Unfortunately, he brought his own digital rope and his own gun. I had no control over those items or him, but the bullets . . . I was able to affect the physics of the room. I couldn't affect the gravity though, as much as I tried. I thought I could send his digital creation a million miles into the space above. I just needed him to fire the bullet, so I could manipulate it to go into his digital head. I won't lie; it felt good to do that. I believe I'm owed some redemption."

"Why did my head bleed though? Why my head and not Mikal's?"

"Mikal was just a digital body. If he had shot me in there, I wouldn't have had any blood either, but that would have been the end of me. That was the only existence I had remaining. You were connected, Dillon. This was not a memory you were watching. This was real time, and your mind was connected to it. He had the gun pushed into your head, and when he pulled the trigger, I had to turn the bullet away from you as quickly as possible. If the bullet had hit your brain while you were plugged in, you would have died. You risked your life, Dillon. I owe you. And I'll repay you. You were brave. I've never seen anything like it, honestly."

Dillon's feelings had been appropriate. He could have died. His life actually was hanging in the balance, as he had thought in that moment. What he felt was genuine.

The feeling of dying and the thought of his kids being involved in this mess overwhelmed him. He wanted to get back home as soon as possible.

"When we go back, what's the plan?" Dillon asked.

"I have decided that, when we return, we are first going to get your kids and make sure they are safe," Elizabeth replied. "They will come with us."

Dillon applauded that move in his mind. That was the best first move he could think of making himself.

"Then we will go to PAstREAM to save Jillian. We will ultimately face Mikal and have to deal with him."

Dillon had no other questions. The plan was set. He went to dial his kids to let them know he was on his way to get them, punching the numbers into his sleeve.

After three rings, Rebecca answered. "Hey, Dad, what's up? When are you coming home?"

Dillon was gratified to hear her voice. "Becca, honey. I'm about seven hours away. I'm coming to get you and Jacob. Something's happened."

"Daddy, what happened? Are you okay?"

Dillon didn't want to scare her, but he wanted her and Jacob to know that the next handful of hours were extremely important. "Baby doll, where's Jacob?"

"He's in his room. Dad, what's going on?"

"I just want you to stay on the line with me, okay? Something has happened. I'm going to come and pick you up. You need to listen to me, hun. You need to stay on the line with me, okay?"

"Dad, you're scaring me. What's going on?"

"Rebecca, I need you to trust me. I'm coming to get you and your brother. Can you go to him, so I can talk to you both, please?"

"Okay, Dad, but you're freaking me out! What's going on?"

"Just go to your brother. I want to talk to you both."

Dillon heard her walking. He needed to make sure his kids understood that they needed to be ready to go.

"Jacob, Dad's acting crazy and said he's coming to pick us up. He wants us to stay on the phone with him."

Dillon didn't care what they thought. He may have been acting crazy, but he wasn't going to apologize for it.

"What? No. Where is he?" Jacob said.

"Dad, where are you?" Rebecca asked.

"I'm in a car on my way back to you. Now, I need you to listen. I'm coming to pick you up. I need you to stay on the line with me until I get to you." Dillon thought he was as clear as he could be.

"How far away are you?" Jacob asked.

"About seven hours away. I'll be home around eight."

"Seven hours? And you want us to stay on the line for that entire time? What the hell is going on, Dad?" Jacob knew that staying on the phone for seven hours was ridiculous. There had to be a valid reason.

"We're in danger, okay? I need you both to make sure the doors are locked and stay on the line with me until I get to you. I need you to promise me you'll do that."

"Dad. What the hell is happening? You're freaking us out!" Jacob said.

"I can't explain it now. I'll tell you in person. I just need you to trust me right now."

"Okay, Dad. We trust you. But when you get here, you'd better have a good explanation for us," Rebecca replied.

As the siblings sat together in the living room watching TV, Dillon listened to them breathing and commenting on whatever they were viewing. He also watched as Elizabeth kept working on Kael. He muted his phone at times, so his kids wouldn't hear Elizabeth in the background. He wasn't ready to share a slimmed-down version of that story until they were together.

Hours passed. As the sun rested on the mountaintops, they were within an hour of their destination.

Dillon was so amped up to get his kids. As every minute passed, he felt a sense of relief that he was closer to being able to protect them again. Every few minutes, Dillon checked in with them.

"How are you guys holding up?"

"We're still good, Dad. Just getting tired of waiting. Jacob is eating some disgusting canned fish, and it's stinking up the living room."

Dillon laughed to himself. That sounded like something Jacob would do. It brought some normalcy to the situation.

Dillon looked at the map on the console screen. Fifty-three minutes left before they would arrive at his apartment. He was relieved, knowing he was just a stone's throw away. The buildings and scenery were starting to look familiar again.

Elizabeth continued working on Kael. It was amazing how much more mobile he seemed to be. He could move his hands a million times better than when they first got in the car. Elizabeth's voice was easy on the ears, so all the talking she did to Kael throughout the ride didn't feel like a punishment in any way. It was almost a meditation as they got through the journey.

Kael's face was starting to look less like that of someone who'd just been downloaded into a body. He could smirk and grin, furrow his brows, and dimple his cheeks. Whatever Elizabeth was doing, it was helping.

Dillon's mind floated between hearing the kids on the line and listening to Elizabeth work on Kael when he heard a loud bang.

"Dad, is that you?" Rebecca asked.

"No, Rebecca! That's not me!" An unpleasant wave pulsed through Dillon.

"Someone's at the elevator door," Jacob said in the background.

"Don't answer it, whatever you do! Just stay where you are. I'm almost there!" Dillon was only fifty minutes away, but fifty minutes now felt like ten hours.

Someone was at his home right now.

"I'll check the monitor, see who it is." Jacob's voice grew more distant over the call.

"What do you see? Jacob, what do you see?" Dillon asked in a panic.

Elizabeth and Kael, who could hear everything, focused on Dillon.

Jacob talked as he viewed the elevator camera. "It's Mikal from PAstREAM and a tall guy. They have a tablet with a cable plugged into where the elevator scanner is."

Dillon's heart sank into his stomach.

"Don't let them in! Put something in front of the doors. The couch— move the couch in front of the door. Block it."

Jacob ran back to Rebecca and spoke quietly. "Dad, what the hell? You can't block elevator doors. Won't they just go away if we don't let them in?"

As Jacob finished his sentence, Dillon heard a voice.

"Hello, children."

"Holy shit!" Jacob said.

"What? What's going on? Jacob!"

"They're inside. They're in our home!" Rebecca said.

"Why are you here? What do you want?" Jacob yelled. The part that disturbed Dillon the most was the terrified scream coming from his daughter. Dillon was losing his mind with terror.

Elizabeth jumped into the driver's seat and took control of the car. "Buckle up tight."

CHΔPΓER
FORΓY-ΓWO

Dillon could barely breathe. His kids were in trouble, and he didn't know what to do. Elizabeth was driving excessively fast, passing other vehicles as if they were traffic cones.

"Are you on the line with someone, my dear?" Mikal asked. "Is your father on the other side?"

"Leave my kids alone, Mikal!" Dillon yelled.

"So, you made it out alive, Mr. Murphy. How nice. Your building scanners were harder to hack than I expected. Took us a tad longer to get in." In the background, Dillon heard muffled screams coming from his kids. "How are Elizabeth and Kael? I imagine they are with you. I'll be taking your kids to the garage at PAstREAM. Elizabeth knows where it is. I'll meet you there. Don't do anything stupid. You can still save your kids."

Click.

Kael clamped his hand on Dillon's shoulder. "We're with you, Dillon. We'll get your kids back."

"What's he going to do with them?" Dillon's mind went to a dark place. "If he wants me dead, I'll let him kill me if it means my kids will be safe. I just don't want them hurt." Dillon put his head between his legs, struggling to think clearly. The only thing he could think about was getting to the garage at PAstREAM.

Elizabeth reached over Dillon's leg and pulled out a small gun that was hidden in an upper compartment in the glove box. She drove the vehicle with her knees and pulled out her tablet. Her fingers pummeled the screen while her eyes moved constantly between the road and whatever she was programming on the tablet.

She gave the gun to Kael. "Take this. Put it in your mouth, and tuck the barrel down your throat."

Kael stared at the gun for a moment before opening his mouth wider than any human could, sliding the gun into it and then twisting it around, so he was able to close his mouth again.

As the car slowed to a crawl, Dillon felt like an eternity had passed over the last thirty minutes.

"We're here." Elizabeth pressed a button on her tablet to open the bay door to the empty garage.

The three got out of the car and walked over to the mezzanine. Elizabeth led them to the office that she had used many times to do Mikal's dirty work. Without hesitation, she opened the door and walked in. Inside, Jacob and Rebecca were tied to chairs facing away from the desk. Mikal was standing at the far end of the room looking out toward the PAstREAM pods through the tinted windows. Another man was in the room, pointing a gun at Dillon's kids.

Rebecca and Jacob both started making noises through the gags in their mouths. Their helpless facial expressions grasped at hope now that their father was there. Dillon was relieved to see them still alive, but he was angry at how they were bound like prisoners.

Elizabeth spoke first. "You built another one of us, I see, Mikal. Did you program this one to kill children?"

Dillon didn't like hearing the words "kill children" in a sentence, but he was anxious to hear the response.

Mikal turned around. "You've disappointed me, Elizabeth. I created you. I made you!" His voice grew progressively agitated as he spoke. "I needed an android that would obey me. I built this one to comply with my commands only. He is not self-aware. He will not stab me in the back like you, and his mind cannot be broken like Kendy's. Let me demonstrate. Calix, prepare to shoot our captives."

Immediately, the android cocked his gun and stepped toward Jacob, pressing the barrel into his forehead. Jacob retracted his head back as far as he could, but the gun followed his movement.

"No, Mikal, take me! Kill me! Please don't hurt my children," Dillon said as he hurried toward his kids.

"Take another step, and they will die right now. I'm not in the mood to hear your pleas of desperation. I do not want to kill your children. I want Kendy back, so I can fulfill his destiny, so I can fulfill *my* destiny. I can wipe your kids' minds of this afterwards. It will be like it never happened."

Mikal went and poured himself a drink. He took a swig of it and then set the glass on the desk.

Dillon looked at Elizabeth for a clue as to what to do next. He was open to the idea of giving Kendy back to Mikal and conceding that the plan hadn't worked. He just wanted his kids back. He would be happy with having his mind wiped of this moment and going back to his regular life.

As he thought it through, however, there was still the unknown about Jillian. Dillon figured he would rather have his kids back alive over taking the chance that he could get their mother back, considering the circumstances.

"We can't do that, Mikal," Elizabeth said.

"You can and you will, or the kids die, Elizabeth," Mikal retorted. "You don't have any options here. You're out of time."

Mikal walked over to Calix, took the gun, and pointed it at the kids.

"Calix, please pat down our guests. Make sure they don't have any weapons. I'm not looking for anyone to be a hero tonight."

Calix walked over to Kael and patted him down aggressively, causing Kael to fall to one knee on three occasions.

"Not used to the new body yet, Kael?" Mikal chuckled. "I'll admit I'm rather impressed that you were able to stay alive the way you did. I enjoyed learning about how you uploaded your mind into the system. We made a good team, the two of us."

Kael didn't speak.

"I didn't get a chance to finish building his voice for him yet," Elizabeth replied on behalf of Kael, who had the gun in his mouth. "I corrupted Kendy's voice box when I was deleting him."

"Fuck you, Elizabeth. You're lucky I've been keeping an active backup program of Kendy. I had worried there could be glitches but not that someone would go in and delete him. That really pisses me off." Mikal waved his gun around in frustration before aiming it back at Jacob's head. "I should have built him a second body. There's not enough time now, so you're going to give me this one back."

Dillon saw sweat drip off his son's brow next to the imprint of the muzzle from the gun. That, plus the whimpers coming through Rebecca's gag, filled Dillon with rage. It was the same feeling he'd had when he lunged at Mikal in the PAstREAM device, only exponentially increased. This time, however, he didn't want to risk Mikal pulling the trigger. It was more than his own life at risk, and there would be no way to affect the physics of the room like Kael did last time.

Calix finished patting down the subjects. He returned to Mikal, retaking his position with the firearm, placing it firmly against Jacob's forehead.

Mikal walked back over to the desk and finished his drink. "We're just wasting time here. I need Kendy's body back, and Kael needs to go back to being dead. Now I'm only going to demand it one last time, or I start killing the kids." Mikal looked at Dillon. "And believe me, it's not something I want to do. You're forcing my hand."

Jacob and Rebecca squirmed in their seats. Dillon looked at Elizabeth, hoping for some sort of answer. These were his children. He was not going to stand by and watch them die. As he stared desperately at Elizabeth, he saw her tapping her thigh quickly. Dillon had seen Elizabeth wrap the tablet around her leg under her dress before they got out of the car. He prayed she was putting a plan into action.

Suddenly, Kael pulled the gun out of his mouth and shot Calix between his eyes and again in the chest. The kids screamed at the sound of gunshots and watched as Calix fell to the floor beside them.

Dillon saw Elizabeth tap her thigh again. Within seconds, Kael aimed at Mikal, who dove behind the desk. Kael shot Mikal in the thigh, and Mikal yelled out a profanity as he hit the floor in agony. Dillon ran over to his kids. He took out their gags and started untying them.

"Dad!" Rebecca screamed, hugging her father as they both let out an array of emotions. Dillon finished untying Jacob's legs while Rebecca held him in a death grip.

Elizabeth grabbed the gun from Kael and aimed it at Mikal. She rushed over to the desk keeping the weapon pointed at Mikal's head. As she approached him lying on the floor holding his wounded leg, Elizabeth opened the lowest desk drawer closest to her. She reached in and took out a charcoal-colored device the size of a beer can.

"Dillon, catch. We're going to need this." Elizabeth tossed the object to Dillon, who juggled it before gripping it.

Dillon held it up and realized what it was. His kids had shown him a story he had reported on regarding a black-market device called a "Perpetuator" that would keep severed fingers and thumbs alive for scanning. It was originally created for hospitals, so they had time to reattach fingers and toes that were accidently cut off, but others used it for more appalling purposes. Dillon wondered if this particular Perpetuator had been previously used.

Elizabeth returned her attention to Mikal, the gun aimed between his eyes.

Mikal smirked at her despite the pain in his leg. "I don't know whether I should be proud or infuriated that I built you."

"You brought this on yourself, Mikal," Elizabeth replied. "I would have followed you and Kael to the ends of the earth, but you got greedy. You're an insane genius. Your work will be an inspiration to many. It does not have to end this way."

Mikal feigned dejection before reaching out to grab Elizabeth's ankle. He had some sort of mechanism in his hand that caused Elizabeth to shake rapidly, dropping the gun.

Kael was the first to realize what was happening. He stumbled toward Calix, took the gun from his cold, dead robotic hand, and pointed it at Mikal. Now in possession of the gun that Elizabeth dropped, Mikal got everyone's attention by putting it into her ear while propping himself up against the desk. Elizabeth was twitching in Mikal's arms from whatever surge of electricity he had used on her. They were in a stand-off.

"I'm still the creator. I've built weaknesses into these wretched machines, even if you've tried to bypass them, Kael. This isn't going to end the way you want it to."

Kael finally spoke now that he didn't have a gun in his mouth. "Mikal, enough. What do you hope will happen here? That I'm going to give up my mind and body so you can have Kendy back? If you kill Elizabeth, I'll kill you."

Mikal laughed. "Has it come to this? After all we've been through, Kael? You were nothing without me. I made you a shit ton of money."

"And you took it all away from me when you killed me. Don't talk to me like I owe you something. You took everything from me, and you did it for your own benefit. Hard for me to spend money with a bullet in the back of my head."

As Kael spoke, he positioned himself in front of Dillon's kids to protect them in case Mikal did anything stupid. Dillon stood beside Kael to build a wall in front of Rebecca and Jacob, who both looked on, traumatized.

"You're not dead, Kael. You managed to stay alive," Mikal said as he struggled to stay upright. "If you were dead, you wouldn't be pointing a gun at me. Now let's cut the bullshit and work out a deal. I can build another body for you. We can transfer your mind to a new, more improved system. I can make you a fantastic one, and you can have input into how you want it to be built. Think about it. Well, not for too long—we're a little short on time at the moment."

Kael contemplated the idea. If he stayed inside Kendy's body, he wouldn't be able to go out in public without some sort of facial modification. People would instantly recognize who he was. On the other hand, he would have to trust Mikal again. Trust him to fulfill his promise to build a new and improved body. Trust him to download his mind and upload it again. It wasn't worth the risk. Plus, Kael knew something Mikal didn't.

Kael pulled the trigger and shot Elizabeth. Mikal used Elizabeth as a shield as bullets began peppering her face and forehead, killing her. Kael kept shooting, finally getting Mikal in the chest and shoulder. His gun empty, he surged toward Mikal, who had dropped his weapon in agony.

Mikal's breathing was labored as Kael grabbed him in a chokehold and picked up his gun.

"Fuck, Mikal," Kael said, "you deserve whatever happens to you from here. You better pray that Jillian is still alive, or I will come back here and torture whatever is left of you."

Mikal could barely talk due to the wound in his chest, slightly away from his heart but almost assuredly through one of his lungs. He gargled blood and spit it out before he replied. "Fuck you."

At the sound of her mother's name, Rebecca jumped out from behind her father. She couldn't believe what she'd just heard. It didn't register. Jacob felt the same way. Were they talking about their mom, Jillian, or some other woman with the same name?

Dillon turned around and looked at his kids, nodding slightly as if to say, *"Yes, this is about your mother."*

"Dad?" Rebecca screamed with a shaky cry, only this time she wasn't crying because she was scared. She was crying because she could potentially be hearing the best news she could ever think to hear. She had grieved her mother's death for so long that it had become a part of who she was.

"Dad, say something!" Jacob said. "Is this about Mom?"

Dillon grabbed his kids and took them out of the room. He got down on one knee, pushing out the words. "Yes, your mom might be alive, but we don't know. And if she is, she could be worse than how I was after the accident."

Rebecca's eyes became animalistic with rage. She left her dad and brother, went back into the office, and walked aggressively over to Mikal, putting her finger in his chest wound. "Where's my mom?" she screamed. "Where is she? Where?"

Mikal squealed and gargled more blood. He was going to die if he didn't get immediate medical attention.

"Help me, and I'll bring you to her —" he coughed up blood, hitting Rebecca in the face, "I can make things right again . . ." More blood sputtered out of Mikal's mouth.

Kael could see through Mikal's lies. He released the chokehold and grabbed Mikal's wrist. He told Rebecca to stand back and shot at Mikal's thumb before breaking the remaining bone by hand. Mikal passed out in pain. Kael didn't care if he was dead or not. He was going to finish what he had promised Dillon.

Kael placed Mikal's thumb in the hole of the Perpetuator to keep the thumbprint alive. Jacob grabbed the device from Kael and twisted the base to lock the thumb in place, activating it. The Perpetuator lit up and made three pinging noises.

Everyone looked at Jacob, wondering how he knew what to do with it.

Jacob looked at his dad, "Hey, I watched that story you did on it—and a few YouTube videos."

Kael reclaimed the Perpetuator from Jacob and then headed out of the office. "Let's go."

Dillon and his kids followed behind Kael, who struggled to walk normally in his new body. After getting off the mezzanine, Kael led them through the PAstREAM pods to a hallway in the back. Two elevators were on each side of the wall.

Kael motioned everyone inside the left one. "Get in. This will slide us over to the hotel's employee hallway. The service elevator is right around the corner from there. We need to scan Mikal's thumb in the service elevator to get to negative floor two. That's the only way to get to Jillian. I just don't know what room she's in."

He pushed the first button on the panel, which had letters instead of numbers. He depressed H, and Jacob, who was in awe of Kael and everything he had just seen, assumed it stood for 'hotel.' The elevator started going down and then stopped. A few seconds later, it started moving again, only this time it went sideways.

Jacob felt like he was in some sort of Reality Room experience. He had just witnessed potentially three murders and found out his mother might still be alive. He wanted to know how they had gotten to this point.

"So, can someone please explain just what the hell is going on here? What did they do to Mom? You guys just killed three people! Are we all going to go to jail?"

Dillon couldn't answer anything yet. He had only one task on his mind: getting Jillian back.

"I promise you both I'll explain everything, but right now, I just want to get to your mom and see if she's still alive. I'm sorry you got involved in this. I never wanted this to happen to you. I just . . ." Dillon welled up. "I just want to get your mother back for you."

Rebecca started sobbing. She grabbed Dillon around his chest and hugged him as tightly as she could. He had obviously been going behind their backs, but he was doing it and risking his own life to put their family back together.

She didn't fully understand to what extent, but she appreciated her father's efforts based on the small amount she had witnessed.

Kael watched Dillon's interactions with his kids. He knew he was doing the right thing for them. Dillon had risked his life for this moment. He had risked his life to save his kids. He had even risked his life for Kael. He couldn't help but wonder what kind of state Jillian would be in, if she was alive.

Kael tore off a piece of his shirt and handed it to Rebecca. "Wipe that blood from your face."

The elevator stopped its sideways movement and started going up. Finally, as they came to a stop and the doors opened, they found themselves behind the scenes in the employee area of the hotel, bins of linens lining the hallway.

When it didn't appear that anyone was around to see them, they scurried over to the service elevator just around the corner.

The group bunched inside, and Kael scanned Mikal's thumb on the console. They looked at one another wondering if the print from the severed thumb would work. Nothing happened. Kael tried scanning it again, and this time the doors closed in the larger elevator they now occupied, which was used to transport housekeeping bins. They started to descend. The ride felt longer than two floors down, although time was difficult to discern in their desperate attempt to reach Jillian.

Finally, the elevator opened, and the group got out into a corridor housing a dozen metal doors going all the way to the end. Kael walked over and scanned Mikal's thumb on the first door. The metal door clicked. Dillon grabbed the large handle on the front edge and pulled it open. It was empty, other than a toilet and sink.

They scanned the second door and opened it. It too was empty, but it had clothes on the floor.

They opened the third door, and inside was half of a torso with electronic parts hanging out of it. As quickly as they thought it could be a human body, they realized it was an android. Or what was left of one.

Kael scanned the fourth door, and Dillon opened it. Someone was inside.

Rebecca was the first to see her. Her mother was alive, sitting on the edge of a bed. Rebecca grabbed her, followed by Jacob, strangling Jillian with hugs, excitement, ecstasy, and concern.

"Mom!" Rebecca's tears soaked the side of Jillian's gown.

Dillon could barely recognize his wife from the memories. She was not the same bubbly woman he had seen in the PAstREAM device. She was a ghost of that.

Rebecca and Jacob pulled away, looking for some sort of reaction or at least an embrace from their mom, but Jillian just sat there, expressionless, a blank look on her face. Whatever joy the kids had at seeing their mom alive quickly turned to despair.

Jillian just sat on the edge of the small bed, staring blankly at those around her. Dillon's heart dropped into the pit of his stomach. He had just broken his kids' hearts again, and at what cost?

"I have work to do." Kael tapped Dillon's shoulder with his bionic hand and walked over to the kids.

"I'll do whatever I can to help her, but I can't promise anything. Give me time."

CHAPTER
FORTY-THREE

Three days had gone by since Jillian was rescued from her prison, and Jacob and Rebecca had seen things most people should never see: murder, conspiracy, and life hanging in the balance of a single decision. The state of their mother. These were not things anyone should witness in their lifetimes, let alone kids.

Dillon sat in the kitchen of their hotel room. He'd scanned into the elevator and hotel room door to see if he could get access to the same unit that he and the kids had stayed in multiple times before. Apparently, Mikal's graciousness extended past his death.

News stories lined the globe at the sudden disappearance of the presidential candidate. Elizabeth had been identified by the many users of PAstREAM who had recognized her. She, and her rock-star appearing accomplice, were the prime suspects after video leaked of the pair in the same elevator as Kendy back at the convention center hotel. Dillon had yet to be identified, but it was only a matter of time.

Later that same evening after the standoff, Kael gave Dillon access to the mezzanine office to make sure the guns were in the hands of the right persons. He also removed the ropes and gags from the chairs where the kids had been tied up. The only blood in the room was Mikal's.

They wanted to give the appearance of an artificial intelligence shoot-out with its creator. They weren't sure if it was believable enough, although at this point, none of it was believable anyway.

Kael didn't like leaving Elizabeth's legacy as a murdering robot. Something about it seemed unfair, even though Elizabeth herself wouldn't care.

Dillon also grabbed the tablet from Elizabeth's thigh and the PAstREAM device from the car, as per Kael's instructions.

Kael doctored the security footage and removed any evidence that the family was staying within the hotel. He didn't want Dillon or his kids to have to deal with any investigations until the time was right. They would eventually have to face the FBI when it came time for the reappearance of their mother after her supposed death.

Kael had been working on Jillian for three days straight, hooking her into the portable PAstREAM device, first removing the latest trash Mikal had inputted into her. Kael then began logging memories in her brain. Memories she had in her mind prior to the day she was kidnapped by Mikal. Kael did it as quickly as he could without hurting her. He had seen what Mikal had done to Dillon, recording, scanning, and altering his memories at insane speeds, causing him to go into a coma. He wanted to avoid a similar result.

If whatever process Kael used actually worked for Jillian, Dillon wondered if he would consider doing it, but quickly decided against the idea for a number of reasons. Plus, Dillon wanted to keep the attention focused on his wife.

Jillian was attached to an IV bag with the same stand she'd had in Mikal's underground room. She would eat small amounts of food that Rebecca or Jacob gave her. She was conscious, but she was an empty shell.

Rebecca didn't leave her mom's side. Dillon didn't even know if his daughter had slept since they found her mom.

Jacob spent a lot of time with Kael, learning about artificial intelligence, how they got to this point, and what was potentially wrong with his mother. Kael answered him as much as he could, but some answers had to come from their dad. Dillon explained how the car crash didn't actually happen and the intricacies of how they got into this position. It was Dillon's knowledge of Kendy, prior to the faked accident, that had led to much of this. The kids were infuriated, and Dillon shouldered the blame.

Kael felt that he and Elizabeth were the ones the kids should be upset with. They'd involved Dillon in their consequential issues with Mikal, albeit for a righteous purpose.

Regardless of fault, Rebecca had not spoken to her father since he told them everything he knew. She was angry with him. Rebecca held him accountable for their current situation. She thought he was selfish, narcissistic, and an asshole of a human being. In her mind, this entire ordeal could have been avoided if he'd just kept himself out of whatever was happening at PAstREAM.

Jacob didn't feel the same way as Rebecca. He sat with his father as they drowned their sorrows in wine.

"I get it, Dad. You were given information that you didn't necessarily want, and you got stuck on what to do with it. You should have shared everything with the police or those FBI agents."

Dillon couldn't argue with that logic. "You're right. I should have informed the FBI. That's a big regret. I screwed up on that. Jacob, I'm not that man anymore. The memories I watched, the decisions I made, that is not who I want to be going forward."

Jacob appreciated what his dad was saying, but he had a hard time believing him. "Dad, you lied to us before and after your coma. I know your intentions were good this time, and I think you'll learn from this. At least, I hope you will."

Dillon didn't have any excuses to offer. He knew he had to take responsibility for his actions, or lack thereof.

Jacob could tell his father was devastated that Rebecca hadn't spoken to him since spilling every detail he had learned about himself and what he had done. He'd worn it on his face ever since.

"Rebecca will come around, Dad. She's upset with you, and you know what? She has a legitimate reason to be. You need to give her some space. She just wants to focus on Mom."

"When did you grow up?" Dillon asked.

Jacob shrugged. "Mom's funeral. I stood in your closet, picking one of your suits to wear. I thought I was going to have to be a father figure to my little sister. I looked in the mirror, and I knew then that I had to become a man. I didn't want to. Not yet. I wasn't ready." Jacob swallowed deeply, choking back whatever sentiment he felt toward the life lessons that had molded who he was and what he was going to become. The wine only added to his emotion.

Dillon put his hand on his son's shoulder. "I'm sorry you had to go through all this. I want you to know that I'm proud of you. You're my hero. I . . . I hope one day I can repay you. And I'll do my damnedest to make it up to you and Rebecca."

Jacob hugged his dad. The emotions that passed through them at that moment were free from judgement.

Kael walked into the kitchen and stood across from the two men. Jacob decided he would go be present for Rebecca and check if she needed anything.

"I can't read your face at all. You need to work on that," Dillon said to Kael as he sipped his drink.

Kael launched into an update of what he was doing. "I'm still recording Jillian's old memories and implanting them as new ones. She's in a similar state as you were. It's like her soul is . . . gone. I want to get as many memories as possible, but I also don't want to be downloading for the next month. I don't know if her brain could handle that. I'm getting as much as I can from the time you two met. Rebecca gave me a list of dates that has been really helpful. I don't know if this is going to work, but it's the best chance we have right now."

Kael leaned against the edge of the sink. Dillon noticed that Kael was still trying to figure out how to use his body. His movements were clunky, but they were improving. He lacked human dynamics, even though he had a human mind. Applying them to an android body didn't transfer over very easily.

"I just appreciate you trying. Rebecca sees what you're doing to help her mom. She argued with me to take her to the hospital but realized fairly quickly that they don't have the same technology to help her that you do here. Her mind has been abused by whatever experiments Mikal did, and I can't imagine a better person to try and fix it."

Kael acknowledged his appreciation for Dillon's belief in him, but he didn't know how this was going to end up. "Dillon. I'll do my best. I'll do everything I can to give your kids back their mom. But if I can't figure this out, she'll just end up in the medical system. Maybe her mind will come back eventually. I don't know. That's the part I can't control. I can upload a million memories into her, but if she isn't there—if her *being* isn't there—I don't know what more I can do."

Dillon nodded in understanding. He started walking through his mind how he would tell his kids that their mother's spirit may never return.

Seven more days went by.

Rebecca continued to stay with her mom and Kael as the process continued at the appropriate speed. Jillian still hadn't spoken a word since they found her. She would eat soft foods and supplement drinks, and Rebecca was there to make sure she swallowed it down. Hour after hour. Day after day.

Rebecca had giant bags under her eyes. She looked like she was a teenager going on fifty. Jacob fell into a depression. Seeing Rebecca go into this fixation, the same unending mindset that besieged her when their dad was in the coma, was eating him inside.

Dillon stayed away from Rebecca and Jillian throughout the day. He didn't want to upset his daughter any more than he already had. He had done what he set out to do: save Jillian no matter what state she was in.

Darkness fell upon the city in yet another wave of time that eluded the members in the hotel room. Dillon walked over to the living room, where Rebecca and Kael had been working on getting Jillian's mind back. The late evening was the only time he felt comfortable checking on them without Rebecca's scorn. Rebecca was lying half on her mom's makeshift bed and half on the couch. Kael was sitting there with his eyes open, but he didn't acknowledge Dillon's arrival. He just stared off into space.

Dillon had previously asked Kael if he required sleep in his new body. Kael had told him that his mind would just shut off for a while. It wasn't needed every night, but every couple of nights, his mind would turn off and dream for about four hours while he charged. Dillon figured it was happening at that moment.

Dillon sat next to Jillian. Looking at her, even though she was a ghost of herself, he still felt she was beautiful. He wondered how such an amazing woman could have been his wife and want to create kids with him. Dillon didn't think very much of who he was prior to the accident. He was extremely judgmental of all the garbage he had seen from his past. He was sitting next to a woman he didn't believe he deserved.

Dillon took Jillian's hand and placed it next to his face. Getting her back wasn't for him. He didn't merit her as a partner—not in his current mind. He wanted her back for his kids.

Dillon turned his attention to Rebecca, who was asleep, her head next to her mother's. His daughter was his reason to keep going. Jacob too.

Hours went by. Dillon was bobbing in and out of sleep, one hand on his daughter's arm, one hand holding his wife. He started dreaming. He had watched a lot of memories of Jillian, and it had given him a new love for a woman that he didn't remember. The kisses, the hugs, the laughs, the sex. He had seen it all at PAstREAM.

Dillon laid his head on Jillian's lap. Not on purpose; it just happened that way with the tiredness that hit him. His mind went to a memory of them on a beach in Jamaica. The white sand, the snorkeling. The constant touch between him and his wife. There was love there. Dillon felt undeserving, but he couldn't help but feel the intensity when reliving the memory.

Dillon snapped back awake and realized he needed to go to bed. He kissed Rebecca goodnight on the top of her head. He knew she couldn't get mad at him when she was sleeping. He loved her so much. He wanted to be a dad again for her and Jacob. He stared at her for a few moments before turning his attention to his wife.

Dillon kissed Jillian's forehead. He didn't feel like he deserved to kiss her on her lips. As he pulled his head back, Jillian's brow furled, almost into an angry expression. Dillon didn't think anything of it. He imagined that Jillian made many facial expressions while sleeping. What he didn't anticipate was her hand grabbing his head sharply, pulling his hair.

In the darkness, a light in the background flickered off Jillian's eyes.

She was awake, and she looked terrified.

CHAPTER
FORTY-FOUR

Dillon stared into his wife's eyes. He didn't know if she was aware of her surroundings, but he saw an essence behind her pupils that wasn't there before.

Their eyes stayed locked on each other. Neither one said anything. Jillian released Dillon's head, water cresting within her eyes. She sat up, and Dillon held her in case she fell back.

Rebecca awoke immediately at the forceful movement. "Mom?"

Jacob ran into the room and flicked the light on. He had obviously been awake in his room, and the sounds from the living room had him jumping into action. Jacob and Rebecca saw their mom sitting up. Her hands were on her face. She was confused.

"Where am I?" Jillian asked. Rebecca wrapped her arms around her mom's chest, tears streaming from her eyes. "Mommy! Mommy, I missed you!"

Jillian lifted her arm and put it around her daughter. It seemed more difficult than it should have been, but Rebecca didn't care. Her mom was embracing her.

Jacob sat beside Rebecca and hugged his mom and his sister. Whatever this was, a start of something more or the acme of what their mom would be, hugging her when she was hugging them back was something both kids could've only dreamed of. They would have given anything for this moment when they thought she was dead, and they didn't let it go to waste.

Kael awoke from his slumber and watched, unblinking, as the family enjoyed their moment. He didn't know what to expect from Jillian at this point. Her mind had been abused, broken.

"What . . . what happened?" Jillian asked.

"Mom, you had an accident," Rebecca said. "Well, actually, your mind was altered. But you're back now. You're okay. We're a family again."

Jillian sat there holding her kids. Part of them felt like she cared, but part of them could feel something was still missing.

They remained touching each other. Whispers and hugs, words of encouragement, and appreciation echoed through the next hour. They didn't want to force anything with Jillian. They just stayed together. Jacob started thinking about the Reality Room. No matter how amazing it was to get away from real life, no absence from reality could top the feeling he had at that moment.

The sun started to come up as the kids talked to each other and held their mom. Dillon was talking with Kael, who was acting like a doctor going over all of Jillian's vitals.

"You need to take her to a hospital now. I've done all I can do. She needs professional medical help to work toward a recovery."

Dillon continued to do everything he could to make sure Jillian had the best chance of success, whatever the outcome would be. He called an ambulance and told the kids to get ready. They were going to the hospital.

EPILOGUE

Kael stayed hidden back at the hotel for a multitude of reasons. For one, he was Kendy to everyone else. With Kendy missing from the presidential race, many people were trying to find him—at least until news broke that Kendy wasn't human. The FBI had scoured Mikal's office after finding his lifeless body and came across the blueprints for all of the AI he had created.

Second, Kael had something of great importance that he needed to do. He disguised himself, shaved his head and grossly distorted his facial features, so he could access his old office without being recognized. He made sure to keep hidden through the employee walkways.

Kael's desktop computer was gone, and it looked like his office had been ransacked. However, the laptop in the hidden floor compartment remained untouched. Other than that, the only items that were left behind were some of his pictures and his robotic dog.

Kael logged in and pulled out a flash drive. He loaded it into a program that Mikal had created when he was building the framework for his AI. It was a program that allowed for an evolving, sentient mind. A collaboration of stolen information, back-door deals, money transfers, and legitimate work from Mikal to put it together. It was where Elizabeth's mind was born.

Kael always had a reverence for Mikal and the work he did. Mikal was beyond brilliant when it came to programming and invention, but in the end, he just wasn't a good person.

Kael and Mikal had grown together, building PAstREAM from nothing. Their relationship had a brotherly quality to it. They would bicker, laugh, scream at each other, and cheer each other on.

But then something happened. Something changed within Mikal, and he became obsessed with power. He wanted to use their inventions for control and authority over others.

As Kael's flash drive finished loading into the computer, he picked up his robotic dog and placed it on his lap, activating it by petting its head. The small dog looked real from an outsider's perspective. Even its movements were smooth. The only noticeable robotic aspect of it was its glowing eyes. Kael wanted his version to have LED lights and work as a Bluetooth speaker.

A pop-up alerted Kael that his file transfer was complete. He turned up the volume on his computer and spoke toward the built-in microphone.

"Elizabeth?" Kael moved his mouse and adjusted a few settings. "Elizabeth, are you there?"

"Yes, I'm here. You did it."

"I did what you told me to do. Now we just need to get a body for you."

Elizabeth had downloaded the data from her body on the ride back into the city in case anything happened to her. That was why Kael did not hesitate to shoot her when Mikal was holding her at gunpoint, though he still didn't like the idea of destroying the computer and processors in her head.

"I have the plans from my old body," Elizabeth replied. "We can use them and make some improvements."

* * *

Back at the hospital, Teddy was the first public authority to be on site regarding the Murphy family. He wanted to be the first one to talk to the woman who was supposedly killed in a car accident, only to be found alive in an underground room at PAstREAM.

Dillon and the kids had spoken with Kael about getting their stories straight. They had over a week together to make sure they were all on the same page. Everyone agreed Mikal deserved his fate. Calix was just a pawn in

Mikal's system, and Elizabeth was the collateral damage hero who deserved a better outcome, although Kael was going to change the latter's destiny.

Dillon told Teddy that Mikal had deceived his family into staying in one of his underground hotel rooms, in which they became trapped for over a week in the same room as Jillian. Kael had added scans into the system, so that when they were checked, they would corroborate Dillon's story.

Teddy didn't like Dillon. He knew there was always more than what was offered to him. There were too many storylines for things to be so easily explained.

Teddy stayed with Dillon and his family, avoiding the kids as much as possible with his questions for the time being, considering he didn't think they knew about anything other than getting their mother back.

Jonathon arrived at the hospital with Shyla and his wife, Dionna. Both families had basically stayed away from each other since Dillon and Dionna had cheated on their spouses. Dionna had a big bouquet of flowers, which she set down on the table in the Murphys' hospital room. Teddy began walking out, nodding at Dillon to acknowledge he would give them a moment of privacy. He wasn't going to give him much of a leash, however.

Jonathon walked up to Dillon and gave him a hug. Dillon embraced him. As much as he tried to hold back his emotion, Dillon had been through a lot. Although he had been an awful friend to Jonathon, he'd still watched many memories that included him. He felt a familiarity and kinship that allowed him to show some vulnerability with his former best friend.

Jonathon pulled free, keeping one hand on Dillon's shoulders. "H-h-how is this possible?"

Dillon looked over at Jillian, who was sleeping, hooked up to monitors. She was frail, her face sunken in. Dionna was hugging Rebecca. Dillon was glad his daughter was getting some additional love. He wasn't able to give it to her, because she was still upset with him.

"It's a long, arduous story, and I'll tell you all about it. Just not right now." Dillon wanted to be honest with his friend, but he wasn't ready to talk about it at this moment after getting grilled by the FBI.

"You know there's a news story here," Jonathon said.

Dillon nodded. "I know."

Shyla was over by the window with Jacob, both of them staring out at the park across the street. "How are you holding up, Jacob? How did they find your mom?"

"She was locked in a room in PAstREAM. The owner kept her captive there and tricked people into thinking she was dead. There was no car accident." Jacob didn't expect her to understand the logic on the first take. It didn't really make sense when it was explained to him either.

"That's insane. I don't understand why someone could do that or even *how* they would do that. I'm sorry your family has had to go through all this." Shyla kept her hands held in front of her, looking at Jacob's face through the reflection on the window.

"Yeah, and we don't know if she'll be okay. I guess they really fucked up her mind somehow when she was in there. At least she's speaking now."

Jacob looked over at Rebecca. He had a habit of checking on her as often as he could. She was the only other person who could truly understand what they had been through.

He looked back at Shyla's reflection. The light from the window shone on her left hand as she swayed nervously. Jacob pointed to the shining object on her finger. "That a new piece of jewelry? I don't remember you wearing something that big in school."

Shyla blushed anxiously. "Well, actually, yes. Kind of. I mean . . . Jacob, I got engaged. It's only been like two weeks, I think. But it's not a big deal. I mean, there's so much going on."

Jacob felt like he had been punched in the gut. A knot tied up in his stomach. He had always had feelings for Shyla. He wished he hadn't asked about the ring. There was already enough happening in his life. He still wanted to offer something to her. It should be a happy time for someone who had been his best friend while they were growing up.

"I'm . . . that's great, Shy. You deserve that. Happiness." Jacob could spill out the words; he just couldn't couple it with any enthusiasm.

As both families grouped together prior to the Winters leaving, they promised they would try and get together again soon, at least to check up on Jillian and bring food for the kids. Jacob didn't like the idea; he didn't want to have to meet or hang out with Shyla's fiancé. He figured he would just make himself busy in the Reality Room, although the PAstREAM building was shut down after Jillian's emergence.

* * *

Over the next week, time seemed to alternate between dragging and racing. The kids watched as their mom went through a battery of tests. She had made significant improvement with her coordination and movements. She could take herself to the bathroom and answer basic questions. When the kids asked if she remembered them, she would simply answer: "yes."

But something was missing. She was aware, but the spirit within her was absent. Mikal had broken her. Something had been removed from who she was, from who Rebecca remembered her mom to be.

As the family sat around the hospital bed at night, eating gourmet cafeteria food, Jacob and Rebecca joked about how it was better than the last meal Jacob made when they were back at home. Jacob was still trying to explain exactly what it was. That memory felt like a lifetime ago.

Dillon kept staring at his wife, which was a constant theme for him. Even though it had been over two weeks since they found Jillian, he still felt like he was meeting her for the first time and learning about the person in front of him. He had not remembered her other than from the memories he had watched at PAstREAM, but she was not the same woman, for obvious reasons.

As Dillon kept peering into Jillian's eyes, he saw something was happening within her. Something in this exact moment. Her eyebrows were raised and her face started changing from the blank expression he was used to seeing. Even Rebecca noticed, and pushed her brother's shoulder to face their mother. Jacob pressed the button beside the bed to call for the nurse.

As the nurse walked in, she too caught on to the family's fixation.

Something inside Jillian clicked. "Mikal, stop. Please," she begged. Tears formed in her eyes. She looked around at those in the room with her.

The nurse called her station and told the family that their doctor would be back later in the evening to check on Jillian but could come sooner if needed. The nurse remained in the room next to Jillian, checking her vitals and monitoring her.

Jillian's mouth opened as if preparing to say something.

Rebecca encouraged her to speak. "Mom?"

Jillian's eyes lit up. "Becca?"

Rebecca could not only see it; she *felt* her mother's spirit return.

"Mom! I'm here. I'm here." Rebecca sat on the edge of the bed, stroking strands of her mom's hair away from her face.

"Jacob." Jillian turned her head with a loving expression to see her son sitting on the other side. He was holding her hand.

Then she looked at the man sitting near the foot of the bed. "Dilly."

Dillon smiled. "Welcome back, Jillian."

CPSIA information can be obtained
at www.ICGtesting.com
Printed in the USA
LVHW110205270521
688656LV00005B/109

9 781525 586026